CW01426023

Starting Over in Maple Bay

A MAPLE BAY NOVEL

Brittney Joy

Copyright © 2021 by **Brittney Joy**

All rights reserved. No part of this publication may be reproduced, distributed or transmitted in any form or by any means, without prior written permission.

Brittney Joy/Horse Girl LLC
www.brittneyjoybooks.com

Publisher's Note: This is a work of fiction. Names, characters, places, and incidents are a product of the author's imagination. Locales and public names are sometimes used for atmospheric purposes. Any resemblance to actual people, living or dead, or to businesses, companies, events, institutions, or locales is completely coincidental.

Cover design by The Red Leaf Book Design / www.redleafbookdesign.com
Book Layout © 2017 BookDesignTemplates.com

Starting Over in Maple Bay / Brittney Joy -- 1st ed.
ISBN 9798594125308

Dedicated to my parents, brother, grandparents, aunts, uncles, and cousins. Thank you for showing me that home is where the heart is. Love you all.

CHAPTER ONE

If Hazel had known the rooster was going to chase her, she would've stayed in her car. Instead, she unclicked her seatbelt and turned to her ten-year-old daughter, Grace.

"Stay here. This won't take long." Hazel opened her door, but Grace protested.

"Can't I come with?" Grace's sweet eyes were a mix of curiosity and impatience.

"Just stay here until I find Mr. Church." Hazel swept her eyes across the country property, looking for the man that sent her a letter a week ago. She didn't see a soul. The front porch of the big sunshine-yellow farmhouse was empty but for a few rocking chairs. No one milled around the red barn behind the home. The only sign of life was a few horses who lingered lazily in green pastures. "Stay put while I take care of this. Okay, sweetie?"

Grace sighed, but Hazel knew her daughter would stay put. Grace was a rule-follower like her mother. Thankfully, she didn't inherit her father's impulsive streak.

Hazel walked up the gravel driveway, an array of questions bombarding her mind. She was looking at Rose Lovell's house—her biological mother's home, and a house which Hazel had never seen before today. In all her thirty-seven years, Hazel never met her biological mother, and had spent more than half her life wondering what Rose Lovell was like. Did Hazel get her auburn-red hair from her mom? Her freckles? Her laugh? Did they have the same mannerisms? The same favorite foods? If they met would there be an instant connection? Or would Rose feel like a stranger?

Now Hazel would never know.

Last week, as Hazel begrudgingly sifted through a stack of mail—mostly bills she couldn't pay—she plucked an envelope from the pile and opened it only because the return address boasted the name of a law firm. She assumed the letter had something to do with her ex-husband, but when Hazel opened the envelope and set her eyes on the letter, her heart stopped. It didn't have a thing to do with her ex. Instead, in two short paragraphs, Hazel learned that her biological mother had passed away a few months ago.

Suddenly, an entire lifetime of wondering was brought to a screeching halt by typed words on a fancy sheet of legal paper. And the very last sentence nearly swiped her off her feet. Hazel's presence was requested in the small northern Minnesota town of Maple Bay . . . at Rose's home, where Hazel could claim her inheritance.

Now, as Hazel stood in front of a foreign house, she wondered why Rose—someone related to her only by blood—would leave Hazel an inheritance when she didn't even give Hazel the respect of a phone call while she was still alive. If it hadn't been for her *real* mother's persistence, Hazel might not have even taken the time to travel to Maple Bay for the reading of the will. Sandy, Hazel's adopted mother and the only mother she'd ever known, was the first person Hazel called after reading the letter. It was Sandy that convinced Hazel to take a day, drive the four hours north from Minneapolis, and see what the lawyer had to say.

Sandy insisted that Hazel do this for herself, that she needed closure. And Sandy was persistent enough that Hazel ultimately gave in and made the trip.

Just hear the lawyer out and then you can get back on the road, Hazel thought, and strode toward the porch steps. She intended to knock on the front door, but slowed her stride when a hefty rooster appeared on the porch. Hazel wasn't sure how she'd missed the chicken. He was the size of a small child and the color of blood. His beady little eyes zoned in on her like she was most definitely an intruder.

"What are you . . . a guard bird?" Hazel asked under her breath, not wanting to offend the rooster who had now puffed himself up and was beating his wings.

She looked over her shoulder, checking to make sure Grace was still in the car. Through the windshield, Hazel could see that her daughter's head was tipped down, probably reading her book, but there still wasn't another person in sight. *Come on, Mr. Church. Where are you?* Hazel was only fifteen minutes early for their noon appointment. Hoping she was at the right place, Hazel double-checked the house number, which was painted in scrolling numbers next to the front door.

877 Maple Bay Drive. This is it.

"Could you skootch over just a bit?" Hazel asked sweetly, and shooed the rooster with her hands, thinking the chicken would respect her request and move to the side so she could safely approach the door. Her gesture instigated the opposite reaction. Instead of shuffling off, the rooster tipped its beak to the summer sky and crowed louder than a police siren. When it finished yelling, the rooster soared down the stairs and ran at Hazel like a deranged T-Rex.

Hazel screamed, startled by the chicken's sudden aggression, but she wasn't about to stick around to find out what else the feathered monster was capable of. Hazel turned and ran, cursing her choice of footwear. Her gold sandals were a good choice for an early June road trip, but they were *not* appropriate for dashing across gravel to get to your car before being mauled by a crazy farm animal.

"Mom, run!" Grace yelled, now hanging out the car window, wide-eyed.

Hazel thought about reiterating that she was already doing that. Instead she yelled back, "Stay in the car!" The last thing Hazel needed was the crazy rooster finding a new target in her daughter.

Glancing behind her, Hazel yelped as she realized the red-feathered monster was at her heels. The bird was half the size of her leg and she was still a few long strides from her car. It was *really* going to hurt when this thing pecked her bare legs with his sharp beak. Hazel cursed the white Bermuda shorts she'd chosen to wear this morning.

Knowing there was no way she was going to make it inside her car without getting mauled, Hazel leapt for the hood. Her decision to jump to safety seemed like a better option than getting lacerated by a chicken, but when she landed, Hazel managed to slam both knees and one elbow against the hard metal of the hood. As she shrieked in pain and flailed about, one gold sandal flew through the air like a frisbee and landed somewhere off in the distance. Regardless, Hazel scrambled up to the windshield and looked back, certain the rooster was going to fly up onto the car with her. Grabbing the only weapon she could think of, Hazel snatched the other sandal off her foot and raised it like a bat. She was not above beating a bird with her shoe.

As she prepared to defend herself with the cute sandal she'd splurged on at Target, a savior came to her rescue. A shaggy black-and-white dog darted in and intercepted the rooster's attack. The dog ran at the rooster, and the big bird retreated without so much as a squabble. The dog continued to tail the rooster, pushing him toward the barn with a silent threat, and only broke his focus when a sharp whistle came from the horse pasture.

Hazel followed the whistle and discovered a tall man walking her way. He looked like he'd just strolled straight out of a country music video. The man wore a dusty ballcap, t-shirt, jeans, and cowboy boots. A rope was slung over his shoulder. Coal-black hair peeked out from under his ballcap. A rough stubble adorned his jaw.

A gate clanged shut behind him.

"Pen 'em up," the man instructed, and pointed toward the barn. The dog stalked the rooster again, forcing it away with salty stares. And that dang bird-monster listened. The red devil zigzagged and hightailed it across the lawn toward the barn.

Hazel blew out a breath and lowered her sandal-filled hand.

"Mom, you okay?" Grace asked, still hanging out the window. She pushed her rainbow-colored sunglasses to the top of her head.

Hazel took stock of her body parts. Other than the bruises that were certain to grow on her knees and elbow, she was fine. "I'm okay." She took another breath and forced a smile, so Grace wouldn't know her heart still beat in her throat.

The dog-whistle-guy approached the car. Hazel expected him to apologize for his attack-bird.

Instead, he said, "The next time you encounter a rooster, I highly suggest *not* staring it down. They take that as a sign of aggression. And running away only fuels their fire."

What? Hazel was completely offended. She was trying to recover from being chased by a crazy farm animal, and this man decided to school her on rooster interactions?

"Excuse me?" Hazel pulled her limbs closer to her body, retracting from her sprawled-across-the-car-hood look. "I wasn't trying to fight with your bird. I was just trying to get to the front door."

Who was this guy? He certainly couldn't be Mr. Church. A lawyer wouldn't show up to a professional meeting in jeans, boots, and a ballcap. Not even a small-town lawyer.

"Are you looking for Frankie?" The cowboy's question was curt, as though Hazel had interrupted his afternoon and he needed to get back to whatever he was doing.

"I was looking for Mr. Church. Daniel Church. I have an appointment with him, and he gave me this address." Who was Frankie?

The man raised an eyebrow and gave her a once-over, judging her for something other than her lack of rooster-knowledge.

Just then the farmhouse's front door opened, and three little boys spilled out in a blaze of shouts and wrestling. The cowboy whistled and grabbed their attention, just like he had with the dog.

"Jesse!" the boys called as they ran across the lawn, like the man had offered them candy.

"Who was in charge of getting the eggs today?" the cowboy—apparently, Jesse—asked the three little kids.

There was a flurry of pointing fingers, before the oldest boy spoke. He looked to be about Grace's age. "Noah got the eggs, I fed the chickens, and Wyatt cleaned the coop."

"Then we played tag in the pen," the littlest boy, who was maybe five or six years old, added like he was excited to tell Jesse about their game. The two older children gave him a glare.

Jesse tipped his head at the boys. "Well, did anyone manage to shut the door to the coop when you were done playing tag?"

The boys looked like they were trying to remember.

"Nope!" the littlest boy replied.

Jesse gestured toward Hazel. "Well, you let the rooster out and he chased this lady. What do you have to say for yourselves?"

The boys all looked at Hazel, surprised. "Sorry, Ma'am," they said in unison. Hazel closed her mouth, not able to scowl at the children.

Before she had a chance to say anything in return, the littlest boy asked, "Is that why you're sitting on your car?"

The oldest added, "Oh, Mother Clucker is the worst!" He made a face like he felt sorry for Hazel. "He chased me through the barn last week and I had to climb up into the hay loft to get away."

"Which is why we always remember to close the coop, right boys?" Jesse interjected. The boys agreed with vigorous head shaking.

"The rooster's name is Mother Clucker?" Hazel asked, a little dumbfounded.

"Yep," the littlest boy replied just as a woman and a man exited the house. The boy jerked a thumb at them as they walked across the lawn to join the debacle. "Momma named him. He chases her too."

The woman gave Hazel a concerned looked as she neared. "Oh no, did that Mother Clucker chase you?"

Hazel was stunned, but it wasn't due to the horribly named rooster. As the woman neared, Hazel was flooded with a strange sense of déjà vu. The woman looked familiar. Her warm strawberry-blonde hair, the band of freckles that speckled her nose, and her high cheekbones reminded Hazel of someone. She just couldn't place who.

"Are you Hazel?" the woman asked.

Hazel nodded and tried to gracefully remove herself from the hood of her car. Instead, she scooted along like a toddler on a plastic slide. How embarrassing.

"Let me help you, Hazel." The clean-cut man who'd arrived with the woman offered his hand to assist Hazel off her car. "I'm Daniel Church. We talked on the phone. I'm so glad you were able to make it here today."

The lawyer. Hazel took Daniel's hand and set her bare feet on the ground. She didn't even have a chance to stand up before the woman reached out and introduced herself, sending Hazel's world completely off balance.

"And I'm Frankie Barnes. Your sister."

CHAPTER TWO

"What'd you say?" Hazel asked Frankie. Her fingers went slack, and she lost her grip on the gold sandal. It fell to the gravel and Hazel glanced around, waiting for someone to admit that this was all a bad joke. "Did you say you're my sister?"

"Half-sister." Frankie let her outstretched hand fall back to her side when Hazel didn't grab it. "Mom said you didn't know. I didn't know, either. Not until Mom got sick. She told me I had a sister not long after her cancer diagnosis."

Every sentence carried a piece of information Hazel wasn't sure she could process. *I have a sister? Rose died of cancer? She knew she was sick and still didn't reach out to me?*

"I . . ." Hazel started, not sure she had a response. Hazel knew today would be emotionally taxing, but she never imagined this scenario.

"Why don't we sit on the porch and talk?" Daniel offered, trying to regroup the conversation. "I have some documents I need to go through with the both of you."

A car door opened and closed. Hazel straightened, even before her daughter talked.

"Mom?" Hazel heard the worry in Grace's question.

Swallowing, Hazel went into Mom-mode. "It's okay, Grace. This won't take long. I need to hear what Mr. Church has to say and then we'll head back home. We'll get dinner at the Pizza Parlor, okay?"

The Pizza Parlor was Grace's favorite restaurant. Hazel took her there at least once a month, usually after cheer practice or to celebrate good grades. Sometimes just to brighten her day. Hazel hoped the meatball pizza would be enough to make Grace forget the fiasco Hazel was exposing her to today. "Can you read your book in the car for a little longer?"

Grace looked confused.

"Do you want to see my pony?" the littlest boy asked Grace with sudden enthusiasm. He seemed completely unaware of the heavy adult-talk going on around him.

"Noah," Frankie started and ran her fingers through the boy's blond hair, tousling it. "I'm not sure this is a good time for that."

Noah's excited face fell, and Jesse piped up. He'd been quiet as Frankie and Daniel had talked. "I'll watch them,"

Jesse offered. "Noah's pony is just over there. You can watch your daughter from the porch."

Behind Jesse, a potbellied white pony grazed in one of the paddocks. He was the smallest horse Hazel had ever seen. Grace's eyes lit up. Maybe a tiny horse would be a better distraction than pizza.

"Okay, but please stay where I can see you. And watch your fingers and toes." Horses bit and kicked, didn't they? Even a tiny one had teeth and hooves. Although, at least Grace was more prepared than her mother. She was wearing black Converse tennis shoes.

Noah bounced like a spring and grabbed Grace's hand. "Come on! Come meet Mister Pepper!"

Grace smiled shyly and went with the little boy. His brothers raced in front of them. Jesse gave a tip of his ballcap before exchanging a strange look with Frankie. Then he followed the kids.

One of the boys called back to Jesse. "Come on, Uncle Jesse!"

"I'm right behind you, Tommy," Jesse replied.

Hazel's heart lurched and the shock must've hit her face. *Uncle Jesse?*

"He's not your brother, if that's what you're thinking," Frankie offered quickly. "Jesse is a family friend. Known him since I was little. The boys call him Uncle Jesse because he might as well be family."

Hazel's chest gave a heave, glad her heart didn't have to withstand one more jolt. Then she gathered her sandals and slid them back onto her feet. "If you don't mind, can we get this conversation started? I'd like to be back on the road soon so I can avoid rush hour in Minneapolis."

Once Hazel was sitting in a rocking chair on the porch, she tried not to stare at Frankie. It was nearly impossible. There was no doubt Frankie and Hazel were related. Frankie looked to be maybe thirty . . . a younger, more vibrant version of herself. The same person Hazel had been ten years ago, before life and a divorce beat her down.

"Here you go." Frankie placed a mason jar filled with iced tea on the table next to Hazel. She handed another glass to Daniel who stood before them both, perched against the porch railing, a thick file in his hands.

"Thank you." Hazel took a sip, wetting her stunned, dry mouth as Frankie took a seat in the rocking chair beside her. Frankie ran her fingers through her strawberry-blonde hair, pushing it from her face. Doing so better exposed her emerald green eyes and the spray of freckles over her nose and cheeks. Hazel shared the same features. Her hair was just a darker shade of red.

"Do you want to wait for Garrett?" Daniel asked Frankie. She shook her head.

"No, it's fine. Garrett won't be home until late. He's working on a project over in Elm Grove." Frankie took a drink of iced tea and caught Hazel's stare, seeming to realize

Hazel had no idea who Garrett was. She set the mason jar down on the table. "That's my husband. Garrett. He works for his uncle's excavating company. They're clearing property for a developer over in Elm Grove and have been working until sunset every day. He won't be home until nine or so. I'll fill him in later tonight, when he gets home."

Daniel pulled eyeglasses from the front pocket of his polo shirt and situated them on his nose. Then he cracked open the daunting file in his hands. "Rose asked me to read her will to you both, together."

Frankie started rocking her chair, looking nervous. But why? Wouldn't she know her mother's final wishes? Daniel adjusted his glasses. "Rose Lovell left her property, homes, all structures and their contents to her two daughters, Francine Barnes and Hazel March."

Daniel continued talking but his voice was muffled by Hazel's shock. She shifted forward and nearly fell out of her rocking chair. "She left her home . . . this place . . . to us?" Hazel was pointing between Frankie, herself, the porch, and the house attached to it. Her finger moved in a jerky blur.

"She did," Daniel replied, simply.

Frankie kept rocking.

"Why?" It was the only sensible word Hazel could utter. She had many other questions, but they all seemed to be rooted in one word . . . why?

Daniel looked stumped but proceeded. "You're Rose's only family. The two of you are her daughters. She left—"

"No," Hazel interrupted, a dull fiery starting in her gut. "No, *we* are not her daughters. Frankie is Rose Lovell's daughter. This is Frankie's inheritance. I never even met Rose. Not once in my entire life. I *have* a mother and a father. Great ones, actually. Rose chose to give me up over thirty-seven years ago and I never even knew her last name. Not until a week ago when I received your letter."

Frankie's face was frozen.

Hazel got up from her chair, feeling unhinged and not wanting to take out a lifetime of resentment on a sister she met fifteen minutes ago. "I'm sorry. This isn't your fault. I think I need to go." She started walking across the porch, wanting to gather her thoughts and deal with this another day.

"Ms. March." Daniel stood from his resting spot against the railing. "You really do need to hear the rest of Ms. Lovell's will."

In any other situation, magically inheriting a beautiful home and a sprawling property would be enough to make Hazel jump for joy and do cartwheels across the lawn. Especially since she was still recovering from how her ex-husband, Bill, had broken her financially. He'd racked up credit cards and taken a second mortgage on their house without her knowledge. In fact, in the past few years, Hazel had discovered a lot of things Bill had done without her knowledge.

But today, Hazel thought she was going to show up in Maple Bay, see the house her biological mother had lived in, and put some things to rest. Hazel wanted closure. Not a house. Walls, windows, and a roof certainly wouldn't make up for being abandoned.

"I'll have to politely disagree, Mr. Church. I don't think I need to hear the rest of Ms. Lovell's will." Hazel looked at Frankie. "This is yours." What kind of mother would deny her daughter—the one she raised—her inheritance?

Frankie opened her mouth but didn't utter a response.

"I'm afraid you can't do that," Daniel said.

Hazel gave him the same look she gave Grace every time her daughter dunked French fries in her chocolate milkshake.

"There's a clause," Daniel added. Frankie had stopped rocking. "Ms. Lovell put a clause in her will. Her property is a total of twenty acres and a few years ago Rose had the property lines readjusted. The twenty acres were split into two ten-acre parcels. She left this parcel to Frankie," Daniel waved a hand at the house, barn, and pastures. "She left the ten-acres with the carriage house to you."

"On the condition that we *both* live on the property for the summer," Frankie revealed, looking at Hazel like she was trying to read her mind. "That's the clause."

"She did *what*?" Hazel nearly shouted.

Daniel closed his file like Frankie had properly summed up the rest of the will. "The clause states that both of Ms.

Lovell's daughters must take up residence on the property from the day the will is read until the day after Labor Day. If either of you does not honor the clause, the entire property will go up for auction and the proceeds will be given to charity. Neither of you will get a red cent."

Hazel couldn't believe what she was hearing. She looked back and forth between Daniel and Frankie. "So, if I don't uproot my entire life and move to Maple Bay for the rest of the summer, then this poor girl gets absolutely nothing?" Hazel meant to look at Frankie, but couldn't bring herself to do so in that moment.

"Yes. Exactly that," Daniel replied.

Hazel laughed. Not because it was funny. Because she felt trapped. She couldn't believe someone who'd never been a part of her life now wanted full control of it. "That's absurd." She walked across the porch and down the stairs, needing to put some space between herself and the insanity of Rose's will. "Grace? Honey? Let's go."

Grace was crouched next to the paddock fence, feeding the white pony handfuls of grass she'd ripped from the ground. Noah was helping her. The other two boys were chasing each other around a tree. Jesse was leaning against a fence post watching them.

Grace looked up, obviously disappointed by her mother's request, but before Hazel could call her daughter's name again, Frankie caught up to Hazel on the lawn.

Frankie grabbed her arm. "Please," she said, and Hazel reluctantly stopped. Her stomach clenched at the plea in Frankie's eyes. "I know I'm basically a stranger, but I need you to consider this."

Hazel took a beat to calm down. "Look, I can't just uproot my whole life. And Grace's." The latter was more important to her. Grace's life had been uprooted and smacked around because her parents couldn't make their marriage work. Hazel wasn't about to throw another wrench in her daughter's life when they were just getting settled. Even if "getting settled" meant they were living in Hazel's parents' basement.

"I get it," Frankie said, and let go of Hazel's arm. "But it's just three months. You only need to live here for the summer, and then you'll inherit the ten acres on the lake. The carriage house is beautiful. Needs some restoring, but I can help you. And come September, you'll own the property and you can sell it. It's a coveted piece of property. It's on Maple Leaf Lake and right on the edge of town. After restoring the carriage house, it could be worth half a million dollars."

Hazel blinked at Frankie, not sure how to continue explaining herself. Hazel also blinked at the possibility of making that much money in one summer. "I just . . ." she stammered.

"I don't know what we'll do if we lose this place." Tears welled in Frankie's eyes, and her obvious strife immediately pulled at Hazel's heart strings.

"Oh, no. Don't cry." Hazel couldn't handle crying. She was an empathizer. If Frankie started crying, Hazel was sure to follow. Then they'd really have a mess on their hands.

Frankie wiped at her eyes. "Mother to mother, I need you to think about this. I need this place for my family. For my boys. It's only one summer."

A lump formed in Hazel's throat and she swallowed it, knowing Frankie had hit her in her Achille's heel—children. Even though she didn't know Frankie, she knew what was standing before her. Frankie was a mother pleading for her children, for her family, for her sanity. That she understood, probably a whole lot more than Frankie knew.

"Momma?" Grace asked, jogging toward Hazel. Her chestnut ponytail bounced behind her. "Can we stay just a little longer? Jesse said I can brush Mister Pepper. Noah went to get his brushes from the barn."

Hazel saw the little boy running toward the barn like his feet were on fire. She pressed her lips together, thinking hard about her words before she let them out. "Five minutes, baby. You can brush Pepper for five minutes, and then we've got to get going."

Grace immediately tried to negotiate a longer time allotment for brushing. "Just five minutes, Grace." Hazel repeated, and Frankie's face fell, like she'd been defeated. "After that, Frankie has a carriage house to show us."

Grace looked unsure if she should be excited about a carriage house or not. "Okay," she decided and jogged back toward the pony.

"I'll take a look at it," Hazel said to Frankie, not sure why she was postponing the inevitable, other than to appease a woman that seemed to be caught in the crossfire of her mother's demands.

Frankie nodded and fought more tears. "Thank you."

CHAPTER THREE

You are just taking a look, Hazel reminded herself as she walked with Frankie to the adjoining property. Grace walked behind them on the dirt road surrounded by woods. She was dragging her feet because Hazel hadn't allowed her a few more minutes to brush the pony. Daniel and Jesse stayed at the farmhouse with the boys.

"What's a carriage house?" Grace asked, breaking the strained silence. "And why are we going to look at it?"

Hazel didn't answer. Not because she didn't know what a carriage house was. Her tongue was tied because she wasn't sure how to answer Grace's second question. Hazel was still trying to comprehend what was happening. She should be on the road by now, headed back to the city, back to Haven Hills.

"It has to do with horses," Frankie said, and Grace perked up.

"It does?"

"Yep." Frankie gave Grace a soft smile. "Before cars were invented, everyone got around using horse-drawn carriages. A carriage house is a building where the carriages and the harnesses were kept. It's like an old-timey garage."

"Oh," Grace said thoughtfully. "Did they keep horses in there too?"

"Sometimes."

Grace pursed her lips, looking more interested in what they were about to discover.

Frankie pointed ahead. "There it is."

They hadn't walked far. The narrow dirt road to the carriage house split off from Frankie and Garrett's driveway. Hazel could still faintly hear Frankie's boys squealing and laughing in the distance. The road curved through tall oak trees and delicate maples, ending at a two-story white building that looked like a cross between a stable and a garage. It boasted a sloping roof and dormer windows. A cupola sat on the roof peak with a metal weathervane. The front featured a huge wooden door. It was big enough to drive a horse and carriage through.

"What do you use it for?" Hazel asked honestly. It didn't look like the carriage house had been inhabited in quite some time. Thick brush edged the building and ivy crawled over much of its grimy siding. The carriage house was in dire need of some TLC.

"Mostly storage now," Frankie said as they reached the door. She grabbed one of the metal handles on the wide wooden door, gave it a yank, and the door split open like shutters.

Hazel didn't know what to expect inside, but when she entered, her sandals clicked against a wood floor and the open space was tidier than she expected. Stacks of tarped boxes took up one wall. The opposite side of the building had a few closed doors and a staircase that went to a second story, but it was the view out the windows on the backside of the building that captured Hazel's attention. There was another large barn door accented by two huge windows that framed Maple Leaf Lake like a painting.

"Wow." Hazel walked over to a window and gazed out at the dark blue water. The shore was maybe a few hundred feet down a sloping hill. A dock and an attached paddle boat swayed gently in the water. An old willow tree draped the base of the dock.

Grace walked up beside her. "You guys have a boat too?" she asked Frankie with pure wonder. "Horses *and* a boat?"

Frankie smiled and nodded at Grace's enthusiasm.

Hazel moved toward the door on the backside of the building. "Can we go outside?"

"Absolutely," Frankie replied, seemingly happy with Hazel and Grace's initial reaction.

Hazel grabbed the handle and pressed her shoulder against the heavy door to slide it open. As she did, a stone patio was revealed. It looked to be occupied much more recently than the inside of the carriage house. Colorful Adirondack chairs were scattered across the patio and pointed toward the lake. Well-worn life jackets hung from chairbacks. A set of oars laid on the flat gray stone. A metal fire pit sat in the center, displaying ash and charcoaled logs.

"The boys love the lake. They spend a lot of the summer swimming and fishing," Frankie said.

"I can see why," Hazel said, taking it all in—the fresh lake air, warm summer sun, and the looming sense of a life-altering decision. "Why wouldn't she leave this to you?"

Hazel specifically left out Rose's name, but Grace's face still scrunched up inquisitively. Sometimes Hazel wished she could go back to the days when Grace was a toddler and she couldn't understand *every* conversation she could hear.

"Who?" Grace asked.

Hazel deflected. "Do you want to go checkout the dock while Frankie and I talk?"

Grace bobbed her head. As she meandered off, Hazel reminded her to stay out of the water.

Frankie rested a hand on the back of an Adirondack chair and took a deep breath. When Grace was halfway to the lake, Frankie said, "I don't know."

"You don't know?"

"Not exactly."

"But you knew about the clause?"

"Daniel gave me and Garrett a copy of the will a few weeks ago. I knew Mom wanted to leave some things to you. I just didn't know the details of her will until I read it."

"I see." Hazel watched Grace as she stepped onto the dock, kneeled, and dipped her fingers into the lake. Hazel honestly didn't know what to think of Rose's will.

"Are you married?" Frankie asked, abruptly pulling Hazel from her thoughts.

Hazel looked at Frankie out the corner of her eye, a little sensitive to the question. "Divorced."

"A boyfriend?"

Frankie's questions felt a little invasive, but Hazel answered with a simple "No." She wasn't ready to add a man to her life. Not after the debacle Bill put her through.

"Do you have a job to get back to?" Frankie pressed.

"Yes," Hazel replied, seeing what Frankie was getting at. "I'm a secretary at Grace's school."

When Hazel was married, she was a stay-at-home mom. After the divorce she needed to jump back into the work force to keep her head above water. She'd been volunteering at Grace's elementary school since Grace was enrolled and when a position opened in the front office, Hazel immediately applied. Hazel was delighted when she was offered the job, and it wasn't just the paycheck she was excited about. Her job at Haven Elementary helped Hazel out of her post-divorce slump. Interacting with the kids brought her daily cheer and gave her a new purpose. Plus,

Hazel liked being close to Grace during the school day, and she enjoyed the co-workers she'd gotten to know over the past year. It was the perfect job for Hazel, and she didn't want to lose it.

"So, you have the summer off?" Frankie prodded. "While school is out?"

"I start again at the end of August," Hazel replied, remembering her boss' face when she'd asked for hours over the summer. Her boss wanted to give Hazel the extra hours, but there simply wasn't room in the budget. Hazel was still searching for a job to fill the gap.

"So, what's keeping you in Haven Hills?" Frankie's brow rose and Hazel thought through all the reasons she couldn't just pick up and move, even temporarily. Hazel and her daughter were just getting settled in their new life. They were finding routine again. Grace's last day of fourth grade was a week ago, but she had cheer camp at the end of June and swim lessons scheduled after that. Hazel had gotten acquainted with a few of the women from work and finally had some mommy-friends to hang out with again. She'd lost quite a few of those when Bill and her split. Not to mention, Hazel didn't know how Bill would feel about his daughter being four hours away from him for an entire summer.

Frankie was staring at Hazel in anticipation of an answer.

"I live with my parents." Hazel's response was meant to encompass something she had to get back to. Instead, it came out a little pitiful. Hazel was going to say that her parents needed her help, but they didn't. She loved Sandy and Peter immensely, but she'd moved in with them because *she* was dead broke. She didn't have any other choice. Her parents loved having all the extra time with her and Grace, but they also had their own lives to live. Sandy played bunko, ran a book club, and taught a silver-sneakers-dance class at the YMCA. Peter was still teaching environmental science at the local college, convinced he would die if he ever stopped working. Furthermore, they just bought a camper and planned to tour as many national parks as possible this summer. They didn't *need* her to live with them. "Grace needs stability. I can't just hop around, moving her from place to place. I've already done that once this year. After the divorce."

Frankie nodded, like she was mulling over Hazel's excuses instead of accepting them. "You don't think Grace would love living here for the summer? Living on a lake? With a horse stable in her backyard? It would be like a vacation. For the both of you."

Hazel surprised herself as the idea of conceding to Rose's will slipped into her head. It was just a couple of months. "Where would we live?" she challenged Frankie. Hazel turned back to stare at the carriage house. "This needs some work. We can't just move in here today like the will says." *Or, rather demands.*

"It's really not that far from being livable. The second story originally was a hayloft, but Mom started converting it into an apartment. It's even setup for a small kitchen. Just needs the appliances. Mom wanted to convert the carriage house into a bed-and-breakfast. She was going to live in the hayloft. She also planned to make the feed room, tack room, and the two stableboy rooms into rentable bedrooms." Frankie paused. "That was her plan anyhow. Before she got sick."

Hazel could see that Frankie was hurting. "I'm sorry for your loss." Regardless of how Hazel felt about Rose, the woman standing before her was dealing with the loss of a parent.

Frankie gave her a quick smile and changed the subject. "As I said, we'll help you fix it up. Both Garrett and I are handy. And until it's livable, you and Grace can live with us. We have a guest room on the third floor. Used to be an attic. It's nice and quiet up there and away from the boys' bedrooms."

Hazel wasn't sure what to think of that. "I couldn't impose—"

"You wouldn't be. You'd be doing me a favor by honoring the clause." Frankie bit her bottom lip, looking worried.

Hazel was running out of reasons as to why she couldn't move to Maple Bay. Her parents would be fine. In fact, they'd probably encourage the change—especially since it was just for the summer. As for her job, Hazel figured her boss would work with her. She'd only miss a week of work and could use vacation-days, if needed. Plus, Hazel stood to make a significant profit by honoring the terms of Rose's will. She'd also be helping Frankie and her family keep their home.

Lost in her wavering thoughts, Hazel looked toward the lake. Her daughter was gleefully spinning on a tire swing that hung from the willow tree. Her giggle carried up the hill and Hazel reveled in it. Grace had always been a shy child, but the divorce had pushed her even further into her shell. She rarely was this outgoing around strangers. Maybe they both needed a break from Haven Hills—from the gossip and pitiful glares they'd been receiving since Bill ran off with a woman half his age. Not to mention, this could be the opportunity Hazel needed to make a fresh start. With some hard work and elbow-grease, the carriage house could be brought back to life. It could be converted into a home, or even an inn like Rose had intended. Then, come September, Hazel could put the property on the market and use the money to buy a home back in Haven Hills. This place could be the start of a fresh, new life for her and Grace.

It was just a summer. Just a few months.

What a day, Hazel admitted to herself. She turned to Frankie. "We'll stay. I just—"

Frankie snatched Hazel into a hug, hushing the rest of Hazel's sentence. Hazel stiffened at first, but then hugged Frankie back, hoping she hadn't spoken too soon. Obviously, Frankie was happy with her choice, but Hazel still had one hurdle to jump. She wasn't married to Bill any longer, but he still had a say in any decision that involved Grace. They shared custody. Hazel hoped she could convince Bill to allow Grace to stay with her in Maple Bay. Because there was absolutely no way Hazel would be apart from her daughter for the entire summer. There was no amount of money that could make that happen.

CHAPTER FOUR

Frankie stood in her kitchen—alone, dirty, tired, and not wanting to scrub the frying pan that sat in the sink. She stared down at a mysterious stain she'd just discovered on her t-shirt and wondered how long it had been there. *Got to be dirt, poop, or chocolate*, she told herself. All three had been part of her day.

The door that led to the garage clicked open. Frankie looked up from her shirt, deciding the stain was a smear of chocolate. She'd dipped into her secret stash today, desperately needing the sweet rush of happiness. Apparently, she hadn't been that sneaky.

Her husband, Garrett, stepped through the door and into the kitchen, finally getting home from work. "You're still up?" He quietly closed the door behind him.

Everyone else in the house was already doing what Frankie wished she was—sleeping. After a surreal day in which she met her long-lost sister, Frankie still had all her usual chores to do. This evening, she'd cleaned the stable, fed the horses, tucked her boys into bed after dinner and showers, and she made sure Hazel and Grace were comfortable in the guest room. Frankie started her day well before the sun was up. Now, it was nearly eleven o'clock at night and she had yet to take a shower.

Frankie pulled a chair out from the kitchen table and sat. She put her head in her hands.

Garrett set his lunch cooler on the counter and walked over, taking a chair himself. He looked just as dirty as she was. "I tried calling you this afternoon. What happened? What did Hazel say about the will?"

Frankie peeked at Garrett through her fingers—at the face she'd known since they were kids. His brown eyes were concerned, but she was still mad at him. She wished he'd been here with her today, to support her when she finally met Hazel. But no. He had to work. He always had to work.

"If you'd taken a day off, you'd already know," Frankie replied, knowing she'd sent his calls to voicemail on purpose.

"Baby," Garrett started and reached for her, touching her elbow. She didn't offer him her hand. "You know how hard I've been working on this project. Fred put me in charge of it, and I need to show him I can handle it. It would've been different if we'd gotten more than a day's notice of the meeting with Hazel."

Garrett had been working for his uncle Fred's excavating business since he was eighteen, and Fred was a hard man to work for. Frankie knew it. He was fickle and stubborn, but he taught Garrett everything he knew about the construction business. A few months ago, Fred told Garrett he was planning to retire in another year and that he'd consider selling the business to Garrett, if he could handle it. Frankie knew what that meant to Garrett, what it would mean to their family, but she also didn't like all the long days he'd been putting in. Especially with what she'd been through recently, with losing her mother. Rose had been Frankie's best friend, her righthand woman. Now Frankie felt like she was running a household, a family, her stable, and her riding lesson business all by herself.

"I know it was last minute, but I wish you would've made time." Hazel closed her fingers over her face like shutters.

"What did she say about the will?" Garrett prodded, avoiding her last comment.

"She's going to do it. She'll stay for the summer."

Garrett sighed, like he'd been waiting all day to do so. "That's great news."

"Not really." Frankie let her hands fall to the table. "She's going to sell the property this fall, after she meets the clause."

"How do you know?"

"I can tell." After Daniel read Rose's will, Hazel had nearly run out of Maple Bay without looking back. She didn't seem to care about her inheritance one bit. Panicked, Frankie did and said everything she could to make Hazel stay, but at the end of the summer Hazel would surely leave. She'd sell the family property and Frankie would have to say goodbye to all the memories that filled the carriage house and the lakeshore. Hazel didn't have a reason to stay in Maple Bay beyond the summer.

"Your mother was a very smart woman," Garrett offered. "You know she did this for you, right?"

Frankie wasn't mad at her mother. She knew Rose had setup the will to make Frankie happy, to allow her time to get to know her sister. Rose knew how difficult her passing would be for Frankie. Especially because it hadn't been that long since they lost Sarah. In a very short period of time, God had taken two beautiful souls out of Frankie's life. Now she felt lost in a world she once loved.

"I know." Frankie looked over Garrett's shoulder and into the living room where a framed photo hung above the couch. It was a picture from a few years ago—of Frankie, Garrett, Rose, and the boys. It was a warm summer day and they were all sitting on the front porch, indulging in root beer floats that Rose had thrown together with her homemade vanilla ice cream. Noah had most of the float down the front of his shirt, Wyatt had some in his hair, and Tommy was sporting a frothy mustache. The whole family was smiling. All six of them.

God, I miss her, Frankie thought, but she wouldn't say the words aloud. If she did, she would certainly cry.

Garrett put his hand on Frankie's. "She did this for you. Rose wanted you to have your sister in your life."

Frankie nodded, knowing her mother's intensions were good, though Frankie wasn't sure how a stranger could possibly fill the hole in her heart. Especially since Hazel would only be around temporarily.

"I'm tired," Frankie said, and closed her eyes, letting her husband's touch and the quiet of a sleeping house cradle her.

"Go take a hot shower and get in bed," Garrett said. "I'll take one after you're done."

Frankie rose from the chair, knowing that wallowing in her pain only made it worse. The morning would come fast. It always did. And she needed to wash away her worries and get some sleep.

CHAPTER FIVE

Hazel was awake. She laid in bed, gazing at her daughter. Grace was sleeping hard. Her cheek smashed against the pillow, one leg thrown out of the covers. She was always a beast to sleep with, rolling and tossing all night like a tornado, but Hazel loved it. Since the divorce, Grace often crawled into bed with Hazel, both seeking comfort and finding it in late night talks and plenty of snuggles.

Through the drawn curtains, pale morning light peeked into the bedroom. Hazel reached for her phone on the nightstand. She figured it was probably about seven o'clock. She gasped when she saw that it was almost nine.

Grace stirred. "Mom? What's wrong?"

Hazel set her phone back down. "Sorry, sweetie. I was just looking at the time and we really slept in."

Seven o'clock was sleeping in for Hazel. Yesterday must have completely done her in.

Grace rolled to her back and stretched her arms above her, touching the rails of the oak headboard. She pushed wispy hair from her forehead. "What are we going to eat for breakfast? I'm hungry."

"Why don't you brush your teeth and I'll see what Frankie is up to downstairs. Maybe we can run into town and get donuts for everyone?"

"Yum." Grace pushed the covers back and sat up.

Last night, Frankie had retrieved toiletries for Hazel and Grace to use. She also found t-shirts and shorts for them to sleep in. She'd even offered to throw their clothes in the wash. Hazel felt like she was imposing, but she also hadn't planned to stay overnight in Maple Bay . . . or for the entire summer. She and Grace had arrived with only the clothes on their backs, so Hazel was forced to take advantage of Frankie's hospitality. Hazel had also called her parents to tell them about her decision to stay in Maple Bay. Before Hazel could even ask, they offered to pack and deliver suitcases the next day. Hazel was looking forward to seeing her parents' faces.

"Grandma and Grandpa are going to be here this afternoon. They're bringing our clothes and some stuff to get us through the summer."

Grace turned sharply toward Hazel. "You asked them to bring my swimsuit, didn't you?"

"Of course." Hazel grinned at Grace's excitement to go swimming. Last night as they drifted off to sleep, Grace had asked a million questions about the carriage house, the lake, the horses, Frankie, and Rose. Hazel tried to answer them as best she could. She had plenty of questions herself and wasn't sure she was ready for the answers.

As Grace brushed her teeth and hair, Hazel tiptoed down the stairs, listening for Frankie or the boys. The house was quiet. In the kitchen, she found a note on the table along with a few boxes of cereal.

Hazel & Grace,
Make yourselves at home. I brewed a pot of coffee. There's milk in the fridge. The boys and I are out in the barn. Join us if you'd like.

-Frankie

Hazel peeked out the kitchen window, taking in the backyard and red barn. Noah was skipping around by the front of the barn, a bucket in hand. Wyatt and Tommy were brushing a horse which was tied to a pasture fence. Frankie sat on the top rail of an arena fence watching a couple girls as they rode horses.

Yesterday, Frankie mentioned she gave horseback riding lessons. Hazel hoped the lesson would be done soon— before Grace had a chance to see the girls riding. Grace would take one look and beg to ride a horse until Hazel's ears bled. But honestly, horses scared Hazel. She'd never been around such big animals, and riding didn't seem like a safe sport for her daughter to take up.

Grace appeared in the stairwell. "Brushed my teeth and my hair!" Grace had smoothed her chestnut tresses into a cute bun on the top of her head. At ten years old, she was starting to look like a mini teenager, growing taller with each passing minute. Hazel wished time would slow down.

"Great," Hazel said, wanting to keep Grace from glancing out the kitchen window. "How about instead of donuts we do cereal this morning?"

Grace wrinkled her nose, but when she saw the brightly colored cereal boxes on the table, she smiled. Hazel didn't keep sugary cereal in the house. Mostly because Hazel knew she'd dip into the boxes for a midnight snack every night.

Grace sat down at the table, and Hazel pulled a gallon of milk from the fridge, setting it on the table next to Grace. She poured herself a cup of coffee and sipped as Grace scanned the cereal boxes, making the hard decision of which she would have for breakfast. The kitchen looked like Frankie had been in a rush this morning. The sink was full of dirty dishes and the counters looked rampaged by a pack of hungry boys. Which it probably was. Looking to keep herself busy, Hazel filled one half of the sink with warm, sudsy water and started scrubbing. She'd made it through all the dishes and was drying off the frying pan when Frankie came in the backdoor.

"Oh, you didn't have to do that," Frankie said, looking surprised as she shut the door.

"I don't mind." Hazel set the pan in the dish rack. "Least I can do considering you housed us and are feeding us this morning. I was going to go into town and get donuts for us all, but then I saw that you guys had already eaten. I didn't realize how late it was. Maybe tomorrow?"

"Uh, sure. The boys would love that. There's an amazing bakery in town—Patty Cakes. Patty makes the best Maple Bars." Frankie stepped out of her cowboy boots. "I was just going to switch the laundry. I totally forgot about your clothes until this morning, but I did get them in the washer."

"I could've switched it," Hazel offered as Frankie vanished into a room off the kitchen. She heard the dryer start up.

"You'll have clean clothes in about an hour," Frankie said as she reappeared in the kitchen.

"Frankie, I want to pull my weight around here if we're going to be taking up your guest room while I prepare the carriage house. Just point me in the right direction and I'll get it done. I'm pretty good at cleaning and cooking." Those were two things Hazel knew she did well. "And it would make me feel useful."

Frankie stepped back into her cowboy boots, and the silver spurs attached to the heels jingled. Grace sat up straight with interest. "Well, you don't have to twist my arm *too* hard." Frankie gave her a polite smile. "Those are two things I'm not too fond of. Mom always helped me in those areas. And thank you for cleaning up the kitchen. I got the boys fed, and we've been out in the barn doing chores and lessons since six."

"You were up early." Hazel knew how late Frankie had been up. Last night, Hazel was having a hard time falling asleep. She'd gotten out of bed, intending to get a glass of water. As she snuck down the stairs to the kitchen, Hazel overheard Frankie talking with a man. Hazel assumed it was her husband, Garrett, and the conversation sounded tense. She didn't want to intrude, so she turned around and headed back upstairs. She hadn't heard much, but knew those types of late-night conversations were only meant for the two people involved. In the last few years of their marriage, she'd had many of those conversations with Bill. "How about I make lunch for us all?"

Frankie looked like she wasn't sure if she should allow Hazel to do so. "I've been meaning to get to the grocery store. . ." Frankie trailed off.

"I'll run to the grocery store. I'm sure I can find it on Google Maps."

Frankie chuckled. "It'd be hard to miss. Just take a right out of the driveway and head into Maple Bay. You'll run right into it."

"Perfect." Hazel set the dish towel on the counter, but realized her clothes were in the dryer. She looked down at the oversized t-shirt and basketball shorts she was sporting and didn't think she should meander into town looking like she'd just crawled out of bed.

Frankie seemed to read her mind. "Do you want to borrow some clothes?"

Hazel hesitated, mostly because she wasn't sure she'd fit into Frankie's clothes. She'd been trying to lose the extra weight she'd put on in the past few years, but the extra pounds were a bit stickier than she'd like.

Frankie didn't let her answer. She walked through the living room and into a bedroom, which must've been the master. A few minutes later she appeared with a stack of clothes and set them on the table. "It's hot today, so I grabbed some shorts and tanks for you to pick from. There's a sports bra here too. You're on your own with the underwear though."

Hazel huffed, hoping her underwear would dry quicker than the rest of her clothes. "Okay, thanks. I'll see if they fit."

"Grace can stay with us while you run to the store." Frankie turned to Grace. "The boys are cleaning pens while I work. I know it's not very glamourous, but you could join them if you want."

Grace shoveled the last few bites of cereal into her mouth before jumping up from her chair and setting her bowl in the sink. "Can I, Mom?"

"I don't know," Hazel replied. Grace was wearing one of the boy's t-shirts and basketball shorts. She'd be just fine running around the farm in that, but Hazel didn't like the idea of Grace being around the horses without supervision. "You've never been around horses before, and I don't want you getting hurt."

"There aren't any horses in the pens they're cleaning, and I'll be able to see them from the arena. Plus, Jesse will keep an eye on them."

Jesse? The cowboy? He was here again? Did he live here, too?

Before Hazel could ask, Grace clamped onto her arm and gave her a pleading look.

"Okay, okay. But you need to listen to the adults, and no petting the horses without asking Frankie, okay?"

Grace ran to the door. She plopped down on the floor and put on her tennis shoes. "Ready," she announced and hopped up.

"Follow me." Frankie opened the door. She and Grace headed out and walked toward the barn. Hazel watched them through the window. They were talking and Grace was nearly skipping. Hazel had never seen anyone so excited to clean a horse pen.

Hazel looked back at the kitchen table and the stack of clothes Frankie had set out. She took a breath. The clock said it was half past nine. If she was going to make lunch, she'd better get to the grocery store. Frankie and the boys ate breakfast early, so they'd surely be starving by eleven.

Hazel took a big slurp of coffee to give herself gumption. She was much more excited to cook than she was to pour herself into Frankie's clothes.

CHAPTER SIX

Jesse stood in the middle of the round corral, nose-to-nose with the big buckskin gelding.

"I won't hurt you, Indy. I promise," Jesse said, just above a whisper. He grasped the lead rope that was attached to the doubtful horse's halter, but the rope carried plenty of slack. Jesse would never try to force a horse to stand still with brute strength. That tactic never earned trust. Instead, Jesse had been working for the past hour to show Indy that time with a human could be pleasant.

Despite Jesse's efforts and patience, Indy's tan coat glistened with nervous sweat, and his stance told Jesse he'd flee at a moment's notice. This was the second time Jesse had worked with Indy. He had the horse in the round pen behind Frankie's barn. Usually, the round pen was used as a safe space to train young horses. It was a much smaller corral than the outdoor arena and if a colt happened to spook or buck, they couldn't run far. However, Indy wasn't a colt. He was thirteen years old and didn't trust a single soul.

Jesse didn't blame him. Indy had been dealt a bad hand by his last owner.

"What do you think of your new home?" Jesse slowly inched his hand toward Indy, giving the gelding ample time to process his approach. When his fingertips finally touched Indy's wet neck, Jesse scratched him in small circles before letting his hand fall back to his side. "Good boy." He repeated the process over and over until Indy started to relax.

Jesse had been riding horses most of his thirty-eight years—starting when he wasn't much more than a toddler. His parents bred and trained Paint Horses and his entire family was involved in the business. At least, they had been. Now it was just Jesse, his father, and his brother, Evan. Evan managed the breeding, sales, and the barn. Jesse did the training. The horses were well-bred so most only needed a few months under-saddle before they were easily sold. The family business—Painted Dreams Ranch—was a small breeding and training facility. Usually, they had four or five foals a year, which was enough to keep Jesse busy and employed part-time. Same for his brother. But where Evan managed the local feed store, Jesse never saw himself doing anything but riding horses. Instead of getting a job in town, Jesse had been taking on outside training projects since he was a teenager. Over the years, he'd made a name for himself. In the area, he was who everyone called concerning their problem horses. *The broncs. The mean ones. The flight risks.* But Jesse didn't mind. He found the biggest rewards in working with the horses no one else wanted.

"You'll make someone a great horse." Jesse scratched Indy's neck again. He continued talking, slow and smooth, as he scratched his way up toward Indy's ears. "You're big, strong, and fast. Maybe you'll be a ranch horse? Or would you like to run barrels? Ride trails?"

He stopped short of touching Indy's ears, not wanting to push the gelding too far. Indy had already made great progress in the short time he'd been in Frankie's barn.

A month ago, Indy was dropped off at Frankie's barn. He was underweight and scared. Frankie and Rose had always worked closely with *Hooves and Hearts*, a local rescue group that worked to rehome neglected horses. Rose started fostering rescued horses when Frankie was a kid and it was a passion they shared, nursing abused horses back to health and finding them a new, happy life. When they got one that proved hard to handle, Frankie always called Jesse. He gladly volunteered his time. Indy was one such case. He was also the first rescue Frankie had agreed to foster since Rose's passing.

"One step at a time. Right, buddy?" Jesse smoothed a hand over Indy's neck, knowing he was talking about Frankie's grieving process as well as the horse's training. It was hard to watch his friend go through such a rough patch. Frankie was like a little sister to him, and Jesse would do anything to protect her. In this instance, with the passing of Frankie's mother, Jesse felt helpless, but he still tried to support her, Garrett, and the boys however he could.

Jesse urged Indy toward the corral gate, deciding it was time to end their training session. Just as he did, Tommy ran around the corner of the barn.

"Lunchtime, Uncle Jesse!" Tommy yelled, and Indy jumped sideways.

"Easy." Jesse stood still and stayed calm. Overreacting with a frightened horse only increased their fear. If Jesse showed courage and kept Indy safe, Indy would start to understand that he could trust Jesse's instincts. "It's just Tommy."

Tommy had stopped cold in his tracks when the horse jumped.

Indy was startled, but he hadn't bolted. That was progress. "Remember to move a little slower around this one, Tommy. For now, anyhow. He's not sure what to think of quick movements." Jesse was sure Indy had been man-handled by his previous owner.

"Sorry. I forgot." Tommy's eyes were wide.

Jesse gave Tommy a reassuring grin. "Do you want to come say hi?"

Tommy nodded and approached the corral slowly. "Hello, Mr. Indy." Tommy neared the fence and Indy watched him with curiosity. The horse wasn't presenting the same fear he showed around adults.

Jesse scratched Indy's neck. "Maybe Indy will have a kid of his own someday." Jesse pictured the big buckskin horse hauling around a little boy or a little girl, everybody happy as clams. "Good job on your approach, Tommy."

Jesse made sure to praise the little boy. Training horses and kids had a lot of similarities. Kindness and praise got you a lot farther than scolding.

"Momma told me to tell you it's lunchtime."

"Thank you. Can you tell her I'll be there in ten minutes?"

Tommy nodded, like he had important instructions. He turned away and kept a calm pace until he disappeared around the side of the barn. Then Jesse heard his little feet sprint into a run. Jesse grinned. Frankie's boys were all-energy, all-the-time. They reminded Jesse of himself and Evan when they were kids.

After putting Indy back in his paddock, Jesse headed toward the house. The boys and Frankie sat at the table on the back deck. Frankie often fed Jesse if he was around for lunch, but if Frankie was cooking, Jesse knew to expect bologna sandwiches or microwaved hot dogs. He didn't discriminate against either, but when he started up the stairs to the deck, he was more than surprised to see the crew mowing down on croissant sandwiches and a side of mixed, chopped fruit.

"That looks good." Jesse adjusted the rim of his ballcap to make sure he was seeing correctly.

"Chicken salad croissants," Frankie replied, halfway through her lunch and looking like she was in heaven.

Noah held his sandwich in front of his face and squinted into the middle. "But the meat sandwich has fruit and nuts in it." He didn't look impressed. Noah was Frankie's picky eater. Jesse knew Noah would've preferred a microwaved hot dog.

"Grapes and pecans," Frankie clarified through a mouthful. "It's delicious. And if you boys eat all your lunch you can have freeze pops."

That was Frankie's bargaining chip and it generally worked. The boys focused on eating.

"Did you make this?" Jesse asked, knowing Frankie would rather scrub stock tanks or clean horse stalls than spend any time in the kitchen.

Frankie laughed. A piece of chicken flew out of her mouth and bounced onto the table. The boys thought their mother's accidental spit was hilarious and they went into a fit of laughter.

Frankie wiped her mouth with a napkin. "Oh, goodness. You know me better than that, Jesse. But thanks for the laugh." She gave him a headshake and a genuine smile. Jesse hadn't seen one of those in a while. "Hazel made us lunch and she's putting together a plate for you too."

Behind Frankie, the sliding glass door opened.

"What's so funny?" Hazel appeared holding two plates of food. Her daughter was right behind her with a third plate.

Jesse gave Hazel a once-over. Yesterday she'd arrived in her fancy car, wearing her fancy clothes. She even ran extra-fancy when the rooster chased her. Granted, the rooster was a mean old thing. Mother Clucker chased everyone. However, Hazel's dramatic reaction only emphasized the city girl that she was, so Jesse was surprised to see Hazel stride out of the kitchen wearing cutoff jean shorts and a black tank top. Her red hair was twisted into a bun on top of her head and she didn't wear a lick of make-up. She looked like she *could* belong on the farm. She must've borrowed some clothes from Frankie, because no city girl owned cutoff Wranglers. Though Jesse had never noticed Frankie filling out those shorts so well.

"The boys are just being silly," Frankie replied, snatching Jesse out of his stare. She took another bite of her chicken salad croissant and gave Hazel a grateful look. "This is *so* good."

"I'm glad you like it." Hazel offered a plate to Jesse. "Frankie said you'd be joining us. I hope you don't have a nut allergy."

Jesse took the plate. "Thank you, Ma'am." Hazel looked at him like she hadn't expected manners. "And, no. I don't have a nut allergy."

Grace took a chair next to Tommy. "When Mom makes snacks for cheer team, there's a whole list of stuff she can't use. Nuts, gluten, high fructose corn syrup, dairy, and . . . " She was trying to think of more, but gave up.

Tommy looked at Grace like she was speaking Chinese. "What's gluten?"

Grace shrugged and all the kids went back to eating.

"That's a lot of restrictions." Jesse took a seat next to Frankie's youngest, Noah, and Hazel sat across from him. Jesse didn't know anyone that refused gluten. Gluten was in all the best things.

"It's a pain, but a lot of kids at Grace's school have allergies so we have to be careful," Hazel explained. Jesse wondered if those kids were allowed to play in the dirt. Dust, dirt, and mud made for a strong immune system, but he opted to keep his opinion to himself.

Hazel popped a blueberry in her mouth, and Jesse continued to size her up. Garrett was a good friend of Jesse's and a few weeks ago, Garrett confided in him. He told Jesse that Rose had another daughter and that she'd willed half her property to a sister Frankie had never met. Furthermore, Rose's will required Hazel to live on the property for the summer, else neither woman would inherit anything. Knowing Rose most of his life, Jesse couldn't wrap his head around this request, and regretfully wondered if Rose had been of sound mind when she last changed her will. Rose was a sweetheart. She was wild and impulsive, but she had a heart bigger than Paul Bunyon. Why would she leave Frankie's happiness in the hands of a woman that had no interest in Maple Bay?

Hazel sipped her iced tea, looking uncomfortable. "Frankie told me that you train horses."

Jesse could tell Hazel was trying to fill the silence. "I do," Jesse confirmed, but didn't expand on his answer. She hadn't really asked him a question.

Tommy expanded for him. "Momma calls him the horse whisperer. Right, Momma?"

Frankie grinned. "I only call him that because he hates it."

"I'm no Robert Redford." Jesse was referring to the *horse-whisperer* title he'd unwillingly picked up sometime in the past ten years.

"Oh, come on," Frankie prodded. "You secretly love the nickname."

Jesse gave his friend a raised eyebrow. "It makes me sound like I'm some kind of horse-therapist."

"You are," Frankie said, and turned to Hazel. "He has a gift. He can figure out even the toughest horses. He works through their problems. He fixes them."

Both Hazel and Grace were looking at Jesse with curiosity, and he was ready to move the conversation in another direction—off him.

"Mom, he's not a *whisperer*." Noah raised his chubby little hand which held a strawberry piece. "He's a cowboy!"

Jesse chuckled at Noah and ruffled the little boy's hair. "Thanks for being on my side, buddy." Noah gave him a toothy smile.

Frankie winked at Noah but brought the conversation back to Jesse. "By the way, c*owboy*, how did Indy do today?"

"Good. He's coming around. I think I'll try saddling him next week, but he's definitely going to need at least a couple of months of work."

"Is he like a wild horse or something?" Grace asked, genuinely.

"Not wild. He's just had some bad experiences with people. Needs to be shown he can trust humans again," Jesse explained. "The local rescue group pulled him out of an abusive home and Frankie is fostering him."

"He was abused?" Hazel asked. "That's horrible."

Grace nodded, agreeing with her mother.

"It is, but he's in the right place now. Frankie is a wizard with nutrition. She'll have him fattened up in no time," Jesse said.

Frankie licked croissant flakes from her fingers. "I focus on his health and Jesse works on his training. Then, when he's in a better place, the rescue group can rehome him."

"That's awesome," Grace said, with the eyes of a kid reaching for an ice cream cone. Jesse's heart swelled. Yesterday he'd watched Grace with Noah's pony. She was so excited to be close to Mister Pepper that Jesse thought she might pop when she touched him. Despite her excitement, she was patient and thoughtful with each movement, doing exactly as she was shown by Noah. She gently brushed Pepper's mane and was even brave enough to give the pony a carrot. Today he saw her vigorously clean a few horse pens with the boys. Grace and Tommy took turns pushing the wheelbarrow and shoveling manure piles from the dirt, while Wyatt and Noah mostly chased each other around the pen. Jesse also noticed how Grace had stared longingly at the girls riding horses in the arena—the ones Frankie was giving lessons to.

"I heard you're staying here for the summer, right?" Jesse asked Grace and she bobbled her head in a quick answer. "Frankie has quite a few horses. Maybe if you help her with some of the barn chores, Frankie could give you some riding lessons."

Grace's mouth dropped open like a nutcracker. Usually, Jesse wouldn't offer up someone else's services, but Frankie was such a good instructor, especially with kids, and she could easily throw Grace in one of her group lessons. He knew Frankie wouldn't mind. Plus, every kid needed a horse. Heck, he'd give Grace lessons himself, but all his horses were young and green-broke. Frankie had a stable full of seasoned, patient horses.

"Totally," Frankie replied like it was no big deal. "If you can scrub buckets and shovel poop, I'm more than happy to give you—"

"Oh, no." Hazel cut Frankie off as though her daughter had just been offered a beer.

Tommy gave Hazel a cockeyed look. Jesse might've done the same.

Hazel quickly defended her response. "Grace has never been around horses before, and I don't want her getting hurt."

Noah leaned over his plate. "I'm around horses all the time and I never got hurt." He spoke through a mouthful of strawberries. "Except that one time when Spot stepped on my toe and Momma had to take me to the doctor. And then the one time I fell off Daisy."

Hazel's eyes widened even more, if that was possible, and Frankie tried to discreetly hush her son.

"Noah, you fell off Daisy because you were trying to ride her backwards," Frankie said.

Noah looked confused and then he laughed. "Oh, yeah! I forgot. That was funny."

"And he was wearing a helmet," Frankie said to Hazel. "All the kids that ride on my property wear helmets. And I always teach safety first. That's a priority. Even if my own kids don't always follow my rules." She gave Noah a glare and he stuck a blueberry in his mouth.

Hazel looked flustered. "I just don't think it's a good idea."

Jesse didn't understand Hazel's hesitation, and was about to tell her so when Grace got up from the table and ran off.

She descended the deck stairs and sprinted across the lawn. Before she retreated, Jesse saw tears pooling in her eyes.

He instinctually rose from his seat, ready to go after Grace and apologize, even though it was Hazel that made her cry.

"I didn't mean to—" he said to Hazel, but she raised her hand, telling him to stay put.

"You've done enough, thank you. I will go talk to my daughter." Hazel stood and pushed her chair back in place. "And please don't offer Grace anything else without running it by me first. Okay?"

Her words were full of proper pleasantries, but her tone was anything but friendly. Jesse nodded, almost involuntarily.

After giving Jesse one more stern glare, Hazel strode across the lawn toward an old oak tree. Grace was sitting on knotted roots. Hazel joined her in the shade.

Jesse looked at Frankie. "I didn't think that conversation would end in tears."

"Neither did I." Frankie seemed worried and Jesse felt responsible for upsetting all the women he'd been having lunch with.

"I'll go apologize." Regardless of what Jesse thought of Hazel's decision, Jesse hadn't intended to upset Grace. In fact, his offer was meant to make her smile. "I'll make it right."

Before he could stand from his chair, a shiny blue truck turned into Frankie's driveway. It was pulling a camper, but Jesse couldn't see who was behind the wheel. It wasn't a vehicle he knew.

Under the oak tree, Grace popped up from the ground and raced toward the approaching truck.

CHAPTER SEVEN

As soon as the truck stopped, Hazel's parents—Sandy and Peter—opened the doors and stepped out. Grace ran to her Grandma and Sandy opened her arms. Peter walked around the truck and joined his wife, worry on his face as he coddled his grandchild. Hazel could hear their concerned questions as she approached.

"What's the matter, my sweet child?" Sandy cooed. Her shoulder-length silver bob sparkled in the sunshine. She tilted Grace's chin up. "Why are you crying?"

Grace sniffled and pressed her face into Sandy's blouse. When Grace didn't answer, Sandy draped her arms around her and looked at Hazel with pleading eyes. "What's wrong?" she mouthed.

Hazel sighed, thinking she might've overreacted when the riding lessons were brought up. She approached and crouched down next to Grace. She put a hand on her daughter's back.

"Grace, it worries me to have you around such big animals. I just don't want you to get hurt."

Grace peeked out from her Grandma's blouse, and her wet eyelashes broke Hazel's heart. Grace wasn't one of those kids that threw tantrums. She didn't cry to get her way. Her feelings had been truly hurt, and Hazel felt horrible for reacting so brashly. She should've taken the time to think it through.

"How about I talk more with Frankie about the lessons?" Hazel brushed a wispy tendril from her daughter's cheek. She could tell how much Grace wanted to ride. "Listen, I promise you'll get time with the horses this summer. I just want to make sure your time with them is safe."

Grace blinked her brown eyes and gave Hazel a sad excuse for a smile. "You'll talk with Frankie?"

"Yes." Hazel kissed Grace on the forehead. "Now give your Grandma and Grandpa big hugs. They packed up our stuff and drove it all the way here."

Grace wiped her eyes before grabbing her grandma around the waist. "Thank you. Are you guys staying here too?" She gave her grandpa a big hug too.

"No, they're headed out on their big camping adventure," Hazel said, knowing her parents had been planning a month-long road trip for the past year.

"Yep," Peter replied. "After we get you two settled, Sandy and I are off to the Boundary Waters for the first stop of the summer. We'll be canoeing by this afternoon." Peter was beyond excited for this camping trip. He was already in his fishing gear. Sandy was less of a fan of the woods and water but agreed to the trip if they bought a camper.

"You guys are going to have so much fun." Hazel kissed her mother on the cheek and hugged her father.

"I sure hope so." Sandy laughed.

"Oh, we sure are," Peter replied. "But you just say the word and we'll setup camp right here."

Hazel smiled, knowing she'd won the lottery when Sandy and Peter adopted her. "No, no. You guys go and have fun. Grace and I are just fine. This will be an adventure for us too." Though Hazel hoped it wouldn't be *too* much of an adventure.

"We're just a call away if you need us. You know we'd come back in a jiffy," Sandy said, and Peter agreed with a serious nod.

Last night when Hazel called her parents to tell them about the will and the property, she knew they'd do everything possible to support her decision. In fact, they would've packed her bags and driven to Maple Bay last night if Hazel hadn't insisted that they get some rest. Her parents were nearing seventy, and didn't need to be on an unnecessary goose-chase down dark country roads.

Sandy patted both Hazel and Grace on the shoulders. "Anything for you two. Now, where should we put your stuff? It's all in the back of the truck. We packed all your summer clothes and a few boxes of household things. The neighbor's son loaded it all up for us this morning."

"We're staying in Frankie's guest room until we can move into the carriage house. Grace and I will take it all up there, but first, let's get you guys some iced tea. Did you eat lunch?"

"We already ate, but iced tea sounds lovely," Sandy replied.

"Grace, can you go get your grandparents some iced tea? I'm going to unload our stuff from the truck."

"Sure." Grace smiled softly, seeming content with the hope Hazel had given her about riding.

When Grace walked toward the deck, Sandy asked, "What was that about?"

"Oh, Grace wants to take riding lessons, but I'm not so sure. Seems dangerous."

Hazel expected her mother to immediately agree with her. Instead she raised an eyebrow.

"Let the child ride a horse," Sandy said. "Isn't that every girl's dream?"

"She'll have a blast," Peter added.

Hazel's mouth popped open. "You guys didn't even let me get a dog when I was a kid." Hazel vividly remembered begging for a dog. She wanted one just like the neighbor's bouncing Golden Retriever.

"Well, that's different. A dog lives inside the house, and I didn't want to clean up after all that hair. But maybe I should've let you get one anyhow." Sandy squeezed Hazel's arm. "Besides, you can't protect Grace from everything. What are you going to do when she starts driving?"

Hazel shuddered at the thought. "I might have to bubble-wrap her."

Sandy and Peter chuckled, but for a second, Hazel seriously considered where she could buy bubble-wrap in bulk. In six short years Grace would be driving. On the road. By herself.

"Life is moving too fast," Hazel admitted, to her parents and to herself.

"It does that. Seems to get faster every year. Wait until you're our age. Months go by in the blink of an eye. That's why you need to savor the moment. Eat the cake. Buy the shoes. Ride the horse." Sandy's eyes crinkled at her last suggestion.

"Okay, Mom. I'll let her ride the horse." Hazel shook her head light-heartedly at her mother's cavalier attitude as a grandmother. There was no way Sandy would've allowed Hazel to ride a horse when she was a child.

Sandy winked at her. "Good choice."

A stampede of quick footsteps grabbed Hazel's attention and she turned to find all three boys running toward her.

Grace was behind them, trying not to spill two mason jars full of iced tea. Jesse walked with her.

Tommy arrived first. "Momma said we need to carry some stuff upstairs." He peeked at the truck and looked excited. Wyatt and Noah were seconds behind him.

"Who are all these handsome little men?" Sandy asked, pressing her hands together.

"I'm Tommy. And these are my little brothers, Wyatt and Noah."

"Very nice to meet you," Sandy said and gave them each a hug. Peter shook their hands like they were little adults. "I'm Sandy, Hazel's mother, and this is Peter, Hazel's father."

Noah pointed behind him. "And that's our Uncle Jesse."

Jesse tipped the brim of his baseball hat at Sandy and shook Peter's hand. "Nice to meet you both. Grace said you have some suitcases to unload?"

"We do," Sandy replied.

"That'd be great if you big strong boys could help us with them," Peter said, and the boys ran to the truck. Jesse opened the tailgate and started unloading suitcases.

Grace offered her grandparents the full mason jars. "Here you go."

"Thank you, Sweets." Sandy took a sip.

"Those might be too heavy for the boys to carry," Hazel said, but Jesse was already delegating boxes.

"We've got it," Jesse replied without looking back. "Why don't you take your parents to the deck to enjoy their iced tea? Frankie would like to meet them."

Hazel had intended to take her parents over and introduce them to Frankie. She also knew Jesse was helping her, but she couldn't help but feel miffed. Why did he keep sticking his nose in her business?

"Thank you, Jesse," Sandy replied, and put her hand on Hazel's arm to steer her toward the deck. "That sounds like a great idea."

As Hazel and her parents walked toward the deck, Hazel glanced back. Jesse had all the kids lined out. Tommy and Wyatt were double-teaming one of the smaller suitcases, each holding an end. Grace had a stack of linens and a quilt. Noah hung tight to two pillows. They all shuffled their way toward the house. Jesse flipped two large suitcases on their sides and grabbed the handles, carrying them like they weighed nothing.

Sandy looked over her shoulder. "He's certainly a tall drink of water." She sipped her tea and side-eyed Hazel as she waited for a response.

"He's something." Hazel looked forward, not wanting *a tall drink of water* in her life. Especially one that inserted himself where he wasn't needed.

"The boys' uncle?"

"A friend."

Sandy made a sound like she was mulling over the meaning of that word. "Could he be your *friend?*"

"Not likely." Hazel gave her mother a look, but figured the question was coming. In the past few months, Sandy had been gently and not-so-gently urging Hazel to date again. But Hazel wasn't ready.

Jesse was a good-looking man. It wasn't like Hazel hadn't noticed. She had eyes. But one act of chivalry wasn't enough to impress Hazel. Hazel had given Bill over fifteen years of her life, and when she married him, she would've never guessed he'd betray her. She thought she knew him. She thought he loved her. But she'd learned from her mistakes, and she wasn't about to make them again.

After lunch, Hazel drove her parents, Frankie, and Grace over to the carriage house. There were a few boxes to drop-off which contained mostly dishes and décor—nothing Hazel or Grace would need while they stayed with Frankie. After hauling the boxes inside, Hazel found she wanted to explore. With her parents here, it somehow felt more real that she and Grace were going to make this their home for the summer.

"This is such a beautiful building. So much history." Sandy brushed her hand over the black leather harnesses that hung on the wall. "When I was a little girl, there were still quite a few working carriage houses in our town. It's a shame so many of them were torn down for new construction."

"This building is over a hundred years old," Frankie said. "Actually, there's a picture upstairs of the original owners not long after they built the carriage house. Helen and Thomas Benson. In the picture, they're all dressed up and sitting in a carriage hitched to a big Belgian horse. Mom found the picture in the library's newspaper files and had it reprinted. It's pretty neat."

"I'd love to see it," Sandy and Peter said at the same time.

"I would too," Hazel added. "Actually, I haven't seen the upstairs yet. Let's go look."

Yesterday had been a whirlwind and Hazel hadn't ventured into the hayloft to assess the state of the apartment. She hoped it wouldn't take too much work. She didn't want to overstay her welcome in Frankie's house.

Grace ran upstairs first, and Hazel wasn't sure what to think of her daughter's silence. When Hazel reached the top of the stairs, she found herself falling in suit with her daughter's stunned face.

"Oh my," Hazel muttered, taking in the open space which looked like . . . an old hayloft.

"This is where we're going to live?" Grace asked, tentatively.

One side of the loft had an angled ceiling and dormer windows. The side that faced the lake had no windows at all, but featured a square wooden door which Hazel guessed was the door that would've been used to fill the loft with hay. There were old kitchen cabinets stacked in a corner, not hung on a wall. A sink sat haphazardly in another corner. There wasn't a bathroom. The only light was a single, bare bulb that hung from the ceiling.

"I thought you said it just needed appliances," Hazel said to Frankie, looking around like she'd stumbled into the wrong room.

"It does." Frankie's voice had gone up an octave, like she was trying to be extra chipper. She started pointing at things. "It's plumbed for a kitchen and a bathroom. All the electrical is in and the far corner is piped for a wood stove. Actually, the wood stove is downstairs under the tarp, along with some furniture Mom had been gathering for the loft and the other rooms she was going to rent out."

Capped pipes and colored wires protruded from walls. Hazel quickly realized how much money and work it was going to take to transform this space into a livable area. Her excitement started to sink.

"It's a blank slate." Frankie was trying to sweeten the pot. "You can make it however you like."

Hazel didn't know what to say. She'd expected to put in a few days, or maybe a week of hard work. At best, it would be a month before the loft would be a functioning space. And how was she going to front the money to fix it up? At the end of the summer Hazel would officially own the carriage house and she could sell the property, but right now, her bank account was practically bare. Hence the reason she was living with her parents.

"It's got good bones," Peter said, and touched one of the big beams that ran along the angled roof.

"And aren't these dormers sweet?" Sandy bent down to peer into one of the dormer windows. She peeked back at Grace. "Would be a great place to curl up with a book."

Sandy was the eternal optimist. Hazel had become a realist, especially over the past few years, and she saw the reality of what lay before her.

"I guess." Grace cocked her head, like she was trying to see what her grandma saw.

Frankie pushed her hands into her jean pockets like she felt bad for overexaggerating the state of the loft. "Like I said, I'm more than happy to help you work on the place. And Garrett is real handy. He actually did the electrical in here."

Hazel looked at Frankie, confused. Frankie had three kids, a barn full of horses, and was a riding instructor. How much extra time could she possibly have? Plus, Hazel hadn't even met Garrett yet.

"This is a lot more work than I thought it would be." Hazel kept herself from saying she was barely squeaking by on the child support Bill *sometimes* paid her. She didn't have any extra cash to support a fixer-upper. Since the divorce, Hazel hadn't even applied for a credit card, knowing her credit had been trashed by all the bad financial decisions made in her marriage. She often wanted to kick herself for letting Bill handle all their finances, for being so naive.

Sandy put her hand on Hazel's arm and guided her across the loft, closer to the stack of cabinets that were in dire need of new paint. "Is it the money you're worried about?"

"I mean—" Hazel started as she looked around the loft. There were projects she knew she could do—cleaning, sanding, painting. She'd even learned some basic plumbing skills. Bill worked long hours, and she'd been in a few watery predicaments before. But where would she come up with the funds to buy all the supplies? The appliances? Hire anyone to help her?

"Your father and I could help you. We could loan you the money."

Hazel broke out of her ricocheting thoughts and looked at her mother. Her sweet, sweet mother. Hazel knew Sandy wanted to help. Her parents had always been there for her, through thick and thin, but they'd never had a ton of money themselves and now they were just starting to enjoy their golden years.

Hazel shook her head. "You and Daddy have worked hard. You deserve to enjoy this time of life. Don't you worry about me. I've got ideas for this place."

"Well, you know we're just a call away." Sandy smiled, but kept her hand on Hazel's arm, like she wasn't quite sure of her answer.

Tomorrow, Hazel would go into Maple Bay and search for a job. There had to be something she could do over the summer. Just as she decided this, Grace turned the latch that secured the square, wooden hay-door. Hinges creaked as the door opened, exposing a breathtaking view of the lake. For a second, Hazel pictured big, tall windows on that side of the loft where she could soak in the picturesque lake view every morning, noon, and night. But her vision was cut short when the hinges somehow burst apart, and the door toppled to the ground. Hazel gasped and put her hand to her mouth as the wooden door crashed against the patio below.

"Oops," Grace said, looking back at her mother with a wide-eyed apology.

Hazel walked over and stuck her head out the opening. The door was still in one piece, but it was now amongst the life jackets and Adirondack chairs below.

Frankie, Sandy, and Peter joined her at the new window.

"Beautiful view," Sandy said.

Hazel tried to channel the optimism of her mother, even as the house she'd just inherited fell apart before her eyes. "I think we better make use of that tarp downstairs to keep the birds out until I can get this fixed."

"I'll go get it, Momma," Grace offered and ran for the stairs.

As she did, Hazel spotted Frankie's boys. They were in swimsuits, splashing in the shallows along the shore. A man was walking toward them, in swim trunks and a white t-shirt. Hazel squinted her eyes at him. Was that Jesse? He had a beach ball under his arm and looked like he'd just come out of the baby-blue cottage on the edge of the water. Hazel had noticed the cottage the first time she visited the carriage house. It was her closest neighbor.

"Or we can ask Jesse to help us put the door back on its hinges," Frankie said, and stuck her head out the opening. She cupped her hands around her mouth and called Jesse's name. He turned, looking confused, and Frankie motioned him over with her arm.

"Can you grab your toolbox? We need your help!" Frankie yelled, and Jesse turned back toward the little blue cottage.

"Does he live there?" Hazel asked, and Frankie confirmed her suspicions.

The meddling cowboy was Hazel's neighbor.

Hazel nodded and sighed, looking from the broken door to the irritating neighbor. She wondered how many more challenges this summer would throw at her.

CHAPTER EIGHT

"Where did I put those contracts?" Frankie asked herself as she dug through another pile of paperwork on her desk. She had about ten minutes until her next client arrived—a little girl coming for her first riding lesson—and she needed an agreement for the girl's parents to sign. Frankie hated paperwork, but it was a necessary evil. She had to have each client's information on file just in case there was an emergency. Plus, there was all the legal mumbo-jumbo in the contract to keep her from getting the pants sued off her if someone accidently got hurt on her property. "I know I made more copies. They're here somewhere."

Frankie picked up a fly mask that had somehow made it onto her desk and moved three empty coffee cups, but didn't see the contracts anywhere. *Ugh.* How was it that she could keep ten horses cared for, three rambunctious boys alive, and her stable spotless, but her tiny office in the barn was continually a mess? The ten-by-ten room looked like the inside of the microwave after a hotdog explosion. Stuff was everywhere.

"You need some help?" a voice asked.

Frankie looked up and found Hazel standing in the open doorway. She was wearing tan capris and a flowy top. Her red hair was curled, and she'd done her makeup. Frankie had barely brushed her teeth this morning.

"Oh, more than you know." Frankie half-chuckled to brush off the reality of her reply.

Hazel offered up a little brown sack. "This might help."

Frankie immediately recognized the stamped logo on the sack. "You went to Patty Cakes?"

"I did. And I remembered what you said about the Maple Bars." Hazel took two steps to Frankie's desk and handed the sack to her. "There's a half dozen in there. Grace and I each had one at the bakery. They're to die for."

Frankie's mouth watered as she opened the bag and pulled out the rectangular pastry. She took a big bite and closed her eyes, savoring the flakey sweetness and creamy maple frosting. It was like biting into a stack of pancakes. "These are my absolute favorite." She held up the donut like it was an award. "Thank you. You just made my day."

"It's a little thank you for letting us stay in your house."

"If you plan on continuing to feed me chicken croissant sandwiches and maple bars, you can live with me forever." Frankie was kidding . . . but not really.

Hazel smiled, but there was an awkward silence that followed.

"Did you need something?" Frankie knew she should be searching her files for the paperwork she needed, but Hazel looked out of place. And it wasn't just the beige-colored pants she sported in the barn. If Frankie had worn those she'd already have horse slobber on them.

"No, I—" Hazel shifted her weight from foot to foot. "Well, actually, I was wondering if you know of anyone looking for help."

"Help?"

"I need a job." Hazel seemed sheepish about her statement.

"Oh," Frankie replied. "What kind of job?"

"Anything really. I stopped by the diner, but they don't have any openings right now. I also swung by the grocery store, bookstore, feedstore, coffee shop. Even asked at Patty Cakes. Everyone was real sweet and took my information, but no one seems to be hiring right now."

Frankie wrinkled her forehead, trying to think of options. "Is that what you went into town for?"

Hazel nodded. "Yes. That, and I sold my car."

"You did what?"

"I sold my car. I put it online last night and a woman from the town over messaged me this morning. Met me at Patty Cakes and she ended up buying it."

"Why'd you do that?" Frankie might've been looking at Hazel like she was crazy, because Hazel looked uncomfortable again. Frankie checked her facial expression.

"I mentioned yesterday that Grace's father and I got a divorce about a year ago. Well, the whole thing left my bank account a little thinner than I'd like. And after seeing all the work that needs to be done on the carriage house, I figured selling my car would be a good way to get a big chunk of cash. I can use it to buy supplies, appliances, fix up the carriage house. That, and getting a job for the summer."

"Oh, that's horrible," Frankie said, and Hazel pressed her lips together. "The divorce-thing, I mean. Not that you had to sell your car or need a job. I mean, you can always drive my truck." Frankie knew she was babbling.

"Thanks, but it's a short walk into town. Only the distance of a few city blocks. I was just hoping to get a job I could easily walk to. Maybe an administrative job? I'm good with a computer. I never finished college, but I've been a secretary at Grace's elementary school for the past year. I've also been part of parent-teacher organizations since Grace started school. I've organized fundraisers, bake sales, field trips. I helped my ex with his real estate business when he needed paperwork filed, appointments made, or data plugged into spreadsheets."

Hazel continued listing all the things that might help her get a job, but Frankie started to tune her out. Instead, she glanced around, taking in the cluttered desk, overstuffed file drawers, and the computer that was collecting dust. Forget the diner and the grocery store. Frankie was the one that needed help. Rose had always been there to help Frankie with her business, but now, Frankie was more than overwhelmed. "What would you think about helping me for the summer?"

Hazel stopped talking. Her mouth was stuck open. "You mean here, with the horses?"

"Mostly this." Frankie circled both hands around the office, still holding tight to her half-eaten donut. "Ever since Mom passed, I barely have time to think. She used to help me with everything. With the boys, the house, the horses."

Hazel closed her mouth, looking somber. "I didn't mean to ask for another favor." She looked like she might turn around.

"It wouldn't be a favor, Hazel. I need the help and I can afford to pay you a few dollars over minimum wage. I need someone to get my files out of this . . . this state of chaos," Frankie stuttered, knowing there were years of papers scattered around the room. "And I've got summer riding camps scheduled every Monday through Friday from next week until the end of August. Do you think you could help me organize the day camps? Could you wrangle kids too?"

"Wrangle them?" Hazel had a mix of alarm and curiosity on her face.

"I'll handle all the horse stuff, but I need someone to make lunches, help with the kids, organize activities like crafts and reading and games."

The alarm started melting from Hazel's face. "I can do that."

"Really?"

"Yeah. Actually, I'd love to. I love kids. Wish I'd had a boatload myself. And I love to organize."

Frankie blinked, feeling a heavy weight lifting from her shoulders. "Well, I'm glad someone enjoys it . . . organizing, that is. I'd much rather clean a stall or a horse than sit at a desk."

"I didn't expect you to offer me a job," Hazel said. "I guess those Maple Bars really are magic." She smiled.

"They are one-hundred percent magic." Frankie took another bite and licked a dab of maple frosting from her lip. "Can you start today? Like right now?"

"Um, sure. What would you like me to do?"

"I've got a riding lesson that's supposed to start in a few minutes, and I need to go get Daisy out of the pasture. Would you mind digging through this mess and see if you can find a blank copy of a contract called a Lesson Agreement? I need a copy for this little girl's parents to fill out. Otherwise, you can print a new copy. The file is on the computer desktop, but my printer has a mind of its own. The last time I tried to use it the stupid thing jammed and then spit out blank sheets."

Hazel joined Frankie behind the desk, looking like she wasn't quite sure where to start. "Alright. Yes. Go get your horse ready." She started flipping through a few papers. "I'll get you a copy of the Lesson Agreement."

"Great." Frankie stepped away from the clutter. "Just come find me if you have questions."

Hazel nodded but didn't look up from the desk. She looked intent on finding her target. Frankie took another bite of her donut and thought the morning was already looking brighter.

Printer paper, paper clips, notepads, file folders. Hazel made a list of supplies Frankie needed for her office. It was the middle of the afternoon, and in her first day Hazel had managed to sift through all the loose papers on Frankie's desk. She now had them divided into neat piles. She hadn't found blank copies of the Lesson Agreement, but managed to get the printer working. She created ten fresh copies, one of which now had Frankie's newest client's information scribbled on it. Hazel wasn't a genius with technology, but she had one trick that worked ninety-nine percent of the time—press the restart button. After unplugging and restarting the printer, the machine quickly spit out ten fresh copies. Now, if only that trick applied to life's mistakes. There were a few things Hazel would like to press the restart button on.

Since the paperwork was organized and ready to file— once Hazel got file folders—she thought the office could use a cleaning. It was in a barn, but if Hazel would be overseeing this space for the summer, she would keep it tidy. Finding a rag in one of the desk drawers, Hazel started wiping down the computer, desk, and the pictures which filled the walls. Behind the desk there was a colorful painting of mountains and running horses. The other walls were full of family photos, ribbons, and shelves of trophies from years past. Hazel glanced at each picture as she dusted off the frames. There were many different horses in the pictures, but what stuck out to Hazel was the joy in each photograph. There were pictures of the boys when they were tiny, riding horses and laughing, posing for the camera with silly faces. There were pictures of Frankie at rodeos and horse shows. There were a couple of pictures from Frankie and Garrett's wedding, even one where both Frankie and Garrett were riding horses and holding hands. And there was a common theme that popped up in most every picture—Rose.

It was obvious that Rose was very close to Frankie. In the pictures, she looked like a beaming mother, a doting grandmother. She looked to be an important and constant part of Frankie's life. Hazel found her gut twist with this realization, knowing that Rose had chosen not to be a part of Hazel's life, or Grace's.

Instead of torturing herself, Hazel pulled her eyes from the pictures and focused on a thick wooden cross that hung on the other wall. The cross was covered in colorful leather pieces that boasted intricate stitching and were attached to the wood by metal grommets. Turquoise stones decorated the center. Hazel wiped down the edges of the cross, thinking it was truly a piece of art. She wondered who made it.

"I haven't seen the top of that desk in ten years," Frankie said, walking through the door. She was leading a horse. The horse popped its head into the office like it needed to see what Frankie was talking about.

Hazel had been so in her head that she hadn't even noticed the clip-clip of horse hooves down the barn aisle. "I've got a list of things I need to get you at the store, but once I have more files, I can completely clean off your desk."

"Looks great. Thank you." Frankie's eyes went to Hazel's hand which still had the rag pressed against the leather-clad cross. There was a quick flash of emotion that grazed Frankie's face.

Hazel dropped her hand. "I thought I'd do some cleaning, but is there anything else you'd like me to get done today?"

Instead of answering her question, Frankie said, "Those were Mom's."

Hazel looked at the wall and then back at Frankie. "What were?"

"The leather pieces on the cross." Frankie stepped toward Hazel and touched the cross that Hazel had been dusting. "Each of these leather pieces came from one of Mom's cowboy boots." Frankie's finger grazed over the red, brown, and black leather. Suddenly Hazel could see that each layered piece was the top of a boot. "She loved her cowboy boots."

Hazel could physically feel Frankie's pain. It hung between them, and Hazel couldn't help but back away. She wasn't sure if she wanted to give Frankie space or if she just couldn't absorb the intimacy of the moment. There were pieces of Hazel that would never understand what Rose did, how she abandoned one daughter but loved another. Somehow, the knowledge of the pictures and the boots made those pieces a little more jagged.

But none of that was Frankie's fault, so Hazel dipped her eyes and said, "It's beautiful."

Frankie shook herself out of her thoughts. "Jesse's mom made it for me. You'll have to meet her one of these days. Joyce was Mom's best friend. She has a place next to Jesse's. Can craft and quilt with the best of them."

Hazel felt stuck. She wanted to know more about her biological mother, but each new piece of information was overwhelming her. "Are you thirsty? I'm going to get a water from the house. Do you want one?"

Giggles and footfalls headed down the barn aisle and one of the boys yelled for Frankie.

"Mom!" He lengthened the word out like it had multiple syllables, and Tommy showed up in the doorway.

"Hi, Daisy." Tommy rubbed the horse on its nose.

"You guys all done with your chores?" Frankie asked.

"We've got two more buckets to scrub," Tommy said. Noah, Wyatt, and Grace showed up behind him.

"You better hurry. I'm going to untack Daisy and brush her, and then I'm done with lessons. If all the buckets are clean, we can get out the sprinkler."

All three boys lite up like Christmas lights and disappeared from the doorway. Grace pet Daisy gently on the shoulder before running off.

Frankie gathered the lead rope in her hands. "Your parents brought Grace a swimsuit, right?"

"They did."

"Good. It's about hot enough to fry an egg on a sidewalk. I've got popsicles and a sprinkler the kids can run through. Grace is welcome to join. You too."

"To run through the sprinkler?" Hazel was sweaty, but that didn't mean she wanted to put on a swimsuit and run around the yard.

Frankie shrugged. "If you want. Sometimes I join the kids, but I'll probably just sit on the deck with a cold glass of wine."

Hazel set the dust rag down on the desk. "That sounds really nice."

Then she remembered the other thing she was going to ask Frankie. She spit it out before she thought too much more about it. "I've also been meaning to talk to you about riding lessons for Grace."

"Jesse and I didn't mean to get in the middle of anything," Frankie started right away. "He shouldn't have offered the lessons to Grace without asking you, but I know he meant well. And, if you change your mind about Grace riding, the offer is still on the table. I'm happy to give her lessons. In fact, she could join in on the summer camps. That way you'd be around to watch her ride too."

Hazel gave her a crooked smile. Frankie had a really big heart, and Hazel felt bad for lumping her in with all her feelings about Rose.

"My mind has been changed," Hazel said. "But I want to pay you for the lessons and the camp."

"Nope," Frankie said, matter-of-factly. "Grace can help the boys with their chores around here and that will be the payment. I won't accept anything else."

Hazel was grateful, but uncomfortable with the offer. She was already living in Frankie's house and under her employment. But instead of arguing, Hazel started thinking about what else she could do to help Frankie and the kids. If Frankie wouldn't let her pay for riding camp, Hazel was prepared to cook up a storm. "Well, I hope you're hungry. Because I plan to do a lot of cooking. And I won't take no for an answer."

Frankie's eyes twinkled. "I'm always hungry." She joined Daisy in the barn aisle. "Meet you on the deck?"

"Meet you there," Hazel replied. A popsicle and a glass of wine sounded like the perfect combination to take the edge off the humid afternoon.

CHAPTER NINE

"Stay," Jesse said to Blue, his black-and-white border collie. The dog laid down obediently on the patio, and Jesse slid open the carriage house door. He slipped inside, intending to drop off the new door hinges and then head over to Frankie's to work with Indy. He'd spent most of the afternoon working with a few Thoroughbreds that were fresh off the racetrack. They were high-strung and fast, but not fast enough to bring in the money, so a client of his snatched them up at auction. She hoped to eventually turn them into barrel horses. Jesse would be working with the Thoroughbreds for the next few months to undo everything they'd learned on the track. Today, he'd spent a few hours with each horse, using patience to ease their anxieties. However, the afternoon had gotten away from him, and now it was nearly five o'clock. He'd only have an hour to work with Indy. Jesse didn't like to rush his training sessions, because horses picked up on stress and that was the last thing he wanted to give them. But this morning Jesse told his mother, Joyce, he would be over for dinner, and being late to supper was not acceptable in the Weston family.

Heading up the carriage house stairs, Jesse paused when he heard a *thump*. Was someone here? He didn't see Hazel's car parked outside when he pulled into the driveway.

"Knock, knock," Jesse called up the stairs. "Hello? Hazel?"

No reply. Maybe the boys were playing hide and seek? Jesse climbed the rest of the stairs, hoping he wouldn't have to chase out a racoon like he did last summer when Noah left the carriage house door open overnight. But when Jesse got to the top of the stairs, it wasn't a wily racoon he discovered. It was a dancing Hazel.

Jesse paused, his hand still on the railing.

Hazel had her back to him. She was standing in front of a kitchen cabinet that was propped up on two sawhorses. Her red hair was whipped into a messy bun. She wore black athletic shorts and a t-shirt that was tied into a knot on her side, exposing her bare middle. She was sanding the edges of the cabinet by hand and dancing as she did so.

Jesse quickly realized why Hazel hadn't heard him. She had white ear buds in. The cord dangled down her back and led to a pocket in her shorts. Her shoulders and hips swayed to a beat Jesse couldn't hear. He knew he shouldn't be watching, but for a few seconds he couldn't help himself.

Hazel was having a good ole' time. She must've been listening to a dang good song because she raised her sandpaper in the air and gave it a few sways, like a flag. Jesse found himself smiling at her carefree shimmies, but when Hazel started to sing, she must've caught a glimpse of him. She yelped and jumped around to face Jesse.

"What are you doing?" She pressed her hand to her chest like he'd given her a heart attack. Then she untied the knot in her t-shirt as though her stomach was on fire and her shirt was the only thing that could put it out. The gray cotton spilled down and covered her middle. She pulled the buds from her ears—all while looking at him like he was some peeping Tom. "You can't just come in here. What if I was changing or . . . or something?"

Or something? "But you were just dancing, right?"

Hazel looked offended. "It doesn't matter if I was *just* dancing. I wasn't expecting company, and this is my place now. You can't just barge in here whenever you feel like it."

Jesse was confused by Hazel's reaction. How had the carefree-dancing Hazel turned so quickly into a fire-breathing dragon? Besides, the carriage house wasn't her place yet. Hazel would have to make it through the summer, and judging by the way her blood pressure had skyrocketed in her first few days in Maple Bay, Jesse wasn't so sure she'd make it to September. "I didn't see your car outside. I was just going to drop off new hinges for the hay door." Jesse held up the hardware as proof. "Had some extra in my barn and thought you could use them."

Hazel squinted at him.

"For the hay door," he added. "The one that fell off yesterday."

She looked at him like he was another rooster coming to spur her in the leg. Continuing to clarify, Jesse pointed to the heavy wooden door he'd picked up off the patio yesterday and carried back into the loft.

Her shoulders relaxed. She set the sandpaper down on the cabinet, next to a few other tools and an electronic sander. "Let me grab my purse. How much do I owe you?"

"You don't owe me anything," Jesse replied, but that stiffened her up again.

"No, let me get my purse. I can't just take those from you." She looked around the loft, apparently for her purse, and Jesse wondered why she was so resistant to accepting help. Frankly, it was annoying.

"Think of it as a welcome-to-the-neighborhood present," Jesse offered. That's what people did in Maple Bay. They helped each other. Maybe the city had taught Hazel otherwise. "When Garrett is home this weekend, we'll put the hinges on and hang it for you."

Hazel made a dismissive motion with her hands. "That's okay. I'm sure I can do it."

He raised a brow at her. "You think you can lift that door and slide it into its hinges? It has to be a hundred pounds."

Even Jesse knew he should wait for a second set of hands to conquer that job.

"I mean, I could hire a handyman or something."

"Why? It's not a big deal. I promise. Garrett and I can do it." Jesse felt like he was convincing Hazel to take a polar plunge in the lake come December. He was just about to give up, leave the hinges, and head out to finish his workday when Hazel walked toward him.

"I must've left my purse downstairs. Please, just let me pay you for the hinges. I insist—"

Her last word came out in a squeak, and suddenly Hazel was on her way to the floor. In her misguided search for her purse, she'd wrapped an ankle in the sander cord and tripped herself.

The yellow cord acted like a snare and Hazel toppled forward in an awkward blaze of hands and knees. Jesse immediately lurched up the last stair and managed to catch Hazel under her arms. She slammed into his chest, but Jesse kept them both upright, avoiding a disastrous tumble down the stairs.

Hazel went ridged in his arms, and Jesse half-expected to get blamed for tripping her.

Then she put a hand on his chest, lifted her head, and looked him straight in the eye. They were close enough to breathe the same air. "I can't believe I just did that. I'm so sorry. Did I hurt you?" she asked.

Up close Hazel didn't look like a fire-breathing dragon. Her emerald green eyes were soft, worried. They searched his face.

Jesse held her close, making sure she got her balance. "No, I'm fine." Though he found himself a little dazed by her proximity. She smelled sweet—like strawberry shortcake—even though she'd been working and dancing in a stuffy, hot loft. Her freckled face glistened. A few strands of red hair were loose from her bun and stuck to her face and neck. "Are you okay?"

"I stubbed my toe pretty good, but otherwise I'm okay." Hazel leaned into him and shook her leg, trying to get her foot free from the electrical cord. She clung to his shoulders until she shook free of the cord. When it slapped the ground, she looked back at Jesse and his eyes must've held all the shock he was feeling as he held her.

Hazel quickly put both feet on the ground and dropped her hands like he'd stung her. "Oh, I—"

A little voice from downstairs cut Hazel off. "Daddy?"

Jesse glanced down the stairs to see his little girl, Charlie, bouncing up the staircase toward him. She was followed by Jesse's mother, Joyce, and his dog. "What you do?" Charlie asked.

He kind of wondered that himself.

Charlie sprung up the rest of the stairs, and Jesse scooped her into his arms. "Hey, Princess." She wore leggings and the rainbow-colored tutu Joyce had given her this year for her fifth birthday. The outfit was perfectly accented with rubber boots—at least, the outfit was perfect in Jesse's eye. He brushed Charlie's white-blonde curls from her face. "Did you drag your Grandma all the way over to the house to get your tutu?"

Charlie gave him a smile, like she knew she wasn't supposed to do that but couldn't resist.

"I told her we'd come get it if she helped me pull weeds," Joyce said, now halfway up the stairs. Blue followed behind her. "When we were at your house, Charlie spotted Blue laying outside the carriage house door. Figured you were in here."

"Hi!" Charlie waved at Hazel.

"Hi, there," Hazel replied with a smile, though she still looked dazed.

"Hazel, this is my daughter, Charlie, and my mom, Joyce."

Charlie waved at Hazel again. Hazel waved back, warmth returning to her face.

Jesse switched Charlie to his other hip and met Joyce on the stairs, helping her the rest of the way up. She gasped when she got to the top.

"As I live and breathe," Joyce started. "You're Rose's daughter, aren't you? Hazel?"

Hazel nodded and stepped forward to offer her hand. "I am. Very nice to meet you, Joyce."

Joyce ignored Hazel's hand and snatched her into a big hug, rocking her back and forth as she squeezed her. Jesse chuckled. Hazel was obviously not used to being greeted like that by a stranger.

Joyce pulled back from the hug but kept her hands on Hazel's arms. "My, oh, my. You look just like Rose." Joyce paused for a few long beats. "We are so very glad to have you here." She rubbed Hazel's arms like she was warming her up. Maybe she was, because Hazel didn't look nearly as flustered as when Jesse had barged into the carriage house.

"Thank you," Hazel replied.

"I want to give her a hug too." Charlie squirmed and Jesse set her down. As soon as her feet hit the floor, Charlie ran to Hazel. Hazel didn't miss a beat. She squatted down and picked Jesse's daughter up like she'd known her forever. Charlie's blonde curls bounced.

"I love your tutu." Hazel brushed the fluffy fabric with her fingers.

Charlie giggled and pressed her hands to her face. "Grandma gave me this one. Daddy got me a pink one and a purple one and a sparkly one."

A big smile grew on Hazel's face. "Well, those are pretty special presents."

"Do you want to see them all?" Charlie asked.

Hazel looked a little flustered, like she didn't want to let Charlie down. For a split-second, Jesse's heart skipped a beat.

Jesse held an arm out to Charlie. "Hazel has some work to do right now. Let's let her get back to it."

Charlie pouted her lips, but then said, "Okay."

"I'd love to see them another time." Hazel set Charlie down, and the little girl skipped over to Jesse.

Joyce patted Charlie's head. "Would you like to join us for dinner?" Joyce asked Hazel. "I'm making ribs, mashed potatoes, and green bean casserole."

"Oh, thank you very much, but I'm a sweaty mess and I should finish the project I started." Hazel pointed back toward the partially sanded cabinets.

"Maybe this weekend then?" Joyce prodded. "For Sunday dinner?"

"Of course. I'd love to." Hazel tucked a loose strand of hair behind her ear. "It was very nice to meet you, Joyce. You too, Charlie."

"Yeah," Charlie said. "Glad we could all give you hugs."

His daughter's comment reminded Jesse of how Hazel had accidently tossed herself into his arms. He looked back at Hazel, expecting her chilly demeanor to return.

Instead, she replied matter-of-factly to Charlie. "Me too." Then she gave Jesse a tight-lipped smile. "Thank you for your help."

Jesse nodded and followed Charlie and Joyce down the stairs. He thought he might've just received a truce from the fire-breathing, rooster-fighting city-lady. But he wasn't exactly sure what to do with that truce.

.

CHAPTER TEN

Hazel's first full day on the job was surprisingly fun. Frankie put her in charge of preparations for the summer riding camps, which were set to start next week. While Frankie taught lessons and took care of the horses, Hazel did some of her favorite things—planning and organizing. She made lists, planned meals, grocery shopped, and created activities to keep the kids busy when they wouldn't be with the horses. The first group of campers would be five kids that had little to no experience with horses, and it was the perfect group for Grace to join to learn all the basics of horse care and riding. Hazel was still worried for Grace's safety, but her anxieties waned as she watched Frankie give lessons and handle the horses. Frankie could've been a teacher. She was amazing with the kids. And all of Frankie's horses were extremely well-mannered and gentle. Plus, it helped that Hazel was now part of the riding camp. She'd be around to experience it all with her daughter. Surprisingly, Hazel found herself excited for Grace's first ride.

"What do you say to Hazel?" Frankie said to her boys as they put the last of the dirty dishes on the kitchen counter next to the sink.

"Thank you for dinner!" All three boys replied in a chorus. Grace and the boys had cleared the table. Hazel and Frankie were washing the dishes.

Hazel rinsed off the last bowl and handed it to Frankie. "You're welcome. I'm so glad you liked it." Hazel had made one of her and Grace's favorites, homemade macaroni and cheese with grilled chicken. She loved seeing it get gobbled up through smiles.

Frankie dried off the bowl and put it in the cupboard. "Where'd you learn to cook?"

"My mom," Hazel answered. "I used to help her a lot in the kitchen growing up. She loves to cook and always made it fun. We'd pick out recipes together, and she always made me a part of the cooking process, even when I was little. Some of my earliest memories are of Mom and I in the kitchen. We still cook a lot together. Grace loves to help too."

"That's really sweet."

Hazel drained the sink of the warm, bubbly water. "Did Rose like to cook?" Hazel was picking up bits and pieces of information about Rose from pictures and a few short conversations, but had generally shied away from the topic of her biological mother. It was the first time she'd asked a direct question to Frankie about Rose.

"She liked to bake more than cook, but she was good at both. I used to help her, too, but not because I liked it. I'd rather do just about anything outside than spend an hour in the kitchen." Frankie shrugged. "Cooking and cleaning aren't my thing. Guess I missed out on that gene."

Hazel was wiping down the counter, but stopped when she realized Frankie was insinuating that Rose had somehow passed a cooking gene onto Hazel. She felt herself retreating from the conversation. Hazel's love of cooking came solely from her mother, Sandy. Not from Rose. Swallowing the thought, Hazel continued wiping down the counter.

Frankie dried a few forks and put them in the silverware drawer. "She wasn't a fancy cook, but she could whip up a casserole like no other. And, she made a mean margarita."

"Do you have a Tupperware I can borrow?" Hazel asked Frankie, redirecting the conversation.

"Sure, help yourself. They're all in the cabinet to your left."

Hazel bent down and picked out a square container and lid. "I'm going to drop off a few pieces of pie at Jesse's." She cut a few slices from the peanut butter pie she'd made for dessert and slid them into the container.

"Okay." Frankie quirked an eyebrow at Hazel.

"As a thank you." She snapped the lid on the container. "He dropped off new hinges for the hay door yesterday, and offered to hang it this weekend." Hazel wanted to bring him a peace offering. They'd had a rocky introduction, but Jesse was her neighbor. And a friend of Frankie's. Hazel wanted to make nice.

"Well, tell him he should be honored to get a few pieces of that masterpiece. And I'm not so sure it should be wasted on him," Frankie teased, light-heartedly.

"I'll make sure he knows." Hazel grinned, knowing that Frankie and Jesse had a playful relationship. From what she'd seen, they acted more like brother and sister than friends.

"I'll meet you at the carriage house in a half hour? So we can paint the cabinets?" Frankie asked.

Last night, Frankie had come to the carriage house with the kids and helped Hazel finish sanding the kitchen cabinets. She'd brought a pitcher of lemonade and a board game, which kept all four kids occupied and laughing while they worked.

Hazel wiped her hands on the dish towel. "That'd be great. I picked up brushes and a gallon of stain at the hardware store while I was in town today." Frankie was awfully handy with a sander, but Hazel was also enjoying her company. She'd almost forgotten how nice it was to have a girlfriend to talk to. Hazel had lost touch with most of her close girlfriends after she married Bill. She'd allowed herself to get wrapped up in his life while accidentally letting go of her own. "See you in just a bit. Come on, Grace. Let's go deliver this pie."

Hazel and Grace left Frankie's and followed the dirt road to the carriage house before skirting around the back. As they walked toward the lake and Jesse's quaint cottage, Hazel wondered if Jesse lived alone. Would his wife or girlfriend answer the door? Should she have brought three pieces of pie? Hazel hadn't noticed a wedding ring, but she hadn't really been looking. He had a daughter, so there was a woman in the picture—whether it was present or past. Was it strange that she was showing up at his doorstep late in the evening with a container of pie?

Before she could get too lost in her head, Grace skipped ahead and called out, "I'll knock."

A deck wrapped around the house and expanded off the back to overlook the lake. Jesse's truck was parked in the drive so Hazel figured he was home. Grace tromped up onto the deck and rapped on the screen door. By the time Hazel joined her, Jesse was approaching the door. He looked like he'd just finished work as he was still in jeans, a black t-shirt, and his signature baseball cap. His dark hair flipped out the bottom of the cap.

"Hey," he said, opening the screen door and looking confused.

Hazel gave a wave. "Hey. Wanted to drop off some peanut butter pie as a thank-you for the hinges and the offer of fixing my door." She raised the Tupperware.

He stepped out onto the deck and Hazel heard someone inside. It might've been his daughter. Hazel felt out of sorts, like she was interrupting his evening. "I hope you like it." She awkwardly pushed it toward him. When he took it, Hazel started backing up. "If you don't eat it tonight, make sure to put it in the fridge. There's cream cheese and whip cream in it, so it'll go bad if you leave it out. Okay, Grace. Let's get going. Say good night to Jesse." Hazel was babbling, but couldn't stop herself.

"Wait," Jesse said. "You made this?"

Hazel nodded.

"It's my favorite," Grace added, ignoring Hazel's cues to retreat. "It's basically a peanut butter cheesecake."

Jesse's eyes widened and he stared through the container lid.

"It's my Mom's recipe. Homemade graham cracker crust and all," Hazel said.

"Wow, thank you." He looked up from the pie. "Charlie and I love peanut butter."

Footsteps pattered toward the door. "Who here, Daddy?" The little blonde girl peered through the screen door. "Hi!"

"Hi, Charlie." Hazel waved back. "This is my daughter, Grace."

"Hi," Grace added.

Charlie bounced and waved her hand, which was holding a small pink bottle. "Daddy, can I paint their nails too?"

Jesse looked slightly flustered. "You caught us in the middle of a spa day." He shrugged his shoulders and that's when Hazel noticed Jesse's hand—the one holding the pie. His fingernails were painted an array of pinks and purples. There were a few extra smears on his knuckles. The polish was a complete contradiction to the rest of him. He was tall, over six feet, and everything about Jesse screamed of a strong cowboy—his dusty clothes, worn boots, and the muscles his t-shirt couldn't hide. But he let his daughter paint his nails? The sweetness of that caught Hazel completely off guard.

Charlie opened the screen door, stepped outside, and reached for Grace's hand. "Can you paint mine?"

Grace took her hand. She'd always been good with younger kids. "Sure." Before Hazel thought-twice about what was happening, Charlie led Grace inside.

Jesse ran his other polished hand over the top of his baseball hat. "Do you want to come inside?"

"Uh, sure. For a few minutes." Hazel awkwardly grinned, feeling like she'd just invited herself over.

Jesse opened the door for Hazel, and she stepped inside, straight into the living room where Charlie and Grace had already made themselves comfortable. They were sitting on the floor next to the coffee table, which was covered in a towel. Five or six polishes sat on the towel. Grace was helping Charlie pick out a color.

Jesse walked into the galley kitchen and opened the fridge door. "I can't wait to try this." He put the pie in the fridge. Hazel glanced at his hand again, which was propped on top of the open door.

Left hand. No ring.

Then she scolded herself for caring. What did it matter if he was married? She was not looking for anything. Not a boyfriend, not a husband, not even a date.

"I take it off after Charlie goes to bed." Jesse closed the refrigerator door, and Hazel realized he thought she was looking at his polished nails. "Most of the time, anyhow. One time I fell asleep on the couch and forgot to set my alarm. I was running late, and by the time I dropped off Charlie at my parents' place, it was too late to do anything about it. I went to four barns that day to work horses."

Hazel pictured Jesse riding and training horses with pink fingernails. "Did anyone notice your manicure?" She stifled a smirk.

"The nice thing about my line of work is that I can wear gloves." He shrugged a shoulder and slid a grin at Hazel. "Can I get you anything to drink? Water? Or—" Jesse opened his fridge again. "A juice box?"

This time Hazel chuckled. "No, I'm okay. We just finished eating over at Frankie's and I need to get going, anyhow. Frankie is going to help me stain cabinets tonight. She'll be over after she gets the boys cleaned up."

Hazel looked around. Jesse's home was tidy and cozy. The living room had an overstuffed couch and armchair. There was a brick fireplace, and the mantle was filled with pictures of Charlie. The backside of the living room was all windows which looked out onto the deck and lake. Blue, Jesse's dog, lay sleeping under the windows. The dog wore a tutu. Hazel thought it looked like Charlie had both males in this house wrapped around her little finger.

Jesse joined Hazel in the living room. "How was your first day?" he asked.

Hazel hadn't seen Jesse at the barn today. "Of work?"

"Frankie said you're going to help her with the summer camps. And that Grace is going to get to ride."

Grace kept her eyes on Charlie's fingers as she painted them, but interjected their conversation. "Frankie said I get to ride Stormy."

The horse's name distracted Hazel from Jesse. "Stormy?"

"Yeah, he's gray and he has a super long, pretty tail. He's a retired police horse," Grace said.

Most animals got their names for a reason. When Hazel was in middle school, they had a neighbor with a cat named "Monster." Monster used to hide in the bushes and lurch out at unsuspecting prey. Usually, it was a bird. Sometimes it was Hazel. "Can't she put you on something with a sweeter name? Like Daisy? Or Butterscotch?"

"Actually, Stormy is a sweetheart," Jesse interjected. "He got his name because of his coat color. Being a retired police horse, he's literally seen everything. Nothing scares him. He'd ride into a burning building if his rider asked him to."

Grace looked triumphant after Jesse's comment. "Plus, he's really cute."

"And there's that." Jesse smiled. "Haven't you met Stormy yet? While you were working?"

"I don't really do much with the horses, but I've gotten to know a few of them. Mostly I'm helping with the administrative stuff, and I'll be *wrangling* children during the camps." Hazel used Frankie's word.

"Sorry I startled you yesterday," Jesse offered, and Hazel was thrown off by his quick topic change. She remembered how she'd reacted when he'd shown up in the hayloft and gave her a heart attack. If she'd had something more significant than sandpaper in her hand, she would've thrown it at him. "I know that's your place now and I shouldn't have taken it upon myself to just walk in. Although, I promise I looked for your car before I went in. I didn't see it, so I figured you weren't there. And I called for you, but you obviously couldn't hear me with your headphones in. Won't happen again."

Hazel knew she shouldn't have reacted so strongly to his simple act of kindness. It was just that she didn't want a man to feel like he could encroach on her space as he saw fit.

She'd gone through a lot to recover from the last man that had consumed her life and then ripped it to shreds.

She pursed her lips. "I believe you. Just please try not to scare me to death again. Like, yell louder next time."

Jesse huffed. "Okay."

"And you didn't see my car because I sold it."

"You sold it?" The ease on Jesse's face faded. "Why?"

"To pay for the repairs for the carriage house." That was all she was about to tell him. She wasn't about to elaborate and explain that she had a few hundred dollars in her bank account before she sold the car. "Grace, honey. Are you almost done? Frankie will be over soon, so we need to get going."

Grace screwed the top back on the coral-colored polish and blew gently on Charlie's nails. "Now, don't touch anything until your dad says you can. Okay?"

Charlie nodded her head in immediate agreeance.

Hazel started to turn for the door.

"Thank you for the pie," Jesse said. "And if you're around this weekend, I can get that hay door fixed for you."

"I'll be around."

"Daddy, you said we'd watch a movie this weekend." Charlie had her hands out and fingers splayed.

"We will, sweetie. Friday night." Jesse looked back at Hazel. "We're having a pizza and movie night. You and Grace are welcome to join us."

Hazel's heart lurched, but Charlie squealed, delighted by her dad's suggestion.

"Please," Charlie said, and she pressed her little hands together like she was praying, careful not to touch the polish. "Can you and Grace watch a movie with me?"

Hazel was ready to spew out excuses when Jesse mentioned pizza and a movie, but the offer was completely different coming out of Charlie's mouth.

"We haven't done that in a while," Grace said, looking eager. Hazel was effectively trapped.

Hazel pressed her lips together, but ultimately gave in. "Sure."

Charlie hopped and squealed. Grace smiled. And Hazel told herself she'd just made a playdate with her neighbor. Because there was no way she was going on a *real* date with the way-too-handsome-for-his-own-good cowboy. Even if he did let his daughter paint his nails.

CHAPTER ELEVEN

When Jesse saw Hazel in her flowy flowered skirt and white tank, he knew he shouldn't have invited her for pizza and a movie. It was one thing to invite Grace and the boys to join him and Charlie for a movie night, but inviting Hazel felt way too close to a date. And Jesse hadn't been on a date in a long time—since he lost Sarah, Charlie's mom. He'd meant to be friendly. To offer an olive branch. Jesse blamed his impulsive invitation on the pie. His sweet tooth had a way of luring him to temptations that weren't always good for him. And Hazel had a sweetness hidden below her coat of armor. He'd seen it, even if it wasn't always aimed at him.

Now, as Jesse and Hazel walked along main street—a row of familiar businesses on his right and the blue waters of Maple Leaf Lake on his left—he knew he'd gotten himself in a pickle.

"Mom, look at all that fudge!" Grace stopped and pointed at the big front window of Kandi's Candy. Grace was holding Charlie's hand and had been since they parked Jesse's truck and started walking on the sidewalk. Charlie beamed up at Grace the same way that Grace was looking at the fudge.

Hazel joined the girls at the window. "Oh, my goodness." She lengthened out each word like it was its own sentence.

Inside the shop, Kandi waved from behind the counter. Jesse waved back.

"Fudge is good with pizza," Jesse said, and opened the door. Grace and Charlie scooted through and ran to the glass countertop to ogle the many different flavors of fudge. "Don't you agree?" He held the door open for Hazel.

She cracked a smile. "Actually, yes. I don't think there's a single thing that fudge doesn't compliment."

They entered and joined the girls at the counter.

"Jesse Weston." Kandi greeted him with joyful energy that matched her signature pink and white striped apron. Her long white hair was twisted into a bun. Kandi had owned the candy shop since Jesse was little, and she'd always reminded him of Mrs. Claus. "Did you bring the newcomers in for some of my fudge?"

"Sure did," Jesse replied. "On our way to pick up a movie and pizza, but just couldn't walk by the best fudge in the world."

"You'd better not." Kandi shook her finger, but was eating up his compliment.

It really was the best fudge he'd ever tasted.

"Have you met my neighbor, Hazel March, and her daughter, Grace?" Jesse asked.

"No, but the pleasure is all mine." Kandi reached over the counter and shook Hazel's hand and then Grace's. "Welcome to Maple Bay."

"Thank you," Hazel replied with a smile.

"And I'm so sorry about your mother. Rose was a pillar of the community, and we all miss her. Please accept my condolences." Kandi was completely sincere with her sympathy, but the smile wiped from Hazel's face. She looked shell-shocked.

Jesse wasn't sure how Hazel felt about Rose, but he'd never heard Rose mentioned a second daughter. His gut told him that even though Rose was Hazel's biological mother, Hazel didn't think of Rose as her mom.

"That's very kind of you, Kandi," Jesse replied. Hazel pushed a tight smile onto her face.

Jesse redirected the conversation. "What are your specials this week? I think we'll need a variety pack to take with us."

Kandi rattled off her weekly fudge specials, recommending the Key Lime Pie, Malt Ball Swirl, and Lemon Berry. As Kandi continued listing flavors, Hazel relaxed more and more until she put both hands on Grace's shoulders.

"Why don't we each pick out a flavor? Then we can share," Hazel said, and both girls quickly agreed. "What would you girls like?"

"Root Beer, please." Charlie looked back at Jesse and he gave her a grin. He knew she'd pick that. Jesse and Charlie often stopped by Kandi's on the weekend, and Root Beer was her most recent favorite flavor.

Grace pointed through the glass to a cream and red swirled fudge. "Can I do the Cherry Vanilla?"

"Good choices," Kandi said.

Jesse looked at Hazel.

"It's a tough decision. They all look so good." Hazel paused. "I think I'll take the Key Lime, please. No, wait. I'll take the Malt Ball." Hazel was now on her tip toes, peering over Grace's shoulder at the array of sweets.

"She'll take both of them," Jesse said, and Hazel looked at him like he'd just offered her dinner at a five-star restaurant. "And I'll take your Salted Caramel, please."

Kandi filled up a little brown box and slipped it into a pink and white striped bag. "Here you go, sweets." She gave the bag to Grace to carry.

Hazel reached for her purse, but Jesse put his hand on her arm.

"It's my treat." He handed over his card to Kandi before Hazel could protest. If there was one thing Jesse had learned about Hazel, it was that she didn't accept gifts well. So, he was quick with his card. "Charlie and I invited you and Grace out tonight. Pizza, dessert, and the movie are on us."

Hazel looked like she might object, but then thought better of it. "Thank you," she said as she slipped her arms around Grace's shoulders and gave her a hug. Grace smiled and leaned into the embrace.

"Come back soon," Kandi called, and they waved before headed down the block to the movie store.

When they arrived at their next stop, Hazel stopped cold in her tracks. She stared at the neon yellow sign glowing in the window. The scrolled neon words spelled out the shop's name—Movies on Main.

"You have a movie store? Like a *real* movie store?" Hazel's mouth was open. "I didn't think these existed anymore. I thought we were going to stop by a Redbox or something."

Jesse laughed. "No Redbox. I guess we're kind of old school here."

"Retro." Hazel's green eyes did this sparkly thing that reminded Jesse of the summer sun glinting on the lake. "My parents used to take me to Blockbuster. I always loved roaming the aisles, picking out a movie together. It's so much more fun than picking a movie from a computer screen."

"I agree," Jesse said, and they entered the store.

Jesse followed the girls and Hazel as they zigzagged through racks of DVDs. Hazel spent most of the time bent down or balanced on her knees, helping the girls sort through movie options. All three of them chatted and laughed. Jesse had a good time just watching them. Right from his first introduction to Hazel, she'd looked at Jesse like she might slap him if he treaded too close. But now, as he watched her with Charlie and Grace, Hazel's kind, jovial heart was so visible that he didn't know how she could hide it.

Charlie skipped toward Jesse, a DVD in her hands. "We picked *Black Beauty*!"

"Oh, boy. I think you've seen that like a hundred times," Jesse said. *Maybe a thousand.*

"But Grace never seen," Charlie replied.

"I haven't either." Hazel walked up behind Charlie. "Charlie said it's her favorite movie. She said we'll love the part at the end where Black Beauty finds a happy home."

Jesse chuckled and shook his head at Charlie. "You told them what happens at the end?"

Charlie wrinkled her nose, like the happy ending was the obvious selling point to the movie.

"All right. *Black Beauty* it is then," Jesse said, and escorted the girls to the counter to checkout.

A few hours later, the pizza box lay open on Jesse's coffee table. There was only one slice left, and the last scene of the movie played. Grace was curled up in the recliner. Charlie was splayed across her beanbag. Both girls had fallen asleep about a half-hour ago, just as the summer sun had slipped away. Jesse and Hazel were sitting on the couch—on opposite ends—and Jesse caught himself glancing Hazel's way, again. He couldn't help it. He'd seen the movie so many times he could practically recite it, but Hazel had quickly been drawn into the story, watching it like a character might die if she took her eyes off the screen.

She leaned against the armrest, her legs tucked up against her. Her flowery skirt covered all but her bare feet. In the dark room, the television illuminated her face and a tear slipped over her cheek and freckles. She wiped it away, but never took her eyes off the movie.

Jesse leaned over and grabbed a tissue from the side table. "Here," he said, and reached across the couch.

"You didn't tell me this was going to be sad." She took the tissue and gave him a grin.

"It has sad parts." He watched her dab her eyes.

"That poor horse. He had to go through such terrible things."

Jesse thought about the movie. It was hard to watch any animal suffer. Worse yet, he'd witnessed the aftereffects of animal abuse in real life, and could never understand how a person could intentionally hurt any of God's creatures. It was why he did what he did—worked with horses that had endured a rough path. He felt a calling to teach them how to trust again. "But he got his happily ever after."

Hazel crumbled the tissue into her hand. "You must think I'm a complete mess, crying at a children's movie."

"Not at all." He would've been worried if the movie hadn't touched her, but seeing her tears told Jesse how tender Hazel's heart was. "Next time we'll pick a funny one."

He meant it. He wanted a next time. He wanted to get to know this woman.

In the dark, with only the movie credits lighting the room, Jesse thought he saw intrigue claim Hazel's face. But it rushed off quickly. She tightened the tissue in her hand and glanced away, at Grace.

"I better get her home." She paused, and then clarified, "Back to Frankie's."

What was Hazel's story? What had happened in her life to make her instinct to retreat so strong? Jesse wanted to know, but didn't press. He could see she was on the verge of back peddling to the door. "I'll walk you back."

"You don't have to do that. Charlie's sleeping."

Jesse stood and grabbed an afghan from the back of the couch. He draped it over Charlie, scooped her up, and wrapped her like a burrito. When her head was on his shoulder, he said, "Nothing wakes this kid. I'll carry her and walk you and Grace to Frankie's. I won't have it any other way."

He certainly wouldn't let them walk through the night alone, even if they were in the safety of Maple Bay. He'd never forgive himself if something happened.

Hazel succumbed and woke Grace by gently rubbing her arm. "Come on, sweetie. It's time to go to bed."

Grace picked up her head and blinked her eyes. "Is the movie over?"

"Yes, and it's late. It's time to go back to Frankie's."

"You can come over and watch the end tomorrow," Jesse offered to Grace. "I know Charlie would love that. Actually, she'd probably watch the whole movie with you again."

Grace nodded, sleepily. "Okay." She rose from the recliner.

Owls hooted as they walked past the carriage house and followed the road to Frankie's. Amidst the yellow moon and shadowed trees, Hazel draped her arm around Grace's shoulders and planted a kiss on her head, but no one spoke until they reached Frankie's front porch.

"Thank you for tonight," Hazel said, and Jesse wondered what thoughts sat behind her gratitude. He couldn't read her. All evening her body language had waffled between warm and distant. He found himself drawn to her warmth. He wanted to understand her distance.

"Of course." He wanted to see her again, for more than a passing conversation or to wave from their respective houses. He opened his mouth to ask her if they could do this again, but Hazel stopped him. She stepped forward and reached for the blanket that Charlie was wrapped in. The afghan had crept down, exposing her head.

"Don't want her getting cold." Hazel tucked the knitted blanket around Charlie. As she did, the soft edge brushed Jesse's neck. His heart thumped. She gave him one last look and held it like she had something to say. Then she hooked her arm around Grace and led her to the front door.

"Good night, Jesse," Grace called. Hazel gave Jesse a soft smile.

"Good night," he replied.

After Hazel closed the door, Jesse headed back toward the lake and his house. As he walked, Charlie wrapped her little fingers in his collar. She gripped his shirt and snuggled her cheek into his neck. Jesse's stomach clenched and a mix of emotions washed through him. Hazel was in Maple Bay for the summer. That was it. Once she honored the clause in Rose's will, he was sure she'd sell the carriage house and move back to the city. And he couldn't allow Charlie to get attached to someone that would leave. He didn't need that heartbreak again—for Charlie, or for himself.

CHAPTER TWELVE

"Rose collected all this for the carriage house?" Hazel asked Frankie. They had uncovered the tarped boxes and furniture in the ground level of the carriage house. Garrett and Jesse were in the loft, re-hinging and re-hanging the hay door. All the kids were over at Jesse's house watching *Black Beauty*.

Frankie ran a hand over an intricately carved post, which looked to be part of a four-poster bed frame. "She'd been collecting stuff for years. Got most of it from garage and estate sales."

There were end tables, bookshelves, headboards, dressers, and boxes of who-knows-what. The wood stove Frankie previously mentioned was on the far side of the pile, and Hazel rounded the wall of boxes to get a better look. When she did, she also discovered a clawfoot bathtub.

Hazel gasped. "Oh, wow." She pressed her fingertips to the white, rounded edge and marveled at the antiqued iron feet.

Frankie walked up beside her. "Mom and I found this at an estate sale on the way to a rodeo."

"A rodeo?"

"Yeah, it was at least ten years ago, and I still think the estate sale was the only reason Mom left her horse at home and opted not to ride. She wanted to make sure there was room in the trailer for any goodies she found." Frankie cracked a grin at the memory. "My barrel horse wasn't sure what to think when he had to ride home next to a bathtub."

"Rose had a good eye. This is like a piece of art." Hazel had always wanted a clawfoot tub. She imagined bubble baths in the deep tub would be heavenly.

"She loved searching for new pieces for the carriage house," Frankie said. "She called it treasure-hunting."

Hazel eyed the tub, boxes, and furniture. There was more here than she thought. She wouldn't need to purchase much furniture to fill the loft and make it into an apartment for her and Grace. But all this stuff equated to years worth of memories—for Frankie. "I can't accept this. I'm sure each of these pieces remind you of your mother. You need to have this. All of it. I'll get new stuff." Her budget for renovations and furniture would be tight, but she'd prioritize, and maybe Hazel should rip a page from Rose's book and tackle some garage sales this week.

Frankie looked startled by Hazel's suggestion. It was not the reaction Hazel thought she'd receive.

"Mom wanted you to have this," Frankie said. "She hoped you'd use it to fill the carriage house. That was her wish, to see her treasure-hunting put to good use and enjoyed."

Frankie's eyes went glassy and Hazel nodded, not intending to upset Frankie. "Okay. I just didn't want you to feel like I was taking something that was yours." At the end of the summer, how would Frankie feel when Hazel sold this place? She was obviously still hurting after her mother's passing, and the last thing Hazel wanted to do was add to her pain. At the end of the summer, Hazel internally promised to move all of Rose's things out of the carriage house and over to Frankie's, where they belonged.

After a few moments of silence, Frankie said, "I'm going to make sure the kids are behaving themselves. And when I say *kids*, I mean my boys." Frankie turned and started toward the back door. "Some parents run a tight ship. I run a pirate ship. There's always a chance of mutiny with my crew." She gave a tight smile. Hazel wondered if Frankie was trying to avoid how her memories made her feel, or the fact that Rose had left half her world to a stranger, even if that stranger was related by blood.

"Hey, Frankie?" Hazel asked. Frankie stopped and looked back.

Hazel couldn't explain how it felt to be given up, but she distinctly remembered the moment she learned that she'd been adopted. It was a few weeks after her thirteenth birthday—a normal Tuesday night. Dad had taken her to volleyball practice and Mom was home cooking dinner. When Hazel and her dad got home, she ran upstairs to take a quick shower, but when Hazel skipped back through the kitchen door, everything had changed. Hazel expected to sit at the table, talk about her day, and eat two helpings of Sandy's Shepherd's Pie.

Instead, her mom was crying. Sandy sat with her face in her hands. Peter had an arm clasped around her shoulders. Between sobs, Sandy and Peter told Hazel she'd been adopted, and they confessed they weren't sure they were ever going to tell her. They loved her so much that it didn't matter where she came from. She was their daughter. But her biological mother had sent a letter, and they didn't want to chance Rose showing up out of the blue. They wanted the news to come from them, not Hazel's biological mother.

Up until that day, Hazel had never once doubted that she was Sandy and Peter's daughter. Her dad had red hair and freckles, just like Hazel. Her mother had dark green eyes. They both loved her immensely. But on that day, questions seeded in Hazel's head. Over the years they'd grown roots, and Hazel wasn't sure she'd ever be able to dislodge them.

How could Rose abandon one child and choose to raise another? Before Hazel came to Maple Bay, she'd pictured

Rose as an irresponsible, selfish person. She thought maybe her biological mother had been a drug addict, or someone so damaged that she couldn't love a child. But Rose had raised Frankie. And judging by what Hazel knew of Frankie, Rose had done a good job.

Instead of saying all that, Hazel said, "I'm glad I'm here."

Frankie pressed her lips together. "Me too." She stood in the frame of the open door, silhouetted by the afternoon sun, looking like she was grappling with her own demons. "You need to look in the box next to the bathtub."

She slipped away, and Hazel's eyes fell to the box in front of her.

Panic crept over Hazel like static electricity. What was in the box?

Hazel slowly opened the cardboard flaps, not liking the feeling Frankie had left her with. Inside there was another box—a wooden rectangle covered in pretty pictures, like someone would cover the pages of a scrapbook. Hazel gently removed the box and ran her fingers over the glued-on pictures. They weren't of anyone or any place she recognized. It looked like they'd been cut from magazines. There were images of children laughing and families hugging. There was one of a cute cottage surrounded by a white picket fence. Most had been cutout in the shape of a heart. Across the lid, Hazel's name was spelled out in purple felt letters.

Her heart stopped. The big, open carriage house shrunk down so that Hazel could only see the box in her hands.

"What is this?" she whispered to herself and pried open the lid.

Inside, the box was full of envelopes. Hazel fingered through them. Each had a date scrolled across the upper left corner—November 16th—but each envelope noted a different year.

My birthday.

Hazel gingerly removed the envelope that displayed the date that would've been her first birthday. With a shaky sigh, she gathered every ounce of courage she could muster and opened the envelope. Inside was a handwritten letter and a picture of Hazel when she was a baby. She was wearing a frilly dress and a flowered headband. Hazel immediately recognized the picture from the many that were hung in her parents' home.

My Sweet Baby,

Today is your first birthday, and I've been thinking of you since the minute you left my arms. Momma said I wasn't ready to have a baby. That I'm still a baby myself. Maybe she was right. I'm not sure. I know I was barely sixteen when you came into this world, but I also know that I'd never felt true love until I saw you. And I can't imagine a greater pain than what I felt when I let you go.

Momma says you will have a better life now, but I feel like a part of me has been missing since you left. Today the adoption agent stopped by and handed me a picture of you. At first, I cried. For a whole day. But then I thought what great parents you must have, because they were kind enough to send me a picture and a note. They named you Hazel. It's a beautiful name, but it will take me awhile to get used to, calling you by your given name. To me, you've always been Charlotte—a name I picked for you the day you were born. I have been calling you Charlie, for short. I talk to you every day, hoping you hear me, but this is the first letter I am writing to you. I hope that someday you can see this and know how much I have loved you. Even if I only held you in my arms for one day.

Love you always,
Rose

The written words cut into Hazel. They numbed her. She scanned through the rest of the envelopes, looking at the dates. There was a letter for every year that followed her first birthday. The last envelope was written just this past year, on her thirty-seventh birthday.

Hazel set the box and letter down. She placed a hand on the rounded edge of the bathtub and focused on her breathing. Reading Rose's letter, seeing that there were many more, was almost too much to take in. The penned words had ripped open a wound she'd bandaged for years.

"Hazel?" A hand pressed against her back and she jerked. "Are you okay?"

She drew her stare out of the clawfoot tub and up the expanse of Jesse. "I don't know."

His eyes flitted around, looking for the source of whatever had sent her spinning. Before his eyes fell back to her, Hazel's mind shot back to the words in Rose's letter. Rose said she'd given Hazel the name of Charlotte . . . or, *Charlie.*

"Do you want to sit down?" Jesse put a hand on her arm and tried to lead her to the stairs.

Hazel didn't move. "What's Charlie's full name?"

Jesse angled his body back toward her, keeping his hand on her arm. "What?" His gaze shifted and found the open box.

"Is her full name Charlotte?" Hazel asked.

Jesse's gaze flitted back to Hazel. "Yes."

Was it a complete coincidence that Jesse had given his daughter the name that was intended for Hazel? That he called his daughter *Charlie?* From the look on Jesse's face, Hazel knew there was more to the story. It wasn't a coincidence. "Why'd you name her Charlotte?"

Jesse looked like his mind was reeling back, searching memories. From the way his shoulders straightened, Hazel thought she'd poked at a painful recollection, like she wasn't the only one with wounds hidden in the past.

"I didn't name her," he said.

Hazel stared at Jesse, waiting for more, but quick footsteps fell on the patio and Tommy burst through the open door.

"Dad!" Tommy yelled in a tone that forced Hazel upright.

Jesse let go of her arm. "He's upstairs. What's wrong?"

"Are you okay? Is everyone okay?" Hazel took a step toward Tommy. *Where was Grace? The rest of the kids?*

"That lady from the rescue group called Mom," Tommy explained. "Said the police need a whole bunch of horses picked up in Elm Grove. Said it's bad. Mom went to get the trailer. Told me to come get you guys."

Garrett had started down the stairs, and Jesse looked at him.

"I'll call Evan. And Creed. My mom can stay with the kids," Jesse said to Garrett. Then he pulled his phone from his back pocket, pressed the screen once, and put it to his ear. The person on the other end started talking before Jesse said a word. "Okay, I'll meet you at the barn."

Garrett got on his phone too, and after a one sentence conversation, said, "Joyce is already on her way." He jogged down the rest of the stairs. "Tommy, go back to Jesse's house. Joyce is going to stay with you guys. She'll be there in a few minutes. Okay?"

Tommy nodded and headed out, running across the lawn. Hazel watched him out the window and saw that Joyce was already pulling up to Jesse's cottage on a four-wheeler.

The kids all spilled out of the door. She ushered them back inside.

"Hazel, you can ride with us," Garrett said, jogging toward the door, assuming she was coming along. "We'll need all the help we can get."

Jesse looked at Hazel and added, "These type of rescues can be pretty bad." It sounded like a warning—like he was giving her the option to ignore Garrett.

Hazel blinked, letting the secrets she'd just unboxed fall away. There was something more urgent to focus on. "I can help. Just tell me how."

CHAPTER THIRTEEN

By the time Jesse had backed his truck up to the horse trailer, Creed was pulling up to the barn. He threw his rusty Chevy truck into park and jumped out, looking ready to start a fight. To anyone that didn't know him, Creed in that state of mind would be intimidating. He was a big guy and a natural athlete, though he'd always chased the adrenaline of rodeo over the organization of team sports. He liked to walk a tight line between brave and crazy. Though to Jesse, Creed had been a loyal and devoted friend since they met in high school.

"Took the cops long enough to catch those guys," Creed announced as he met Jesse at the trailer hitch. He threw a few lariat ropes in the truck bed.

"I guess they caught them after they stole two more horses from some barn in Iowa. Took the horses right out of their pasture last night." Jesse cranked the jack, lowering the trailer onto the hitch. When it eased onto the ball, Creed reached down to snap on the safety chains and plug in the electrical. They'd hooked up a trailer together about a million times and didn't have to talk to do so.

Creed was a year younger than Jesse and moved to Maple Bay to live with his dad when he was fourteen. He had a rough past and a nonexistent family life. His freshman year of high school, Jesse's dad hired Creed to help around the barn. Over the years, Creed had become like another brother, an honorary member of the Weston family.

Creed cussed. "If I get my hands on them—"

"I know," Jesse replied. Creed hadn't finished his threat, but Jesse knew what he meant. Jesse felt the same.

This past spring, a handful of shady guys showed up at a local rodeo. No one knew them. They claimed they were from Texas, looking to buy some young roping prospects, but they stalked around the grounds and a few saddles went missing. Not long after, a barn just outside of Turtle Lake was broken into and two horses were stolen. Those horses had been at that rodeo. Since then, the same thing had happened at a horse show in Iowa and two rodeos in South Dakota.

"They were right under our noses," Jesse added. "Had been using an abandoned barn outside of Elm Grove to stash the horses until they could offload them. Got sloppy though. Took a few horses to an auction just south of Minneapolis, and the Appaloosas were recognized. The cops came before the scumbags could disappear. One squealed the location of the barn they'd been using. Apparently, there are about ten horses that were seized and need to be picked up. Left the horses with no food or water." Jesse's stomach twisted at the thought.

"They were stealing horses?" Hazel asked. She'd been standing on the far side of the truck near the passenger door, quiet as a mouse.

Creed stood up at her voice, nearly hitting his head on the truck's bumper.

Jesse stuck the pin in the hitch, making sure it was secure, and stood. "Creed, this is Hazel."

Creed and Hazel looked at each other over the truck bed, and recognition slid over Creed's face. "Hazel? The lucky lady you wooed with pizza and a movie?"

Creed asked the question like he knew way more than he did. Jesse hadn't said a word to Creed about his evening with Hazel, but that was the thing about a small town. You couldn't keep much from anyone. Especially if you made an appearance on main street.

"There was no *wooing*, Creed." Jesse slapped Creed on the shoulder a little harder than normal as he passed. "Hazel just moved here. Was showing her the town and taking the girls out for the evening. She has a daughter too."

Creed ran a hand through his blonde hair, pushing it from his face. "I'll have a talk with him," he said to Hazel.

"He's a little rusty. Next time he'll take you on a *real* date. I'll make sure of it."

Jesse opened the driver side door and shot a look at Creed. He pointed at the back door and said, "Let's go."

Creed gave a shrug like he was only trying to help, and then followed Jesse's pointing finger. He opened the backdoor and whispered to Jesse, "What? It's been forever since you've been on a date. And she's really cute."

Creed gave Jesse a sly grin as he slid onto the bench seat and shut the door. Jesse knew his friend was just trying to get him *back in the game*, as Creed had said many times before. They'd been each other's wingmen in their younger, carefree years. But those years seemed like a lifetime ago.

Jesse jumped in the truck and hoped Hazel hadn't heard any more of Creed's *helpfulness*, but when she climbed into the passenger seat, Hazel didn't meet Jesse's eye. He wasn't sure if that had to do with Creed's comments or whatever she'd discovered in the boxes in the carriage house. Hazel's questions about Charlie had surprised him, and he didn't understand what could've upset her that much.

Putting the truck in drive, Jesse eased it forward and focused on the task at hand—not the hurt he'd witnessed on Hazel's face.

"Yes, they were stealing horses," Jesse answered Hazel's original question. "They were making quick money by stealing horses and taking them out of state to sell them. Probably down south. Good thing they got lazy and took the latest to a sale just south of Minneapolis. Otherwise, who knows how long this could've gone on."

"And they abandoned the rest of the horses at the barn we're going to? With no food or water?" Concern grabbed at Hazel's voice and Jesse glanced at her as he drove down the driveway. Worry for the animals had bypassed whatever she'd been upset about.

"They sure did," Creed answered from the backseat. His tone had gone from teasing to seething.

Jesse saw Frankie's truck and trailer on the road ahead, past his parents' house. Frankie was driving and Garrett was with her. She'd pulled over to wait for Jesse.

"The cops got ahold of the rescue group Frankie works with. That's who called. We'll pick the horses up and bring them back to Frankie's until their homes are located. Between my trailer and Frankie's, we should be able to get them all."

Frankie had a big stock trailer that could hold six horses. The trailer that Evan and Jesse shared could haul four. "My brother, Evan, is going to meet us there. He was in Elm Grove, picking up some fencing."

It was only a half-hour drive to the abandoned barn, but the trip felt longer. When they finally turned off a bumpy road to follow Frankie's truck and a cop car through a grassy field, Jesse gripped the steering wheel tight. There was no barn. On the edge of the field, butted up to woods, there was a dilapidated house that looked like it was built well over a century ago. Windows were boarded up or busted. The front porch was caved in. Roof shingles flapped in the warm afternoon wind.

Near the house there were a few small outbuildings, but nothing a horse should be kept in. Hazel and Creed leaned forward at the same time.

Hazel put her hands on the dash. "The horses are in that house?"

There was another cop car parked near the busted front porch. Evan's truck was next to it.

"Looks like it." Anger bubbled inside Jesse and he hadn't even seen the state of the animals yet. He only hoped the horses were still in decent shape. He reminded himself that the thieves intended to sell the horses and couldn't get good money for injured animals. And that's what those scumbags cared about after all—the money.

Jesse parked next to Frankie's rig, and everyone exited the vehicles.

Evan greeted Jesse with a solemn expression. "I went inside. The vet is on his way."

From the look on his brother's face, Jesse knew the situation they were about to encounter was not good.

"How many?" Jesse asked.

"Eight," Evan said.

Frankie pulled a duffle bag from the bed of her truck, unzipped it and handed out eight halters and lead ropes, though she didn't give one to Hazel. Jesse wished Hazel had stayed back with the kids. She didn't need to see this. Furthermore, she didn't have any experience with horses and couldn't jump in to handle scared, injured animals.

Jesse turned to Hazel, deciding on the safest job he could give her. "There's a full water tank in the tack room of my horse trailer. Buckets too. Can you fill them? Once we get the horses out, we'll need to see if they will drink."

Hazel gave a nod and headed toward the trailer.

The two officers showed the rest of them to the back of the house where there was a cracked, dented door.

"Animal control just left Minneapolis but won't be here for another few hours," one officer said. "Didn't want the horses in this mess any longer than they had to be. Thanks for coming so fast."

Frankie walked toward the banged-up door like she'd carry the horses out if she had to. "Let's get them out."

Jesse and Evan were close behind her. Frankie creaked open the dented door and shined a wedge of sunlight into the dark house. Jesse's heart sank as silhouettes came into view. The horses closest to the door sprung back in a clatter of hooves. A few were lying down. The bitter scent of urine assaulted Jesse's nose. Frankie coughed, catching the pungent smell as well.

Jesse put his hand on Frankie's shoulder and stopped her from going inside. "Let me and Evan go first. We'll hand them out as we get them haltered. Don't want to scare them any more than they already are."

Frankie stepped back, agreeing with his plan, and Jesse slid through the door. Evan was behind him.

"Easy, babies," Jesse whispered in his calmest tone. Wide, white-rimmed eyes stared back at him. A horse in the back snorted. "We're here to help."

Jesse guessed the horses were well-trained performance horses. The thieves had been strategic in their targets, picking out their victims at rodeos and horse shows and then coming for them days later, in the cover of night. This wasn't a pack of wild mustangs. If Jesse could show these horses that they weren't in danger, he and Evan should be able to halter and handle them.

Jesse eyed the horse closest to him—a petite Palomino with a gash across its chest. Despite the dark, dried blood on its golden coat, the Palomino eyed Jesse curiously.

"How'd you get that cut?" Jesse asked, like the horse might tell him. It was anyone's guess what had caused the injury considering the horse was standing in a kitchen. Cabinet doors hung off broken hinges. A few busted appliances were scattered across cracked tile. "Are you going to be the bravest of the bunch? The leader?"

Jesse slowly pulled the halter off his shoulder where it hung and stepped toward the Palomino, proceeding with caution. He moved slowly, but sensed that the horse wanted to trust him. When he was a step away and the horse hadn't retreated, Jesse guided the halter over the Palomino's nose and buckled it behind his ears. The little Palomino sighed, like he knew he was one step closer to safety. He followed Jesse without hesitation to the door. When Jesse handed the lead over to Frankie, Evan was able to halter a stocky black Quarter Horse that seemed to be attached to the Palomino. The black horse followed the Palomino to the door.

After the first two horses were outside, the rest of the horses perked up. They jostled nervously, not wanting to be left behind. Jesse and Evan made quick work of catching horses and handing them off to Frankie, Garrett, Creed, and the officers, until only the worse-off of the bunch was left. A lanky chestnut hobbled on three legs. A dark bay mare was laying on the soiled carpet. She hadn't gotten up yet, was sweating, and Jesse had seen her nip at her stomach multiple times since he'd been in the house.

"Probably colic," Jesse said to Evan. His brother agreed with a sympathetic grunt. "Who knows how long these horses have been without food or water."

There were a few buckets, but they were tipped over and empty. Frankly, Jesse was surprised all the horses weren't in the same state as the mare on the ground.

Jesse called for Frankie and asked her to get banamine from his trailer. It was a medication Jesse could give the horse to ease her pain and hopefully remedy the issue. Frankie showed up at the door with something better than the drug.

"Dr. Shiner is here," Frankie announced, and stepped through the door with the veterinarian. "Garrett and I can help the doctor with these two. Can you guys get the rest of the horses loaded?"

Jesse bent down and ran a hand over the bay mare's black mane and whispered, "Everything is going to be okay. Don't give up. We'll get you home." Then he left the two horses in the hands of the vet.

Outside the house, the officers and Creed each held a horse. The other three had been loaded into Frankie's trailer. Creed was attempting to load the big black Quarter Horse who, for whatever reason, didn't want to get in the trailer. The horse danced from side to side, going every which way but into the metal box on wheels. Jesse didn't blame him. The horse didn't know where these strangers were going to take him next.

Someone put a hand on Jesse's arm.

"Only a few drank water," Hazel said, releasing her hand.

"We've got a short ride home," Jesse reassured her. "Hopefully they'll be more comfortable there and will drink then."

Suddenly, the black horse reared into the air and pulled Creed out of the trailer. Jesse instinctively threw an arm across Hazel and moved her back from the activity.

Hazel gasped. "What can I do?"

"Probably best if you stayed back." Jesse could tell she wanted to help, but didn't want her getting hurt.

Hazel went to stand next to one of the outbuildings, and Jesse joined Creed at the trailer to help coax the black horse in. It took another ten minutes and a few more tantrums, but the horse finally conceded and joined the others. As Creed pushed the swinging divider into place and secured the horse, Jesse went to take the lead of the next horse from one of the officers. His hand stopped in midair when he heard his name.

Hazel screamed for Jesse, but when he whipped around, she was nowhere to be found.

"Jesse!" she called again from somewhere behind the outbuilding. Jesse ran, following her voice.

What was happening? Where was she? And why did Hazel sound like she was hurt?

He sprinted toward the tin shed and skated around the corner, kicking up dust as he went. On the backside of the shed, he found Hazel. She was running toward a man dragging a young sorrel horse along by its halter. The man had a lead that was attached to the horse's halter, and ended in a silver chain that wrapped over the horse's nose. The horse was frantically trying to get away from him.

"Hazel, stop!" Jesse shouted as Hazel quickly covered ground and jumped on the man's back. She wrapped her arms around the man's neck, and from the pained sound he made, she did something to seriously hurt him. The man swore and released the horse, focusing instead on Hazel. He grabbed at her arms and spun until Hazel flew off his back and through the air. Her red hair was like a ribbon in the wind until she hit the ground and rolled.

Jesse reached the man just as he lurched toward the horse again.

"Hey!" Jesse shouted, gaining the man's attention and giving him just enough time to see Jesse's fist before it hit his face.

Jesse's knuckles collided with the crook's nose and succeeded in sending the man toppling to his back. He met the man on the ground and landed another punch before they proceeded to tumble across the grass, fighting for leverage. As they wrestled, Jesse threw a knee on top of the scoundrel's chest. He pinned him to the ground, but the man continued to fight. He kicked and flailed, and Jesse was relieved when he heard the familiar sound of a thrown rope.

A lariat whistled through the wind and then snapped. The man stiffened, and Jesse knew exactly what had happened. Sneaking a look over his shoulder, Jesse saw that Creed had roped the crook's booted feet and held the rope tight with gloved hands.

"Yeehaw!" Creed yelled from a distance like he'd just roped a calf. "Got'em, Jesse!"

An officer raced past Creed, his gun drawn.

Jesse stared down at the crook. "I don't know where you're from, but around here we don't take kindly to thieves or anyone that would dare lay a hand on a woman. Now you get to join your lowlife friends in prison." He stood when the man raised his hands in surrender.

"Keep your hands up! Roll onto your belly!" the officer instructed as he got close. The man did as he was told, rolling over like a sausage in a skillet.

Knowing the thief was under control, Jesse moved toward Hazel like a beacon. She was no longer on the ground. She stood maybe ten feet away. Her ponytail was shoved to the side of her head, and grass stains streaked her tank top, but she looked more stunned than scared.

"You okay?" he asked as he neared. She nodded and Jesse unconsciously pulled her into a hug.

Hazel leaned into his embrace, her head fitting perfectly under his chin, and Jesse held her for a few long breaths. With his arms still wrapped around her shoulders, Hazel eased back and looked him in the eye. He was close enough to count the freckles across her nose. He wanted to wipe the dirt smudge from her cheek.

Before he could move or speak, Hazel said, "Evan caught the horse."

Jesse blinked and turned his head to see that his brother had ahold of the terrified colt. He'd snapped another lead to his halter and was removing the chain from his nose. Frankie had arrived with another horse to calm the colt's nerves.

"I heard something moving behind the shed," Hazel explained. "That guy took the horse out of the shed and was trying to leave with him through the woods."

Jesse stared at Hazel like he was looking at her for the first time. "You jumped on that guy's back." He couldn't believe she'd done that.

"First thing I thought of." Hazel blinked up at him. "Mom always said if someone attacks you, poke them in the eye or kick 'em where the sun don't shine. I thought I had a better chance at his eyes."

Jesse laughed, amazed at her bravery. "Good advice." He might've underestimated Hazel. Seemed like she had some cowgirl in her blood after all.

CHAPTER FOURTEEN

By sunset, they'd trailered all nine horses back to Frankie's and got them settled in their safe, temporary home. Because the horses needed veterinary attention, they were each placed in a stall in the barn. Everyone chipped in to prep the barn, even the kids. Wheelbarrows of cedar shavings were filled and dumped into each stall, making soft, clean pillows for the exhausted horses to rest. Fresh water was pumped into buckets, feeders were filled with green hay, and there were plenty of pats and rubs given throughout. As the evening went on, whinnies and pacing turned into chewing and quiet, and Hazel found herself relaxing too. She was dirty and tired, but happy knowing she played a part in rescuing these beautiful animals.

As she walked down the barn aisle, Hazel found Frankie in the stall with the dark brown horse that seemed to be the sickest. Jesse said the mare had colicked—which Hazel learned was a clinical term for abdominal pain that could turn deadly in a short amount of time.

Hazel stopped in the open stall door. "Is she doing better?" Hazel asked, knowing the vet had spent a good part of the evening treating this mare and stitching up the other two horses with deep wounds.

"She is." Frankie petted the mare's shoulder. The horse was standing, but looked exhausted. "But she's going to need monitoring overnight."

"Don't worry about the kids. I'll take care of them. Have they eaten yet? Is there anything else I can do for the horses?"

Frankie gave her a tired smile. "Joyce has the kids in the house. She whipped up some brats and tots. Why don't you go eat and rest? Believe me, Joyce has the kids handled. Garrett will stay here with me. We'll take shifts watching this one overnight."

Hazel felt bad going to get food and take a shower while Frankie stayed in the barn to help the sick horses. "Are you sure there's nothing else I can help with?"

Frankie pursed her lips like she was thinking. "Could you get me and Garratt some brats? And tots?"

"Absolutely." Hazel turned to leave the barn, but Frankie stopped her.

"Hazel?" Frankie asked. Hazel peeked back into the stall. "I didn't mean to drop that bomb on you. Mom's letters, I mean. I knew she left them in the carriage house for you. I just wanted you to find them sooner than later."

Hazel nodded in thought. "Have you read them?"

Frankie shook her head. "Haven't had the courage to go through much of Mom's stuff since she passed."

"I read the first letter . . ." Hazel trailed off and leaned against the wooden stall door.

"What did it say?" Frankie softly prodded.

"That she gave me up for adoption because she was too young, but that she thought of me often."

The two women stared at each other, hurt for different reasons.

"She thought of you all the time," Frankie said, concern wrinkling her forehead. "She told me that before she passed."

Hazel wasn't sure she had the capacity to talk about the letters or Rose tonight. She'd gone through a whole rollercoaster of emotions today, and now she just wanted to rest—her mind and body. "It's just a lot to take in. Too much for tonight, I think."

Frankie ran a hand over the horse's shoulder, petting her. "I'll read them with you if you want." Her offer was tentative, verging on nervous, and it urged a lump into Hazel's throat.

Hazel cleared her throat. "I'd like that." Hazel figured the letters would be hard for Frankie to consume as well. Maybe they could help each other navigate Rose's words? She gave

Frankie a reassuring smile. "I'll be right back with some food for you and Garrett."

Then she walked out of the barn, leaving her conversation about Rose and the letters for another night.

When Hazel entered the house, she saw Joyce and all five kids sitting around the kitchen table. She had the boys, Grace, and Charlie. Everyone was focused on a wooden board game filled with marbles.

Hazel shut the front door and Joyce looked up at her. The kids did not.

"Hey, sweetie," Joyce started, and Hazel's anxiety waned. She liked how Joyce used a term of endearment even though she barely knew Hazel. "You hungry?"

"I am. And I was going to grab some food for Frankie and Garrett too. Frankie said you made some brats?"

Joyce pointed to the kitchen counter. There were tinfoil wrapped paper plates. The rest of the kitchen was spotless. "I've got plates made up for you, Frankie, Garrett, and Jesse. Should still be warm. Would you mind taking a plate to Jesse's? He should be back from our barn soon. He went with Evan to finish chores at our place."

Hazel wondered where Jesse had gone in the past hour. He'd stayed at Frankie's to situate all the horses, and then he went to continue work at his family's barn? He had to be wiped by now. "Sure."

Hazel moved into the kitchen and stacked the warm plates on top of one another. "Thanks so much for cooking and watching the kids, Joyce. Really appreciate it."

Joyce waved a hand at her. "No problem at all. We watch out for each other around here. Besides, I love these little stinkers. Any time with them is a good time." She wrinkled her nose at Charlie, Wyatt, Tommy, Noah, and Grace. "Your turn, Noah."

Noah knelt in his chair and reached over the table to move a marble on the board.

"What are you guys playing?" Hazel asked.

"Joyce is teaching me how to play Chinese Checkers," Grace replied, looking excited as she stared at the board and then moved a white marble.

Hazel smiled and her heart warmed. Growing up in the city, she'd never experienced such a tight-knit community, people willing to help at the drop of a hat. Her graduating class had over six hundred students—many of which she didn't know—and most of her neighbors kept to themselves. But ever since Hazel arrived in Maple Bay, it was like she'd been sucked into a family, even when she resisted it.

"Thank you," she said again to Joyce, and then opened the fridge to grab a few drinks. "Maybe you can teach me how to play another time?"

"You betcha," Joyce replied, as Hazel dug in the fridge. "There's some cool beers in the crisper. Jesse would probably appreciate one."

Hazel grabbed waters for Frankie and Garrett. Then she opened the crisper and grabbed a few bottles of beer as well. They were well-deserved tonight.

After delivering food and drinks to Frankie and Garrett, Hazel made her way to Jesse's house. Cool evening air had snuck in, blowing out the hot day, and a low roll of thunder groaned in the distance. Hazel started jogging down the dirt road when big, sporadic raindrops began falling. By the time she made it to Jesse's cottage, the sky had opened, and rain was falling in sheets.

Hazel bound onto Jesse's porch and whipped open the screen door. The house was dark other than the light above the kitchen sink, so Hazel figured Jesse wasn't back yet. Once inside, she decided to leave his dinner and a beer on the kitchen counter. Should she leave a note? Hazel set the tinfoil plates and two beers on the counter and found a magnetic notepad and pen on his fridge. She put pen to paper but what was she going to write? *Thanks for coming to my rescue today, here's a brat. Your friend, Hazel?* Or, *Glad you punched that guy out. Got you a beer?* Or, *I thought about kissing you today, after you hugged me?*

Hazel shook her head and quickly scribbled, *Have a good night. - Hazel.*

She went to set the pen down, but nearly jumped out of her skin when Jesse burst through the door. The pen went flying and bounced off the cupboards.

"I brought you a brat," Hazel spat out, realizing she'd clutched at her heart at Jesse's entrance. He looked just as surprised to find her standing in his kitchen. "I mean, your mom made dinner. Just dropping it off."

Jesse sighed and ran a hand through his wet, dark hair, pushing it from his face. It looked like he'd been caught in the rain a little longer than she had. His blue jeans were soaked and peppered in mud below the knee, but it was his shirt that captured Hazel's eyes. His cotton t-shirt clung to his chest, looking like a second skin over hard-to-miss muscles. The thin cloth tightened and loosened as he caught his breath.

"Driving the four-wheeler instead of my truck wasn't the smartest decision." Rain dripped from his elbow to the tile floor.

"Here." Hazel grabbed the dish towel on the counter and handed it to him. She might as well have thrown him a napkin. The towel wasn't going to accomplish much, but Jesse took it anyhow. He wiped his neck and face, and she begged her eyes to look away. But as Jesse dabbed the rain away, Hazel noticed the state of his hand.

"Oh my gosh." She stepped toward him and gently pulled his hand from his face. His knuckles were ripped open and bleeding. She could see the start of bruising. "You need to get this cleaned up."

Before Jesse could protest, Hazel led him to the sink and turned on the faucet. She eased his hand under cool water, moving it back and forth, and used her own fingers to gently rub away the dirt and blood. When his hand was washed clean, Hazel turned off the water and looked up. She still held Jesse's hand and didn't realize how close he was to her. His blue eyes were locked on her, as if his knuckles weren't even a thought.

Her brain scrambled and spit out the next logical thought. "You need to get some ice on this." Letting go of his hand, she opened the freezer and removed an ice tray. Cracking it apart, Hazel shook out a few cubes and rolled them into the wet dish towel.

"I'm fine, Hazel."

She ignored him and wrapped his hand in the cold, rolled towel, tying it at his palm. "You're going to need some ibuprofen and antibiotic ointment. Do you have that?"

Jesse grinned. "Yes, I have ibuprofen and ointment, but I what I really need is this."

He leaned toward her, and Hazel's heart slapped her in the face. For a second, she thought he was going to kiss her. Instead, he took a beer from the counter. Holding it with his wrapped hand, he twisted the cap off with his other. "Join me for a beer?"

Hazel pressed her lips together, telling her heart to settle down. *For goodness' sake.* It was like she'd never been alone with a man before.

Jesse offered Hazel the sweating, open bottle. She tried to tell herself that she should head back to Frankie's, but she knew everyone and everything was taken care of there. Besides, she'd planned on drinking that cold beer, with or without company, and spending a little extra time with the man holding it wouldn't be the worst thing in the world.

"Sure." Hazel accepted the bottle. Jesse opened the other.

He raised his arms, as if she needed a reminder of how his clothes clung to his body. "I'm too wet and dirty to sit down in the house. Join me on the deck? There's a covered area."

Hazel took a sip of her beer, swallowing hard. She nodded and Jesse led her out the backside of the house. The wooden deck overlooked the lake and the first ten feet or so was covered by an overhang—which was good because rain continued to fall, hard. They each took a seat in rocking chairs.

Raindrops pounded the roof and slapped the lake. They couldn't hold a conversation over the rain, but it was nice to sit in silence, without any pressure. Hazel enjoyed her drink and breathed in the wet summer air. She let the rhythmic beat of the storm soothe her. By the time she was halfway through her beer, she'd melted into the rocking chair, wondering if she could sleep there.

Eventually, the rain eased and fell to a pitter-patter.

Jesse leaned his head back on the chair and turned his face to her. "What made you ask me about Charlie's name?" His question shook Hazel out of her trance. She'd almost forgotten about the letter.

Hazel rocked a few more times before replying. "A box I opened had a bunch of letters in it." She placed a hand on the wooden armrest and ran her fingers over it like a worry stone. "Letters that Rose wrote to me, but never sent."

Jesse picked his head up tentatively, immediately catching the gravity of her discovery. He patiently waited for Hazel to continue.

Hazel kept rocking, but knew she needed to know the truth, whatever it was. That was why she came to Maple Bay in the first place—to understand a past she hadn't been part of. "In the letter, Rose said she'd named me Charlotte and wanted to call me Charlie, for short." Hazel glanced at Jesse. He leaned against the armrest. His chair had stopped moving.

He shook his head, slowly. "I didn't know."

Hazel scrunched her brow, more confused than before. "You didn't know what?" There was something he wasn't telling her. "Why'd you name your daughter Charlotte? Did it have anything to do with the name that Rose picked out for me?"

Jesse ran his teeth over his bottom lip, considering what he was about to say. "Charlotte is Frankie's middle name. Frankie's full name is Francine Charlotte Barnes. Before she was married, her maiden name was Francine Charlotte Lovell. When Frankie was little and got in trouble, Rose would call her by her full name. Sometimes, she'd even call her Frankie Charlie Lovell. My daughter is named after Frankie."

Hazel had stopped rocking her chair now too. She'd gathered that Frankie and Jesse were close. But that close? Then she remembered what Jesse had told her when she asked about Charlie's name the first time—that he didn't name her. "Was Charlie's mother close with Frankie as well?"

Jesse took some time to answer, and Hazel felt like she shouldn't have asked that question.

"Charlie's mom was my sister," Jesse said after a minute. "She was also Frankie's best friend. My sister, Sarah, named Charlie after Frankie."

Hazel's breath caught in her chest. Her lips parted, and she repeated Jesse's words in her head. Charlie was Jesse's niece? Not his daughter?

"I adopted Charlie after my sister, Sarah, passed." Jesse eased back into his chair. "She died in a horrible riding accident. Charlie's dad was never involved in her life."

"I'm so sorry, Jesse," Hazel offered, stunned.

He reached for his beer and took the last gulp before staring out over the lake. "Charlie has been a complete blessing in my life." He adjusted the dish towel wrapped around his hand. "But she'll never know her mom. Sarah was an incredible person. Beyond incredible. She did everything big. She laughed big. She loved big. And she loved Charlie with every inch of her being. She was so excited to have a little girl. Charlie was just a baby when we lost Sarah."

Hazel closed her eyes, sopping up Jesse's pain, thinking how incredibly hard it must've been to lose a sister and take on the responsibility of her baby at the same time. Her sympathy also stretched over to Frankie. Frankie had lost her best friend *and* her mother?

Opening her eyes, Hazel reached for and grasped Jesse's hand—his uninjured one. "You might not know *yet* what a blessing you are to Charlie, but I can tell you that you are." He looked at her and she tightened her grip. "I see how you are with her, Jesse. I've only known you for a week and I know without a doubt that you're an amazing father. And if anyone knows the importance of adopted parents, it's me. You are the most important thing in that little girl's life, and I'm certain your sister is looking down on you and is so proud of what you've done, of how you love Charlie."

With only the moonlight peering through the rain, it was hard to read Jesse's expression, but Hazel continued to hold his hand.

"Thank you," he said, and his vulnerability pushed a piece of her own past to the surface.

A cricket chirped from below the deck. "I thought about adopting. After Grace." Hazel didn't admit that to many people. She didn't know why. It was almost like there was shame wrapped up in her confession.

"Why?" he asked softly.

Hazel wasn't sure if it was the emotional day, the cover of the storm, or the fact that she was holding Jesse's hand, but she was just comfortable enough to continue. "My ex-husband, Bill, and I tried for five years to get pregnant. I had two miscarriages that were nearly the end of me. Grace is my miracle baby. I didn't think I'd ever get her."

Jesse began making slow circles with his thumb on Hazel's palm, like he was encouraging her to continue. It worked. "I didn't let Grace out of my sight for three years. I never left her. No babysitters. I wouldn't leave her with my parents. I wouldn't even leave her alone with Bill. I was scared something bad would happen to her, that she'd stop breathing and I wouldn't be there to help her. That I'd somehow lose her, and it would be my fault." The last word caught in her throat and she knew she'd said enough.

"Hazel?" Jesse spoke her name like a question and waited for her to look at him. "The miscarriages were *not* your fault."

She couldn't believe he'd picked up on her guilt even though she hadn't specifically mentioned it. Hazel nodded.

It was an obligatory motion. Hazel carried the loss of her miscarriages with her. Even after ten years she couldn't convince herself she hadn't done something to lose her babies. If she'd just been more careful . . . she knew it was why she was overly protective of Grace, but she couldn't help it.

"I wanted to have a houseful of kids. I would've had five, maybe six, but was never able to get pregnant again after Grace. I wanted to adopt, but could never get Bill on board." If she were being honest with herself, all her fears and doubts had slammed a wedge between her and Bill that grew bigger and bigger over the years. Not that there weren't other wedges, but that wedge was a big one. And it was Bill's reluctance to adopt that ultimately distanced Hazel. Years later when Bill cheated on her, Hazel was devastated, but they'd been broken for years. She'd been holding her family together until it literally came apart at the seams.

"What's keeping you from having more kids? From adopting now?" Jesse asked, and Hazel blinked at him. She hadn't expected him to ask her that.

"I've thought about it. Of adopting on my own, but it's scary, you know—parenting by yourself." She gave him a lopsided smile, realizing she was preaching to the choir. "But I guess you know that."

Jesse bobbed his head. "I was certain I wanted to adopt Charlie, but completely terrified at the same time. I'd always been her fun uncle. Wasn't sure I'd know how to be her dad."

"You're a fast learner."

"Not so sure about that," he replied. "Charlie and I lived with my parents for the first six months. I had my own house. Bought this place ten years ago, but Sarah and Charlie had been living with my parents when she passed. I didn't want to take Charlie out of the home she was used to. Not right away."

"It was probably also nice to be there, with your mom and dad." Hazel knew Joyce was a mother hen and was sure she'd been there for Charlie and Jesse, even when she was desperately grieving the loss of her own child. Hazel hadn't met Jesse's father yet, but if he was anything like Jesse, Hazel knew he had a kind, protective soul.

"And your other siblings? Do they live close too?" She'd met Jesse's brother, Evan, today, but had heard Joyce refer to other kids and grandkids. She couldn't help but be curious as to why his other siblings hadn't adopted Charlie.

"Most of them do." He ran a hand through his dark hair. "Dad, Evan, and I run the breeding and training business. Evan has a place on the other side of my parents' property. My oldest sister, Anne, lives in town, with her husband and four kids. But my younger sister, Kat, moved to Chicago the year after Sarah passed. I wished she lived closer."

Jesse shifted in his chair before continuing. "Before the accident, both Kat and Sarah worked in the family business as well. They were really close. Kat took Sarah's death really hard."

Jesse's eyes looked far off, like he wasn't sure if he wanted to continue. Hazel wondered what had happened to his sister, Sarah. Had Jesse witnessed the riding accident? Had Frankie? She continued to hold Jesse's hand, thinking how completely horrible that must've been, no matter how it'd happened.

Jesse sat up, abruptly, jerking Hazel from her thoughts.

"Are you cold?" he asked. "You've got goosebumps all over your arms."

Hazel had been so lost in their conversation that she hadn't noticed she was getting chilled, but at Jesse's suggestion her body gave a shiver. "Maybe a little. But—"

She was going to say she should be getting back to Frankie's, but Jesse got out of his chair and went inside. A few seconds later, he appeared with a flannel shirt.

"Here," he offered, and Hazel stood to take the shirt from him. Instead, Jesse opened it up and threw it around her like a cloak. Soft cotton slid over her bare shoulders. Jesse tugged the shirt gently to cover her arms. "That should warm you up."

Hazel stared up at Jesse. He was backlit by a shimmer of moonlight and it further pronounced his strong features. "Thank you," she said. He hadn't removed his hold from the front of the flannel, and the weight of his grip kept the slightest tension between them.

Hazel didn't move.

Jesse's eyes took her in like they might surround her. It had been a long time since a man looked at her like that. A long time since she'd allowed it. Even though the rain and thunder had stopped, Hazel felt like she was standing at the edge of a thunderstorm. She didn't want to step away.

"Hazel?" Jesse asked.

"Yes," she breathed, wondering if he was going to kiss her. Did she even remember how to kiss a man?

"What were you thinking when you jumped on that guy's back today?"

She studied Jesse's tempting lips, distracted even as she answered his question. "That I wasn't going to let him get away."

A grin spread across his face. "You're a lot tougher than you look."

Hazel blew out a tight breath—along with a laugh—because she knew she looked pretty tough. At least, right now she did. Today she'd been thrown across the ground by a horse-thief, helped save a herd of stolen horses, and ran her dirty-self through the pouring rain. Her wet hair was *mostly* still contained in a ponytail, her tank top had grass and dirt stains all over it, and the mascara she'd stupidly applied this morning was probably smudged under her eyes like a raccoon.

But Jesse was looking at her like she couldn't have been prettier.

Hazel stopped breathing when he released a hand from the flannel shirt. Jesse placed a single finger under her chin and tipped her face up. His ice blue eyes explored her for what felt like hours before he leaned in and pressed his lips to hers. When he fully released his hold on the flannel, Jesse touched her with only his kiss and a single finger at her jaw. It was like he was giving her an out, space to back away if she wanted.

Hazel closed her eyes and kissed him back. She absorbed his sweet, strong scent—like cedar and wildflowers. A hint of the beer they'd shared lingered on his lips, and Hazel knew she was drawn into his kiss because they'd shared much more than a drink. It was like a thread had been sewn, connecting them through a buried past.

Wanting to be just a little closer, Hazel ran a shaky hand up his chest and brushed her fingertips over the dark stubble of his jaw. Jesse deepened the kiss and for that moment, Hazel let herself get lost in him.

But deep down, Hazel knew she couldn't fall for this man. Her life was not in Maple Bay. And she was coming to learn that Jesse deserved a woman that was all-in, someone that wouldn't pack up and leave at the end of the summer.

Reality gave Hazel pause, and she opened her eyes. When she did, Hazel spotted headlights shining through the house. She pulled back just as the front door squeaked open.

From inside the house, a man's voice called, "Jesse?"

Jesse's eyes went wide, though they still held a haze. "It's Garrett," he said, and Hazel instinctively dropped her hand and pulled Jesse's flannel around her like a blanket. "He's probably got Charlie."

Jesse cleared his throat and opened the screen door that led back into the house. "I'm on the deck, Garrett."

Garrett's shadow moved through the living room. As he neared the screen door, Hazel saw that he was carrying a sleeping Charlie.

"Oh, sorry," Garrett said, as he peeked out onto the deck. His eyes flitted over Jesse and Hazel. "I didn't mean to interrupt anything. Was just bringing Charlie home, because she fell asleep playing Chinese Checkers."

"It's fine," Jesse replied, still holding the door open. "Thanks for bringing her home."

Hazel didn't think Garrett saw them kissing, but realized she was standing close to Jesse and wearing his flannel. Her cheeks blazed like hot plates.

"I should be getting to bed too," Hazel said. "It's been a long day. Can I ride home with you, Garrett?"

"Sure." Garrett looked like he wasn't sure what to do next.

Hazel walked into the house. Jesse followed.

"I'll take her." Jesse reached out for Charlie and took his daughter from Garrett. Her little body fell against Jesse like a sack of potatoes.

"Where do you want me to put this?" Hazel started to pull the flannel from her shoulders.

"Keep it," Jesse insisted. "It's cold outside. I can get it from you tomorrow."

Hazel froze with one shoulder exposed. Then she eased the soft cotton back over her skin. "Thanks." She was sure she blushed again. "I'll see you tomorrow then."

"Tomorrow," Jesse replied.

They all said good night and Hazel endured an awkward ride home with Garrett. Thankfully, it was a short drive.

CHAPTER FIFTEEN

Frankie poured the rest of the ginger ale into the pitcher and set the empty liter bottle onto Joyce's packed kitchen island. Joyce, Anne, and one of Joyce's sisters, Judy, zipped through the kitchen like bees around a hive. Frankie knew not to linger long. She dipped a wooden spoon in the pitcher and gave it a swirl, mixing up the ginger ale, Hawaiian punch, pineapple juice, and ice.

"Punch is done," Frankie announced. She tossed the wooden spoon in the sink and the empty bottle in the recycling bin. Joyce whizzed by and gave her a squeeze on the shoulder.

"Perfect, sweetie." Joyce stopped at the counter and tipped the lid off a big, oval crockpot. She stirred the steaming sloppy joe mix and gave an approving nod. Setting the lid back in place, Joyce wiped a hand across her pink floral apron which covered khaki shorts and an even brighter pink floral top. "Go outside. Enjoy."

Joyce gave her a wink and Frankie smiled back. She headed out of the kitchen not because she wasn't wanted or wouldn't offer to help. Frankie just knew that everything was taken care of, and everyone had their job. Hers was to bring the punch.

For as long as Frankie could remember, Sunday afternoons were spent at the Weston household. She didn't remember a time in her life when she didn't know Joyce, Gene, or their kids. Rose and Joyce were thick as thieves. Had been since before Frankie was born. They grew even closer (if that was possible) when Frankie's father abandoned his wife and daughter in order to chase his lofty movie-star dreams somewhere in Los Angeles. Regardless of her father's choices, Frankie never felt like she missed out on a family. The Westons were Frankie's family even though they weren't related by blood, and she'd never appreciated them more than this year, after losing her mom. Outside of her husband, the Westons were what kept Frankie from fully falling apart. They'd been through a lot together.

Frankie stepped out the sliding glass door and onto the deck. Outside, the whole crew was spread out on the wide, grassy area between the house and the barn. They were setting up for a game of kickball. Tommy and Wyatt were discussing where to put third base. Evan prepared to roll a rubber ball to Noah so he could practice kicking. Garrett squatted next to Noah, giving him tips. Creed and Gene were in the outfield with Anne's four teenagers, sipping pops and waiting for the game to commence.

Frankie reached down to open the cooler on the deck, wanting to grab a cold pop before joining the game. Before she reached into the ice, Jesse's truck pulled up alongside the house and parked. He got out and opened the backdoor. Charlie and Grace spilled out of the backseat. Hazel appeared from the other side of the truck, holding a casserole pan covered in foil.

Frankie stood and waved, glad that Hazel and Grace were joining them. Frankie and Hazel had started to find a rhythm together this week between sharing a household, taking care of the kids, and working together. It would've felt strange if Hazel and Grace hadn't joined them for Sunday dinner at the Weston's.

The kids in the backyard yelled to Charlie and Grace, and the two girls ran off to join the kickball game. Hazel walked up the stairs and joined Frankie on the deck. She wore a cute sundress and sandals, and Frankie thought it'd be awfully hard to play kickball in that outfit. But that was okay. Frankie wouldn't judge Hazel for her sense of fashion. Eventually, Hazel would give in to Wranglers and cowboy boots.

"Where should I put the Oreo cheesecake bars?" Hazel asked. Frankie was completely jerked out of her thoughts concerning kickball and clothes.

"Excuse me?" Frankie asked. "Did you say Oreo? And cheesecake? Like together?"

Hazel grinned, sheepishly. "Made it last night. After you went to bed."

"You are a wizard." Frankie opened the sliding door for Hazel. "You can add it to the smorgasbord on the island."

Hazel stepped through the door and Joyce welcomed her from across the kitchen. Frankie had barely closed the door when Jesse handed her a Cherry Coke.

"Thanks," Frankie said, cracking open the pop.

Jesse stood from his crouched position over the cooler and shook his wet arm off. She knew he'd searched the very bottom of the cooler to find her favorite.

"Two more of the horses went home today." Frankie was referring to the horses they'd rescued last week. "The bay mare and the chestnut Thoroughbred."

Jesse grabbed a pop for himself and shut the cooler. "The mare that colicked?"

"Yep." Frankie took a swig of cold, cherry goodness and licked her lips. "I'm so glad she made it through that first night. I was worried about her."

"Me too."

"The horses belonged to a family from Winona. Two teenage girls. You should've seen the girls' faces when they finally saw their horses." Frankie was thankful she was able to help the girls get their horses back. Frankie still had the horse she grew up with—Ruby. Ruby was twenty-nine years old now and had seen Frankie through the roller coaster of life. She could only imagine what she would do if someone tried to steal her heart-horse. No, she didn't have to imagine. She knew. She would've killed that someone.

"How many are left?" Jesse asked.

"Two. Police are still trying to identify their owners."

He nodded, and Frankie looked Jesse up and down. He was disconnected from their conversation, which was weird. If Frankie had been talking about the weather, she would've expected half his attention. But they were talking about horses. They *always* talked about horses. It was their favorite subject. She squinted at him, about to call him out when laughter bubbled out from the kitchen. Frankie peered through the glass door. Joyce was near the sink, waving a ladle through the air like she was telling a story. Anne and Judy were giggling. Hazel was laughing. Full-on laughing. Her head tipped back, a hand to her chest.

"Must've been a good story." Frankie turned back to Jesse to find him engrossed in whatever was going on in the kitchen. "Jesse? Are you really hungry or something?"

He was fully focused on the kitchen. He hadn't even opened his pop yet.

Jesse's gaze returned to Frankie. "What?"

She squinted at him again, and it suddenly dawned on her what he was looking at.

"Holy cow," Frankie uttered. "You like Hazel."

"What? No." Jesse looked down at the can in his hand and popped the tab. He took a long drink, and Frankie knew he was avoiding her comment.

It had been years since Frankie had seen that look on Jesse's face—the one where his heart melted out through his eyes. She hadn't seen him look at a woman like that since before he adopted Charlie—back when he was engaged to Emily. Had Frankie been so wrapped up in work, the horses, and the kids that she hadn't noticed something growing between Jesse and Hazel?

"You totally like her." Now that Frankie thought about it, she had noticed a difference in Jesse in the past week. It wasn't strange that he arrived today with Hazel and Grace. He was a gentleman and had offered them a ride. Besides, his driveway literally passed the carriage house, where Hazel had been all morning, working on projects. In the past week, Jesse had been showing up at Frankie's barn in the mornings, to work with Indy. During the week, he usually showed up in the evenings, after all his regular clients were taken care of. But Hazel wasn't in the barn in the evenings. Now that she was working for Frankie, Hazel was in the barn during the day. Mostly in the office. "I thought it was weird that you kept going into the office to fill up your thermos. I've never seen you drink so much coffee. I thought I was going to have to take out a loan just to keep coffee grounds stocked."

Jesse chuckled, uncomfortably. "I drank a whole pot on Friday. By myself. And I was only at your place for an hour. Had the shakes by noon."

Frankie laughed, knowing she'd hit the nail on the head. Jesse had been making excuses to spend time in the office, to talk with Hazel. "So, you do like her, then?" Frankie posed her statement with less snark this time, trying to get Jesse to confess.

Jesse shrugged. "Not sure liking her is a good idea."

Frankie hooked a thumb in her belt loop. "Why? Because she's going to leave?" It was the exact thing Frankie was worried of. Now that she was getting to know Hazel, Frankie knew she wanted her sister to stay in Maple Bay, to stay a part of her life.

Jesse raised an eyebrow and leaned back against the railing. "I'm not in a place in my life anymore where I can just date or have a fling. If I'm going to get involved with a woman, I need to know there's a good chance she'll stay in my life for . . ."

Jesse trailed off, not finishing his sentence.

"Forever." Frankie abruptly finished his sentence. She knew what Jesse wanted. He was ready for a family and wouldn't let anyone into his heart that wasn't also ready for that commitment. He'd changed after Sarah's death, and Frankie knew it had to do with many things—guilt, responsibility, need.

Frankie had changed as well. She didn't take her family or friends for granted anymore, not for one second. She knew everything could change in an instant.

The door slid open and Hazel joined them on the deck, a big smile on her face.

"I love that you guys get together every Sunday. What a beautiful tradition." Hazel raised her shoulders like she was overflowing with happiness. When neither Jesse nor Frankie responded right away, Hazel's face fell. "Did I interrupt something?"

Jesse stood from the railing. "No, we were just talking about—" He looked like a deer in headlights.

Frankie jumped in. "Corn."

Hazel squinted an eye. "Corn?"

"Yeah, it's going to be a real good year for corn. See how tall it is already?" Frankie pointed to the neighbor's corn field. "Another month and it'll be taller than Jesse."

"And that's good when it's really tall?" Hazel asked.

"Yep, real good." Frankie looked back at Jesse. His eyes were pleading at her to close her mouth. She didn't. Instead, she jumped to a new topic. One that could be good for both her and Jesse. "Hazel, have you ever thought about cooking for a living?"

"Me? Like in a restaurant?" Hazel asked.

"You're an amazing cook, and it seems like you really enjoy it. You could work in a restaurant, start a bakery, or—" Frankie paused to drive home her point. "You could officially turn the carriage house into a bed-and-breakfast. Maple Bay doesn't have an inn, and the carriage house is in a great location, right next to the lake. It's the *perfect* getaway spot. And I honestly think people would come from all across the state just to get your cooking."

Frankie couldn't tell if Hazel was taken aback by her suggestion or considering it, but a shrill ring distracted them both. Pulling a cell phone from a pocket hidden in her sundress, Hazel looked down at the screen. She frowned.

"I have to take this," Hazel said. "Excuse me."

She gave a polite smile and answered the call as she walked off the deck and past Jesse's truck, obviously wanting space for a private conversation. As she did, Frankie's head churned with ways in which she could convince Hazel to stay beyond the summer. And how she could get Jesse and Hazel to spend more time together.

CHAPTER SIXTEEN

Hazel didn't want to talk to her ex-husband. She wanted to listen to Joyce tell another story about Jesse as a rambunctious little boy. She wanted to eat a sloppy joe and get to know the Weston family. She even had a strange urge to play kickball, though she'd never kicked a ball in her entire life. But Hazel and Grace had been in Maple Bay for nearly two weeks, and Hazel had yet to have had a conversation with Bill, other than texts.

"Hi," Hazel answered Bill's call and walked toward a tall oak tree.

"Hey," he replied. "Sorry it took me so long to call you back. Work has been crazy."

Bill always blamed his job for his lack of communication. Hazel knew Bill's real estate business was demanding, but it wasn't like he worked every minute of every day. Plus, his cell phone was practically glued to his hip. He could've easily gotten back to her after her first four calls. She figured his distraction had a lot more to do with Cynthia, the shiny-new toy he'd been dating for the past few months.

"Are you and Grace still out in the boondocks?" he asked.

"Maple Bay, Bill." She rolled her eyes. Hazel had texted Frankie's address to Bill the very first night she and Grace stayed in Maple Bay. He knew where she was.

"That's right. Maple Bay. Cute. You're coming home soon, right?" He asked her the question like she was on vacation.

Hazel hadn't told Bill the whole story. She would've if he'd picked up the phone, but she wasn't about to sum up her biological mother's death and a pending inheritance in a text or two. She took a deep breath and hoped this conversation didn't blow up in her face. She needed to get Bill on board with her plan if she was going to stay in Maple Bay until September. Hazel channeled her sweet voice, instead of the snappy version she wanted to use with Bill.

"A few weeks ago, I found out my biological mother passed away."

There was silence that followed. If nothing else, Bill knew what that would mean to Hazel.

"I'm sorry to hear that."

"Thank you," she continued, wanting to get it all out. "She left me a piece of property. That's why Grace and I came to Maple Bay. For the reading of her will."

"Okay." Bill sounded confused. "Like she left you her house?"

"Kind of." Hazel paced under the shady oak tree. "I also found out I have a sister. A half-sister."

"What? Wow."

"It's been an interesting few weeks," Hazel replied. "There were actually two properties in Rose's will. She left one property to me and one to my half-sister, Frankie. There was also a clause in her will. In order to inherit my property, I have to live here for the entire summer." Hazel squeezed her eyes shut as she finished her sentence, afraid of what Bill might say next.

"You're going to move there? For the summer?"

She rolled her teeth over her bottom lip. "I already did."

"What?" Bill's question was sharp. "You can't just move my daughter wherever you want to."

"*Our* daughter." Hazel's voice went raspy. "And I didn't just take her. I tried calling you for days after I learned about the will and the clause. If you would've picked up or called me back, I could've told you exactly what was happening. Besides, you know she's safe. She's with me, Bill."

Technically, Hazel and Bill had fifty-fifty custody of Grace, but Bill wasn't always good with his fifty percent. On one hand, Hazel wanted Grace with her all the time. On the other hand, she wanted what was best for her daughter. She wished Bill would learn how to prioritize his life and not make work his only commitment.

"I thought you just took her on a little summer vacation," Bill said. "Hazel, we have to make decisions concerning Grace together. You can't just decide for me."

Hazel about lost it. She gripped the phone tight, making sure she didn't spit out the first response that came to her mind. She wanted to tell Bill that since she met him, in her first year of college, Hazel had stupidly made Bill a priority in every major decision in her life. When he proposed, Hazel dropped out of school, never finishing her degree. She wanted so badly to be a wife and a mother. It was all she ever really wanted—to have a family of her own—so she did everything she could to make Bill's life easy and wonderful, forfeiting her own wants and needs. She thought that was what it meant to be a good wife, to make a happy family. It wasn't until later in their marriage, when Bill began checking out, that Hazel realized she couldn't make him feel a certain way about her or their family. It didn't matter how clean the house was, what fancy recipe she made for dinner, or how perfect their child was. It wasn't good enough for Bill. He was focused elsewhere—on a mistress.

"I'm not making decisions for you," Hazel started. "I'm asking you to work with me. For one summer." Hazel couldn't lie to herself. In the past few weeks, some surprising thoughts had crept into her head. She'd found herself wondering what her life would be like if she kept the carriage house, if she and Grace permanently moved to Maple Bay. Hazel was enjoying getting to know her sister and nephews. She was proud of the work she'd completed so far on the carriage house. Grace was blooming around the horses, coming out of her shell. Not to mention, the kiss and conversation she'd shared with Jesse had sparked something inside Hazel she couldn't ignore.

But now, talking with Bill, Hazel was whipped back to reality. She couldn't move to Maple Bay permanently. Her child's father lived in Haven Hills, and that was where Hazel needed to be, at least until Grace was grown. Hazel wouldn't move four hours away from Haven Hills and miss out on time and experiences with her daughter. Even when Grace was with her father, Hazel still attended every cheer practice and school event. Plus, she needed to be close to Grace in case her daughter needed her. What if there was an emergency and it took Hazel four hours to get to her daughter? No. Hazel wouldn't allow that.

Hazel's mind rattled back to her original plan. "If I stay here through Labor Day, the property will be signed over to me and I can sell it." She needed the money. Bill knew that.

"That's fine."

Hazel nearly tripped. "It's fine?"

"It's fine that *you* stay there for the summer," Bill corrected her. "But Grace needs to be with me on my weeks. I'll pick her up from your parents' place Monday morning, like the custody papers say."

"Monday morning? Like, tomorrow morning?" That was exactly what the custody papers said, but that hadn't been the case since the divorce. Bill picked up Grace when it was convenient for him—if he wasn't too busy with work or gallivanting about in his dating life. *Now* he wanted to follow the custody agreement?

"Cynthia and I have been dating for a couple months now and she's only met Grace a few times. It would be nice if she could get to know her over the summer."

Hazel's heart squeezed like it was in a vice. She knew this was part of being divorced, part of co-parenting, that Grace would be introduced to new women in her father's life. But Cynthia was the third girlfriend Bill had introduced to his daughter in the year since the divorce.

"Bill—" Hazel started.

"Cynthia is great with kids," he said casually. "And she'll watch Grace while I work."

That brought a whole new level of anxiety to Hazel. Grace was shy. She was quiet and sensitive, and Hazel knew her daughter wouldn't be comfortable hanging out all day with a woman she didn't know. Grace's sweet little heart was still healing from the divorce and she didn't need to be babysat by her father's twenty-something girlfriend. Especially if Bill could be distracted by a shiny new toy in a month or two. Grace needed to be here, with Hazel, having a carefree summer full of fun. She deserved that.

"It's almost the end of June. I just need you to work with me for two months. Grace is having a great time here. There are horses for her to ride, a lake for her to swim, and I want her to get to know her aunt and her cousins." Hazel was pouring out anything that might change Bill's mind. She didn't even have a car to drive back to the city. She had planned to use every cent from her car's sale to pay for renovations and living expenses.

Bill sighed. "Two months is a long time."

She knew she was asking a lot, but Hazel was trying to start a new life for her and Grace.

"Look," Bill continued. "I've got to get going. I've got a showing in a few minutes. We can talk more about this in the morning, when I pick Grace up at your parents'."

Hazel pushed away any fantasy she might've drummed up about starting fresh in Maple Bay, of owning and running a bed-and-breakfast, of raising Grace in this sweet small town. Hazel knew she couldn't make that happen, but she hadn't yet given up on staying in Maple Bay for the summer.

Pulling out her last bargaining chip, she said, "I'll give you the listing." Hazel knew Bill was in just as tough of a financial spot as she was. He was starting over as well, recovering from their shared debt and the divorce. Furthermore, the housing market in the Haven Hills had been tough in the past year.

"What are you talking about?"

"The property I'm inheriting," Hazel continued. "It's ten acres on a lake. The building is actually a beautiful historic carriage house and I'm fixing it up so it can be sold as an inn or even as a single residence. I think it will sell fast. If Grace and I can stay here for the summer, together, I'll be able to put it on the market right after Labor Day. You can have the listing. And the commission."

Bill's silence told her she'd gotten his attention. Hazel heard a car door open and close.

Hazel tried to sweeten the pot, "And when we move back to Haven Hills, we can work out a schedule to make up for the weeks you gave up, if you'd like."

Bill gave a deep sigh. "You said Grace is having a good time?"

"She is." Hazel held her breath.

"I guess that's okay then." He sounded irritated. "As long as she's having fun."

Hazel closed her eyes, relieved. Bill said he was at his showing and needed to go. She hung up, put her phone back in her pocket, and tried to blow out all the frustrations she was feeling. When that didn't work, she walked back toward the deck.

Jesse was standing in the same place, at the deck railing.

"Everything okay?" he asked, his brows pinched.

"Everything is fine." Hazel pushed a smile onto her face. "I'm going to see if your mom needs any help in the kitchen." Hazel walked into the house, wanting a spatula, spoon, or towel in her hand—something tangible to focus on, outside the whirlwind of emotions that had just shot through her.

CHAPTER SEVENTEEN

Before Sunday dinner, when Hazel's phone rang and she pulled it from her pocket, Jesse saw the name on her screen—Bill—and knew that was Hazel's ex-husband's name. When her face fell and Hazel proceeded to have what looked like a heated conversation, Jesse had a hard time keeping his feet on the deck. He wanted to save Hazel from whatever was making her pace, but didn't think it was his place to push those boundaries. He didn't know enough about Hazel or her previous marriage to step in and help. He also knew past relationships could be complicated. Especially when you had a child together.

Besides, what was he going to do? Go find the guy and set him straight? Make sure he knew how stupid he was for letting Hazel get away?

Whatever was said over the phone had upset Hazel, and Jesse hated that. It upset her enough that she'd gone quiet

Sunday afternoon, at least toward him. The truck ride over to his parents' house had been full of laughter and excitement. The ride home held this strange sense of formality, like Hazel needed distance from Jesse.

Even though he didn't want to, Jesse took her cue and gave her the space she silently asked for. Over the next few days, Jesse continued to work at Frankie's barn in the morning, when Hazel was there, but he kept a respectful distance. At least he tried to. Frankie's first summer camp was in full swing. There were six campers, including Grace, and Hazel marched the kids around the barn and arena like a momma bear. Frankie taught all lessons that involved the horses, but Hazel managed everything in between. She made meals and coordinated activities. Jesse found himself watching her whenever he got a chance. With the kids she was at ease, at home in her own skin. She was relaxed, cheerful, even giddy, and Jesse found himself in a predicament. Even from a distance, he was being drawn in by Hazel.

But he wouldn't pursue her if she wasn't ready for a relationship. So instead of making excuses to spend time with Hazel, Jesse kept to his task. He worked with Indy, helping the gelding regain his confidence so he could eventually find a new home. Thankfully, Jesse was making progress with the horse. By the middle of the week, he was riding Indy in the round pen.

At least Jesse was making steps forward in one area of his life. It just wasn't in his love life.

After untacking Indy and putting him back out in the pasture, Jesse headed toward his truck.

"Hey, Jesse!" Frankie walked out of the barn leading Daisy. The paint mare was saddled and bridled. "Can you help me with something? It'll just take a second."

"Sure. What's up?" he asked, even though he knew he should hit the road. He had two more stables to visit and three colts that needed to be worked at his own barn.

Frankie handed Daisy's reins to Jesse. "Can you take her out in the arena? I want to show the kids the proper way to get on a horse. This afternoon they'll all have their first riding lesson."

"Okay." That was simple enough. "Come on, pretty girl." Jesse led Daisy away from the barn and into the sand arena.

Frankie called to Hazel. She was sitting with the kids at the picnic table under the maple trees. They were working on a craft project that involved horseshoes, glitter, and paint, but the kids eagerly abandoned their crafts when they saw Jesse and Daisy. Hazel led the kids into the arena, and they glowed like spotlights. Jesse grinned at their enthusiasm.

"Kids, this is Jesse." Frankie strode through the gate, tailing the group. All six kids greeted Jesse with waves and eager hellos—even Grace, who obviously already knew Jesse. "Jesse is going to show you the proper, safe way to get in the saddle. You need to pay close attention as you will each be getting up on Daisy after the demonstration. Okay?"

Heads nodded seriously, and Jesse draped Daisy's reins over her neck, preparing to show the crew how to mount a horse. He started to fiddle with the saddle stirrup, making sure it was long enough, but Frankie cleared her throat.

"Actually, I was hoping you could hold the horse and Hazel could get on," Frankie said. "That way I can give play-by-play instructions while you two act it out. Thanks a bunch. This will be *great*."

Frankie didn't wait for anyone's input. She took Hazel by the arm and nudged her toward Jesse. Hazel stepped forward, away from the kids, though she looked like she might run or hide.

Frankie wasn't making a lick of sense. She could've mounted Daisy by herself and given instructions to her students as she did it. The whole scenario was fishy, but Frankie's shifty grin told Jesse all he needed to know. She'd noticed that Jesse and Hazel weren't talking, and Frankie wasn't about to allow that to continue.

"Let's all encourage Hazel, because this will be her very first time getting on a horse. Just like all of you. Isn't that great?" Frankie laid the pressure on thick and her scheme was working. The kids clapped and uttered variations of, "You can do it, Ms. March."

When Grace chimed in with "You got this, Mom," Hazel succumbed with a sigh.

"You don't have to do this if you don't want to," Jesse whispered, hoping only Hazel heard. She stood awkwardly, like she was having a debate with herself. "But you do know they sense fear, right?"

Hazel quirked an eyebrow. "Horses? Or kids?"

Jesse smirked, thinking she was right on both accounts. Horses and kids had an innate sense for sniffing out fear. Then they either ran from it or took advantage of it. He offered his hand in case Hazel wanted to take it. "This will be painless. I promise. Daisy is a veteran. The only time she senses fear is if she thinks her dinner might be late." He tipped his head toward Daisy. The well-fed mare was standing like a statue, her bottom lip droopy as though she'd missed out on her mid-morning nap.

"If there's even the slightest chance that I might fall, I fully expect you to catch me," Hazel warned. Then she set her hand in Jesse's. His heart gave a traitorous thud.

"You won't fall." He would catch her if she did.

From behind, Frankie started giving instructions. "So, the first thing Hazel needs to do is make sure she has control of the reins."

Jesse took Frankie's cue and guided Hazel's hand to the reins that hung over Daisy's neck. Without words, he curled her fingers around the leather. "I've also got ahold of the reins so Daisy won't go anywhere. Now, just put your left foot in the stirrup, grab the saddle horn, and pull yourself up."

Hazel's back was only a few inches from his chest. She turned her head to him, and his eyes ran down the curve of her neck, fully missing whatever Frankie had been babbling about in the background.

"Sure glad I wore jeans today," Hazel whispered, and raised her leg to put a tennis shoe in the stirrup. After a little hop and a grunt, Hazel pulled herself up and swung a leg over Daisy.

She shimmied into the saddle seat, looking surprised by her feat.

"You look like a pro," Jesse said.

Hazel seemed amused by his comment and gave him a grin. It warmed him from the toes up. The kids clapped, and Hazel patted Daisy on the neck.

"Thanks for standing still and not making me look like a *total* city slicker. You're officially my favorite horse," Hazel said.

Jesse patted the mare as well.

"Now, Hazel needs to dismount," Frankie called, and explained the necessary safety tips as Hazel reversed what she'd just done. She swung a leg up, over, and down, but as one foot found the ground, the other got stuck in the stirrup. The hang-up was just enough to make Hazel teeter.

Jesse immediately placed a hand on her lower back.

"I've got you," he said, steadying Hazel and giving her time to loosen her shoe from the stirrup. Hazel pulled her foot out and placed both feet back on the ground. Jesse kept his hand splayed over her back.

"Thank you." Hazel blushed. "Guess there's more than one way to look like a city slicker." She quirked her mouth and Jesse wanted to kiss it.

"You did good." He reluctantly let his hand fall from her back. "You just need practice."

"See, kids," Frankie said. "There's another safety tip for you. That is why we *always* wear cowboy boots when we ride. And we always keep our heels down. We don't want to get our foot hung up in the stirrup, right?" The kids agreed boisterously with Frankie. "But we'll give Hazel a pass today, because I didn't exactly give her a heads-up that she'd be getting on a horse."

"No, you did not," Hazel replied, adding a sassy look for Frankie. Then she said to the kids, "All right, now it's your turn. I want you guys to line up next to me and show me what you've learned."

Jesse kept hold of Daisy as Frankie helped each camper safely mount and dismount. Hazel cheered the kids on like they were practicing for the Olympics, and Jesse forgot why he was keeping his distance from Hazel. He also wondered if Frankie had any safety tips for his heart.

CHAPTER EIGHTEEN

My Sweet Hazel,

Today is your fifth birthday. Your parents still send me a picture of you every year, and I am beyond thankful for their kindness. You're getting so big. I keep comparing this year's picture to last year's, and I can't believe how much you've grown. Your hair is almost the exact same color as mine, and I think you have my nose. I still think of you every day.

For your birthday, I made something for you—a wooden box to hold all the letters I've written to you. For the past few months, I've been cutting pictures from magazines and gluing them to the outside of the box. It's like a collage of wishes . . . blessings that I hope for your life. I picked out pictures of happy families, cozy houses with white picket fences, and any picture that reminded me of love. One day I hope I get the chance to give you my box of letters so you can know how much I've loved you, even from afar.

I also wanted you to know I'm in a better place now. This year I made a big change. I left Minneapolis and moved to a new town. I needed a fresh start, so I opened a map, closed my eyes, and let my finger fall where it might. I know it sounds crazy, but I blindly picked this wonderful little town—Maple Bay. I've got my own apartment above a beautiful flower shop on main street. I can see the lake from my living room. I got a job waitressing at a diner and immediately hit it off with one of the other waitresses, Joyce. She's become my best friend. I've got a steady job, a good home, amazing friends, and I even started going to church. If you had come into my life today, things would've been different. I would've had a good home to raise you in.

Love always,
Rose

"Mom didn't talk a lot about her life before Maple Bay," Frankie said to Hazel. They were sitting side-by-side on the carriage house floor, next to the boxes and furniture that hadn't been touched since Hazel read the first letter from Rose. "Mom said Grandpa passed when she was in elementary school. And I only met our Grandma a few times."

Hazel looked at the letter they'd just read, together. She set the paper on her knee but didn't let it go. "They didn't have a good relationship? Rose and her mom?"

Frankie shook her head. "I never really understood it until she told me about you. For a long time, Mom blamed Grandma for losing you. She wanted to keep you but wasn't given a choice. Mom was only sixteen and Grandma sent her away, to a convent, the day she found out about the pregnancy. Grandma had the adoption setup before you were born."

Hazel's heavy heart collided with the opposition of giggles that echoed into the carriage house from outside. The sliding barn door was wide open, and the kids were playing a game of tag in the setting sun. Grace squealed as Tommy ran by and tagged her.

"I can't picture my life without Grace in it." Hazel didn't even want to think about what it must've felt like to carry a child, give birth, and then give your baby away. Grace's birth was the happiest day of Hazel's life. "That must've been really hard for Rose."

Hazel found herself sympathizing with Rose, comparing her pain to the agony Hazel had felt after each miscarriage. Hazel had grieved each baby she'd lost. Had Rose done the same? Was it worse because she knew her child was somewhere in the world, being raised by someone else?

"I can't even imagine," Frankie said. "I mean, my boys drive me crazy sometimes, but I wouldn't trade them for the world. They're my heart."

They were quiet as they watched the kids play.

Hazel swallowed. "Rose sent me one letter. A few months after my thirteenth birthday. Her letter said that she was happy I had a wonderful home and parents, and that she wished me the best. There wasn't a mention of wanting to meet me or get to know me. At the time, I thought that meant she didn't care. But maybe Rose thought she was giving me a better life by not being in it?"

Frankie looked flustered, like she couldn't find the answer she desperately wanted to give. "The Rose I knew was an amazing person. An amazing mother. And I hope you're able to see that as we read her letters. I think she took a while to find her way in life, but that she truly wanted the best for you."

Hazel soaked up Frankie's words. She took the letter from her lap, folded it, and placed it back in the box, next to the other letters she and Frankie had read tonight. They'd read through the letters written on Hazel's second through fifth birthdays. "I think that's enough for tonight. Let's go out with the kids and enjoy the evening."

Frankie conceded with a soft smile. She rose from the wooden floor and leant a hand to Hazel.

Hazel used Frankie as a crutch and stood. "Nothing will make you feel old like sitting on the hard ground."

Frankie grinned and they walked out of the carriage house, arm in arm, to join the kids.

On the patio, Frankie stacked wood in the raised, metal firepit while Hazel unwrapped graham crackers, marshmallows, and chocolate bars. She set them on the table. When the fire started crackling, the kids flocked to it like moths and each grabbed a stick. The boys roasted their marshmallows quickly, mostly burning them and laughing at each other when the white puffs turned to charcoal and goo. Grace turned hers slowly over the fire, rolling the marshmallow in the heat until it was golden. Hazel reveled in the happy moment, truly thankful for the experiences she was able to share with her daughter here in Maple Bay.

"Here you go, sweetie." Hazel had a graham cracker and a piece of chocolate in her palm. Grace placed her golden marshmallow on top of the chocolate and pushed it off the stick with another cracker. Then she took the sweet sandwich and bit into it, her eyes fluttering in bliss.

As Grace chewed, Hazel ran a hand over her daughter's chestnut ponytail. "You did such an amazing job with the horses today. I'm so proud of you. Such a little cowgirl you are."

"Thanks, Mom. It was so much fun. I can't wait to ride again tomorrow."

"I'm glad. It was so fun to watch you take your very first ride today. Can't wait to watch you again tomorrow."

Grace licked a chocolate smear from her finger. "And I'm proud of you. I never thought you'd ever get on a horse, but you did it!"

Hazel's heart swelled. She put an arm over Grace's shoulders and squeezed. "Thank you, baby. I needed to hear that." How was it that her angel of a daughter knew exactly what to say to soothe her cares? Hazel kissed Grace's forehead. As she did, she noticed a light on in Jesse's house and thought about how he'd helped her get on Daisy today. And how he caught her when she'd stumbled. "Do you think Jesse would like a s'more too?"

"Of course," Grace replied, like that was a silly question. "Everyone loves s'mores."

"Will you help me make him one?"

Grace put another marshmallow on her stick and started the meticulous process of roasting a golden treat. When two picture-perfect s'mores were complete, Hazel set them on napkins and carried them toward Jesse's house, leaving Grace to talk horses with Frankie and the boys. When she was halfway across the lawn, Hazel saw a dark figure strolling down the dock. It had to be Jesse. The figure walked to the end of the dock and took a seat.

Did Jesse want to be alone? He could obviously see that Hazel, Frankie, and the kids were sitting around the fire. Why hadn't he joined them?

Hazel started to turn around, not wanting to intrude, but something inside her made her stop. Maybe it was the way he'd eased her nerves today. Or the way he'd made her feel that rainy night on his deck. Why couldn't she give herself permission to enjoy the company of a man again? It didn't need to be anything more than that.

Today, she'd stepped out of her comfort zone and got on a horse. She put one foot in the stirrup and her butt in the saddle. The horse didn't run, buck, or rear. It didn't reach back and bite her or throw her to the ground like a ragdoll. In fact, her time in the saddle wasn't scary at all. Nothing bad had happened. Instead, Hazel had surprised herself *and* made her daughter proud.

Now there were other chances she needed to take.

Hazel stepped on the wooden dock and padded across it in her bare feet. As she did, Jesse looked back. He was silhouetted by the yellow moon and its reflection off the dark blue waters. Hazel couldn't see his face until she got close. "Mind if I join you?" she asked, only a few steps behind him. His cowboy boots were on the dock, his jeans pulled up to his knees. He must've just got done with work.

Jesse scooted over, making room for her on the edge of the dock. "Not at all. Just taking a breather." He smiled at her and Hazel's heart fluttered.

"Where's Charlie?" Hazel took a seat and shimmied her yoga pants up to her knees so she could dangle her feet in the lake as well. As she did, she tried to remember the last time a man had physically affected her like that—forced her heart to buzz like a hummingbird. Her memory blanked on a result.

"Still with my mom. I'm going to pick her up after they finish their game of Chinese Checkers."

"I love that Joyce plays board games with the grandkids. So many of the kids that Grace has grown up with just bury their heads in electronics."

"That's not really a thing around here. At least, my parents would never allow it. Me either. We've got too many fun things to do around here. No time to waste staring at a phone."

"Lots of fun things. Like campfires." Hazel handed Jesse a s'more wrapped in a napkin. "Speaking of, I brought you a s'more."

Jesse raised his eyebrows and accepted the treat. "Thank you," he said, "And, cheers."

"Cheers." Hazel followed Jesse's lead, touching their s'mores together like two champagne glasses.

"You know, you don't always have to bring me food in order to come talk to me. I mean, I appreciate it, but you can just come talk to me . . . anytime you want to." Hazel had taken a big bite of her s'more but stopped chewing to consume Jesse's comment instead. He'd called her out on something she didn't even realize she was doing. Hazel had been using food as an ice breaker—an excuse to feel needed in a space she wasn't sure how to enter.

"It's my love language," she replied through a mouthful, without thinking. As soon as the words left her lips, her stomach dropped—probably all the way to the bottom of the lake.

Jesse made a sound in his throat like he was clearing marshmallow.

"I mean—" Hazel quickly chewed and swallowed. "I show my love by giving gifts." Had she really just sat down next to Jesse and dropped the L-word in the first two seconds of conversation? "Gifts. Gestures. It's how I show I *care*." She emphasized *care*, backpedaling and trying to distract from her casual use of the word *love*. Could she be any more awkward?

Jesse wiped his mouth with a napkin. In his silence, the cool breeze off the lake turned hot.

"My love language is spending time together," he replied, and Hazel glanced at him. His blue eyes were soft, concealing any judgement she thought she'd find. "Spending quality time together. Making memories. *This*."

Her chest thudded. Jesse not only knew what *his* love language was, he was now talking about how it applied her. *To them.*

"Is that why you like to cook?" he asked, pushing past the over analyzation going on in her head.

Hazel set her napkin-wrapped s'more on the dock, refocusing as she thought about his question. "It's one reason. Probably the biggest." Cooking and baking allowed her to funnel her creativity into a meal or a treat that filled bellies and brought smiles. "Food makes people happy. It brings people together. I like to make my family and friends feel good." She placed her hands next to her knees, folding her fingers over the edge of the dock and swirling her feet in the water.

Jesse watched her like she was telling him a story. "What are the other reasons?"

Hazel made a slow circle with one foot and a water ring spread out around them. "It makes me feel needed. And part of something." Her response poured out of her, but she'd never seen that truth until Jesse had prodded. She got an immense amount of joy watching loved ones enjoy her cooking. And it did make her feel part of something—it had always brought her closer to family and friends. "Wow, you should've been a therapist."

Jesse chuckled. "I think I'm better at reading horses than people."

"I think you're pretty good at reading both," Hazel replied. "You're very intuitive. You see things most people miss."

"I try to pay attention." Jesse brushed off her compliment like his attention to detail didn't make him special. But it was his attention to detail, his attention to her that made her feel seen. Hazel wondered what it would be like to be with someone like Jesse. A man that took the time to see her, that was sensitive to her needs and wants. She'd gotten so used to making everyone else a priority, that she'd almost forgotten what it would be like to be a priority herself.

"Hazel?" Jesse asked. His dark hair was pushed back from his face, showing off the strong angles of his jaw and cheeks. "Is this okay?"

"This?"

"Spending time together," he clarified. "Getting to know each other. Kissing."

Hazel's stomach flip-flopped. She couldn't deny—even to herself—how his kiss had made her feel. Jesse had ignited something inside her that she'd lost long ago. But *this* . . . this wasn't permanent.

"I want it to be." She was being honest. She wanted more of Jesse. She also didn't want to fall into a relationship that would be a memory come fall. She was able to stay here, in Maple Bay, for the next few months. She could enjoy her time with Jesse, but only for the summer. After that, she would need to go back to her life in Haven Hills. Grace needed to be close to her father. And Hazel needed to be close to her daughter, always. "I like spending time with you. And Charlie. And your family."

Jesse considered his next words. He slid his hand around the inside of her elbow and gave a tug. "Lay down with me."

"Here?"

Jesse lowered his back to the dock, keeping his feet in the water.

Hazel followed, and they laid side-by-side across the wooden planks.

"I come out here to decompress," he said. They both stared up at the night sky. It was full of stars, like coarse sugar dumped on a navy plate. "There's something about being between the water and the stars. Reminds me to take a breath and enjoy the moment, because you don't know what tomorrow will bring."

Hazel swallowed, taking that to heart, knowing that Jesse had endured great loss with the death of his sister. She also thought of the letters she'd just read—of what Rose had written to her, but never sent. What would have happened if Rose had taken a chance and reached out to Hazel while she was still alive? Told her the words she had only written? How would both of their lives have been different?

Hazel inched her hand toward Jesse's. She looped her pinky finger over his and confessed what she was really scared of. "I don't want to hurt Grace or Charlie." She tilted her head to him. He did the same. "In the fall, I'll need to move back to Haven Hills, for Grace's sake. I can't keep her from her father. And I won't ever choose to be separated from her."

No matter how much she wanted Jesse to keep looking at her like he was, Grace would always be Hazel's priority, the deciding factor in every decision.

Jesse bent his leg and brought a foot up onto the dock. Droplets cascaded back into the lake, but he never looked away. "I don't want to hurt the girls either." The silence that followed was punctuated by laughter from the campfire.

"Do you think we could just enjoy each other's company for the summer? No promises past that? And no kisses in front of the girls?"

Jesse's offer tempted her. It also frightened her. But maybe she needed to take this step, to open her heart to the possibility of a connection. If they kept their feelings to themselves, she could protect Grace and Charlie from any heartbreak at the end of the summer. Though if she took this chance, she wasn't so sure her heart would be allowed the same protection.

"I do enjoy your company." Hazel tightened her pinky finger around his. "And I'd appreciate it if we stayed friendly in front of the girls." She gave him a smile, trying to convey the nerves and excitement tingling through her. He squeezed her pinky back. Then they both looked up, into the sky, and kept each other company under the summer stars.

CHAPTER NINTEEN

The following weekend brought Maple Bay Days, an annual event which always fell on the weekend closest to the Fourth of July. The whole town looked forward to and participated in the festivities. There was a rodeo, parade, carnival, and a barn dance. Jesse's family had been involved with the town event since it started, nearly a hundred years ago. His great-great grandfather had been on the very first committee that planned and hosted the rodeo, which had grown into a well-respected event that drew competitors from all over the Midwest.

Ever since the beginning of Maple Bay Days, there'd always been a Weston on the rodeo committee. For the past thirty years, it had been Jesse's dad, Gene. However, Gene wasn't the only Weston involved with the festivities. Joyce and her sister, Judy, coordinated the Maple Mercantile—a tented area near the carnival and rodeo which was full of food vendors and shops. Jesse's sister, Anne, organized the barn dance. Evan and Jesse were involved in the rodeo—running bucking chutes, riding as pick-up men, or doing any task to keep the rodeo running smoothly. Creed usually jumped in to help wherever needed as well—when he wasn't competing in rodeo events.

Maple Bay Days was like Christmas in July—an event everyone in the town looked forward to—but Jesse couldn't remember the last time he was *this* excited. Because this year he got to share it with Hazel and the girls.

"Knock, knock," Jesse called loudly as he and Charlie entered the carriage house. He'd let himself in. Hazel had invited that since their conversation on the dock, but he still waited for Hazel to call back before he headed up the stairs to the loft. He didn't want to give her a heart attack like he had before, though he wouldn't mind if she fell into his arms again.

"I'm just finishing up the scones," Hazel called, and Charlie ran for the stairs.

"What's a scone?" Charlie yelled, disappearing into the loft.

Jesse followed and heard Hazel answering Charlie's question.

"Wow," he said, entering the loft. He'd intended to compliment the warm, sweet smell that filled the space, but his eyes landed on Hazel, Grace, and Charlie, and *wow* didn't even describe a fraction of how he felt.

A few days ago, Jesse had helped to move and hook up a fridge and oven in the loft, completing Hazel's kitchen. Hazel and Frankie discovered the almost-new appliances at an estate sale. They fit perfectly with the cabinets Hazel had sanded and stained, and this morning was the first time Hazel had used her new kitchen. A pan of scones sat cooling on the stove. Muffin tins and mixing bowls filled the deep farmhouse sink. Boxes and Tupperware full of goodies covered the counter. And in front of it all, Hazel stood, wearing a flour-dusted apron and a smile that went from ear to ear. Grace wore a matching apron and held a spatula. They both watched Charlie intently as Hazel bent down and popped a piece of a scone into Charlie's mouth.

"What do you think?" Hazel asked as Charlie chewed.

Charlie's eyes got big. "Can I have more?"

Hazel laughed. "Of course. Here, finish this one off." She handed Charlie the rest of the triangular scone.

For a second, Jesse imagined what it would look like to come home to Hazel and the girls every day. To wake up with Hazel and make breakfast. To be a family.

"How about you, Jesse?" Hazel asked, pulling him out of his fantasy. "What do you want to try? I've got vanilla bean scones, chocolate croissants, blueberry lemon bars, and strawberry crumb cake muffins."

"You made all that for the mercantile?" Jesse asked.

"Just four dozen of each. Your aunt said they could go through a few hundred baked goods at the coffee stand each day. I made a little extra. Couldn't help myself." Hazel gave him a slanted smile. "And I'll make more tomorrow morning for the rest of the weekend."

"Judy and Myra will be so excited."

Jesse's aunt, Judy, owned the coffee shop in town— Perkup Coffee—and she always had a very popular booth at the Maple Mercantile. Usually, Judy baked all the pastries for the shop, but she'd been doing less and less because of her bad hip. Her daughter, Myra, helped to run the shop, but barely had time to run the business, let alone bake all the goodies. They were shorthanded and overworked. When Joyce heard they might not have any pastries to offer at Maple Bay Days, she picked up the phone and called Hazel.

"I'm so thankful for the opportunity," Hazel said. "And that your mom thought of me."

"Mom and Judy have *loved* the desserts you've brought to Sunday dinner the past few weeks. They don't hand out compliments easily when it comes to baking, and I've heard them gush over your desserts multiple times."

Hazel glowed at the praise. "That makes me so happy. And I'm glad to help Judy. Plus, the money I make this weekend will help pay for a few more repairs around here."

Jesse glanced around the loft. Outside of the kitchen, the rest of the space was empty. A floor sander and a few other tools sat in the corner where Hazel had started the process of refinishing the wood floor. "This floor is going to look amazing after it's sanded and stained. You sure you don't need help?"

"Honestly, I kind of like sanding," Hazel replied. "With my headphones in, it's actually relaxing. The sander does all the work. I just push it along. But if you're offering, I could use someone to run the edge sander."

"Deal." He gave her a wink, impressed by everything Hazel was tackling by herself. She was getting better about accepting help here and there, but he didn't think she realized what she accomplished daily. She was restoring an old carriage house, raising a respectful and kind daughter, and was working as Frankie's fulltime assistant. Plus, this morning she baked enough pastries to feed the whole town. And it wasn't even eight o'clock yet.

Hazel walked to the counter and snatched a pastry from a box. "Here. I want you to try a chocolate croissant."

"Don't waste that on me." Jesse would gladly gobble up anything Hazel offered, but he didn't want to eat into her profits.

"We can share it. I haven't eaten anything yet this morning. Was too busy baking." Hazel offered up the flaky pastry, but not for Jesse to take. She brought it to his lips, and he took a bite. His eyes nearly rolled back in his head when the butter and chocolate combined in his mouth.

"My goodness," he mumbled.

"Is it good?" Hazel's eyes flickered to his lips and he caught her gaze lingering there.

"Best thing I've ever tasted," Jesse lied, but only because he knew Hazel was the best thing he'd ever tasted.

Hazel's eyes danced, and when she took a bite of the croissant they were sharing, Jesse called on all his self-control to stop from scooping her aproned body into his arms and kissing the butter from her lips. The girls chattered behind Hazel, and their cheery voices kept him in check. Charlie was asking Grace a million questions about the goodies on the counter, her apron, and if she got to lick batter from any spoons. Jesse might've been able to steal a quick kiss from Hazel without them noticing, but he knew his kiss would be anything but quick. He'd been wanting to kiss Hazel again since their lips parted, but after their conversation on the dock, he knew she needed to take things slow. And he wouldn't chance her shutting down again.

Reaching out, Jesse swept his thumb across Hazel's bottom lip, brushing away a pastry flake. "Your croissants will sell out in the first hour of the mercantile. I guarantee it." His voice was gruff, and Hazel's emerald eyes returned his need. At least, he thought so. He wasn't going to find out. Not this morning.

Instead, Jesse cleared his throat and called to the girls. "Let's start loading these boxes, ladies. I've got my truck pulled up to the front of the carriage house. The mercantile waits for no one."

Jesse pulled into the fairgrounds and parked his truck in front of the big, white tent that housed the shops and food vendors. Across from the tent was the bustling arena, full of rodeo contestants who were warming up their horses, getting ready for the first event which was set to start at noon. The mercantile opened at ten o'clock sharp and the vendors were putting the finishing touches on their temporary shops.

Directly in front of the tent, there was a turquoise two-horse trailer that had been converted into a traveling coffee shop. The side had a wide window which popped open to create a counter and passthrough window. The front of the trailer boasted the *Perkup Coffee* logo, painted in black.

"Hey, Myra," Jesse said to his cousin as he walked toward the trailer with Hazel, Grace, and Charlie. Each of them carried boxes of baked goods.

Myra waved at them through the passthrough window, looking relieved as she handed a to-go cup to a customer. She had a line of at least fifteen people, waiting patiently and not-so-patiently for a cup of joe. "Hey, guys," Myra called. "Come on in."

Jesse led his crew into the back of the trailer, which was open and had a ramp. He remembered a few years ago when Myra bought the old rust bucket. Even he raised his brows at her idea to convert the horse trailer into a coffee shop. Her mom, Judy, had practically called her crazy, but Myra had an idea and she ran with it. Jesse had helped her with some of the renovations and now the two-horse trailer was a fully functioning coffee shop, complete with a small fridge and sink. The front of the unit—where horse heads usually resided—had cabinetry which housed supplies, an industrial coffee maker, and an espresso machine. Everything ran off a generator.

"Myra, this is Hazel and her daughter, Grace." Jesse set the boxes he was carrying on top of the small fridge.

"Nice to finally meet you guys. I've heard all about you. Sorry I didn't get a chance to meet you at the past few Sunday dinners. Been at rodeos, but I'll be there next weekend." Myra took cash from a customer with one hand and filled a paper cup with the other. Her black hair was wrapped into a twist and at least three pencils poked out of it, holding the twist together. The turquoise apron she wore over a tank top and jeans looked like it had endured a few coffee spills. "I can't tell you how much I appreciate you bringing the baked goods." She gave Hazel a quick, genuine smile over her shoulder.

"I'm happy to," Hazel replied, and Jesse took the rest of the boxes from Hazel and the girls, finding places for them in the trailer.

"I'll give you cash at the end of the day if that works for you." Myra grabbed a pencil out of her hair to make a note. Part of her hair spilled onto her back.

"That's totally fine." Hazel stepped into the trailer and peeked around. "Do you need some help?"

Myra stopped writing and tilted her head toward Hazel. "I always need help." The laugh she gave sounded a little pained.

"I can't make a latte, but I can definitely take money and clean," Hazel offered.

"I can help too. I don't have to be at the chutes for twenty minutes," Jesse added. Then he turned to the girls. "Charlie, can you take Grace into the tent and go to Grandma's booth?"

Charlie jumped around, then took Grace's hand and pulled her toward the tent. Joyce and Judy were inside. Jesse could see them from the trailer. As organizers of the mercantile, his mom and aunt were the official greeters and loved every minute of it. They had a big space in the front of the tent which was a family activity area for crafts and games. All the grandkids hung out there throughout the day.

"Where do you need us?" Hazel asked. Myra took a huge, thankful breath.

"Anywhere," she replied. "Just jump in."

Hazel stepped up to the window and started taking orders. Jesse went to the sink full of dirty dishes and grabbed a sponge. Myra stayed glued to the front of the trailer, running the espresso machine and coffee maker like a mechanic on an engine. Soon enough, the trailer was tidied, the line of customers was served, and an entire box of Hazel's pastries was gone.

"You guys are a lifesaver." Myra fixed her hair back into a neat twist with another pencil.

Jesse glanced at his watch, feeling guilty as the line in front of the trailer started to grow again. "I've got to get going. They're expecting me at the chutes to help with team roping."

"I can stay," Hazel said, barely looking up as she scribbled the next customer's order on the notepad and punched numbers on the calculator.

"Are you sure?" Myra asked. "I don't want to take up your time."

"It's no problem. I was just going to walk around the mercantile with Grace until Jesse was done." Hazel took the customer's cash. "But Grace looks pretty content right now."

Jesse looked at the tent and saw Grace, Charlie, and all of Frankie's boys lined up with a bunch of other kids, gearing up for a potato sack race. They were all standing in burlap sacks, eager smiles on their faces. "Mom and Judy have a million games for the kids. They'll keep them busy over there."

"Then I'll stay and help Myra." Hazel gave them both a smile.

Jesse dried his hands and inched toward the back of the trailer. "I'll come get you when I'm done then? We could watch the rest of the rodeo together?" Jesse paused at Hazel's side, taking advantage of the small space of the trailer and sliding a hand onto her lower back. Hazel glanced at him and blushed, which only made him want to curl her to his chest.

She nodded and Jesse reluctantly left the trailer, looking forward to coming back this afternoon.

CHAPTER TWENTY

"You two make a cute couple," Myra said as she added cream to two iced coffees.

Hazel was leaning out the trailer window, handing a napkin-wrapped vanilla bean scone to a customer. She nearly dropped it. "What?" Hazel shuffled and managed to save the scone from falling to the grass.

"You and Jesse." Myra clipped tops on the iced coffees, grabbed two straws, and handed them out the window. "Here you go, Beth. How's that new horse of yours doing?"

"Amazing," Beth replied as she took the cups. "Going to run him today."

Myra made small talk with Beth, mostly about their horses. Hazel tidied up the counter, half-listening as she wondered what Jesse had told his cousin. In the past few weeks, Hazel had fantasized about being in a relationship with Jesse, but that's all it was. A fantasy. They simply couldn't make a relationship work long-term, and Hazel wasn't going to broadcast her new feelings for Jesse to the world, even if they were starting to take up a good portion of her thoughts. She wouldn't risk Grace or Charlie's hearts.

Beth walked off and there was a little reprieve, which was good because the coffee pot was empty, and they were on the last box of pastries.

"We're just friends," Hazel said quietly, referring to Myra's cute-couple comment.

Myra pulled a bag of coffee grounds from a cabinet. "I didn't mean to pry." She looked a bit surprised as she opened the top of the coffee maker and removed a full, wet filter. "I just assumed you guys were dating. I haven't seen Jesse look at someone like that in . . . well, ever. And he hasn't brought anyone to Sunday dinner since Emily."

Hazel's heart did this weird pitter-patter thing, and she didn't know if it was excitement from the first part of Myra's comment, or leeriness from the name she dropped. "Emily?" Hazel tried not to look too interested, but Myra made a face at her question, and that only piqued Hazel's interest.

"I need to learn when to keep my big mouth shut." Myra poured a carafe of water into the coffee maker. "Sorry. If you guys haven't talked about that yet, it needs to come from Jesse's mouth. Not mine. Forget I said anything, okay?"

"Sure." Hazel's mind turned. Who was Emily? She wiped down the counter, busying her hands before she started asking questions. Did it matter who Emily was? Jesse had a past, just like Hazel did. He was in his late thirties as well. Of course he'd had serious relationships, but why hadn't he shared anything about them? Had he been married before? Would he keep that to himself, even after she'd confided in him about the downfalls of her own marriage?

"There he is," Myra announced with a trill to her voice. "Here comes that handsome *Prince Charming*." Hazel glanced up from her scrubbing to see who Myra was referring to.

Jesse was riding toward the coffee trailer. On a white horse.

Myra joined Hazel at the window, putting her elbows on the counter, and Hazel felt the need to reiterate that Jesse was just a friend. No matter how handsome he looked smiling at her from under a black cowboy hat.

Instead, she spilled out, "He does kind of have that modern-day prince charming thing down, doesn't he?" Hazel meant it as a joke, especially because he was literally riding a white horse.

Myra laughed and gave Hazel a soft pat on the back, almost like she was consoling her. "Oh, boy. I don't know who you guys think you're fooling." Hazel looked at Myra, who now wore a knowing grin. "If you guys aren't dating yet, you should be." She gave Hazel a wink as Jesse neared.

Jesse stopped the horse in front of the window like he was rolling through a drive-through on horseback. "How you guys doing over here?"

"Amazing," Myra shot back. "Almost sold out of Hazel's pastries and I made one more pot of coffee for the afternoon sippers. Thanks for grabbing my horse for me."

"No problem." Jesse dismounted and gave the horse a rub on the neck. "Frankie tacked him up."

"Perfect. I have just enough time to warm him up before the first round of barrel racing starts." Myra glanced at Hazel. "Hazel, this is my horse, *Prince Charming*. I call him Charm for short."

Hazel's mouth popped open and she laughed nervously, like she'd just been caught in a silly lie. Myra walked out the backside of the trailer, leaving Hazel with her mouth hung open. She slapped it shut when Jesse looked at her, confused.

"Did I miss something?" he asked, just as Charlie and Grace came out of the tent and strode over to pet the horse. Charm lowered his head and sniffed them.

"Nope, not at all." Myra flipped around the chalkboard sign that displayed the specials. The backside of the sign read *In the saddle, come back later*. Myra hopped up on her horse, Charm. "Thanks so much for all your help today, Hazel. Was really nice to get to know you. Enjoy the rodeo, and I'll see you tomorrow."

Hazel reached for words. "I can stay here and watch the trailer while you ride."

"You've done more than enough. You guys go enjoy the rodeo. I'll be back soon enough to serve coffee." Then Myra trotted off on her *Prince Charming,* and Hazel cursed her tongue for speaking the truth.

Hazel sat down on the bleachers next to Jesse and took a bite of her corndog. Grace and Charlie were sitting in front of them, sharing a rainbow-colored cotton candy, laughing at the rodeo clown as he did a skit with a stick horse in the arena. The four of them had spent the afternoon together, riding carnival rides, watching the rodeo, and exploring the barns. Jesse was quite the tour guide and Hazel had eased out of her awkwardness, hoping Myra wouldn't say anything to Jesse about her *Prince Charming* comment.

"The broncs are up next, and Creed is the first rider," Jesse said.

Charlie waved the cotton candy in the air, and yelled, "Yeah!"

"What's a bronc?" Grace asked. She'd been using Jesse as her own personal rodeo encyclopedia all day. He'd been happily giving her answers as fast as she could ask the questions.

"It's a bucking horse," he replied, and she gave him a face, like she didn't understand. "The horses will come out of the blue chutes on the other side of the arena. The rider needs to stay on for eight seconds. If they do, they'll receive a score based on their ride. The highest score wins."

"Eight seconds isn't very long," Grace replied, unimpressed.

Jesse laughed. "Oh, believe me. It's plenty long on a horse that can buck as hard as these broncs do."

This was the first rodeo Hazel and Grace had ever attended, but Hazel had seen rodeos on TV and in movies. Frankly, she thought these men were crazy for getting aboard a horse that was intent on tossing them through the air. It was like getting on a roller coaster and choosing not to buckle your safety belt.

"Seems a little dangerous," Hazel said.

"Oh, it is," Jesse replied.

The announcer introduced Creed, said the name of the horse he was about to ride, and then one of the blue gates burst open to prove Jesse's point. The bronc bound out of the chute like a firecracker shot from a box. It jumped, bucked, and jerked through the air. Creed had one hand on a rope that was connected to the horse's halter. The other hand waved through the air as he endured the wild ride. Hazel put her hand over her mouth as she watched, thinking eight seconds was way too long. She only took a breath again after the buzzer sounded and Creed made it safely to the ground with the help of a pickup man.

Jesse hooted and hollered for his friend, as did the rest of the audience. Creed took off his cowboy hat and waved it at the crowd, looking happy with the score that'd just gone up on the board. Hazel clapped, but mostly because Creed was walking away in one piece.

"Wow." Grace gave Hazel and Jesse a wide-eyed look, and then turned back to the arena to watch the next rider.

Hazel leaned toward Jesse. "And you used to do this?" He'd told her that Creed and he used to rodeo together.

"Not this," he said. "I used to do team roping. No bucking involved there. At least, there shouldn't be."

"Thank goodness," she replied, quickly, and he gave her a curious look. "I mean, I wouldn't want you getting hurt." There was absolutely no way she could watch someone she cared about ride broncs or bulls. She barely knew Creed, and the ride she just witness had sent her blood pressure into the hot summer sun.

Jesse gave her a warm smile. "When I get in the saddle, I always intend to keep my butt on the leather."

"Good plan," she replied.

They watched the rest of the rodeo together, although Hazel found herself putting her hand over her mouth or eyes through each of the bucking events. She pitied these men's wives and mothers. When the rodeo was over, Jesse drove Hazel and Grace back to Frankie's. In the short, ten-minute drive, both Charlie and Grace fell asleep.

"They sure had a lot of excitement today." Hazel glanced at the backseat and smiled to herself. Grace was slumped against the door. Charlie had her head back against the seat. Her mouth was wide open. "I think I'll let Grace sleep in tomorrow while I bake. I'm going to try and get to the fairgrounds by seven-thirty. That's when Myra is going to open the trailer in the morning."

Jesse parked in Frankie's driveway. The house was still dark. It looked like they were the first to get home.

"I can drive you over," Jesse offered.

"Are you sure? I don't want you going out of your way." Hazel knew he didn't have any rodeo duties until ten o'clock. "You don't want to sleep in? It's a Saturday." She planned to be up before four in order to get dressed and bake all the goodies she planned to make, but that didn't mean Jesse needed to be up early as well.

He quirked an eyebrow at her. "Seven o'clock is sleeping in for me. And I'd love to drive you and Grace over. I like spending time with you, Hazel. I had a great time today, and was hoping we could do the same tomorrow."

Jesse tentatively reached for her hand, which lay on the arm rest. She watched as he slid his hand around hers, lacing their fingers together. She looked up and met his gaze. She wanted to kiss him. Badly. Instead, they stared at each other in the dark. The radio played a soft song, and Hazel thought how easily she could fall in love with him. Her head and heart had forged a war. Her head was losing the battle.

"Hazel?" Jesse ran his thumb over hers.

"Yes?" Her breathing increased with every passing second.

"Would you and Grace accompany me and Charlie to the dance tomorrow night? After the rodeo. Would you two be our dates?"

She swallowed. "Yes, we'd love that." Her heart swelled. He hadn't just asked her on a date. He'd asked her and her daughter.

Even in the dark, she could see his blue eyes twinkle. Then he raised their intertwined hands to his mouth and kissed the back of her hand. Hazel closed her eyes and focused solely on his tender kiss, on his lips pressed against her skin.

Until Charlie screamed out, "Yeah! We all going to the dance together!"

Hazel's eyes popped open at Charlie's voice and she lurched backwards, nearly out of her own skin. In the same motion she yanked her hand free of Jesse's, and Jesse somehow managed to hit the steering wheel with a flailing body part. The truck's horn beeped and made them jump, again.

Hazel turned toward the backseat. Charlie was staring at her from her booster seat, wide awake and smiling.

"You guys are funny." Charlie laughed.

How long had she been awake? What had she seen?

Grace stirred and rubbed her eyes with her palms. "Who honked the horn?"

Jesse mouthed, "Whoops."

"Okay, we're here," Hazel said, nervous energy bundling in her chest. She was glad they hadn't kissed on the lips, and that Charlie couldn't read her mind. "Time to go to bed." She opened the door and stepped out. Grace followed and sleepily walked toward the front porch.

"I'll see you in the morning." Hazel gave Jesse a nervous grin and wondered if she should just start baking now. Unlike her daughter, Hazel wasn't sleepy. Not anymore.

CHAPTER TWENTY-ONE

Hazel stayed up late baking double the amount of pastries she had the day before. Despite her lack of sleep, she had another wonderful day at the rodeo. Hazel spent the morning in the Perkup Coffee trailer, helping Myra. She genuinely enjoyed Myra's company, as well as chatting with all the customers. When they sold out of pastries and coffee by noon, Myra decided to close shop early and prep her horse, Charm, for another barrel race that afternoon. During her ride, Hazel cheered her on from the stands, along with Jesse, the girls, and all of Jesse's family. Grace and Charlie screamed the loudest when Myra won first-place and galloped a victory lap. The rest of the afternoon was spent wandering the mercantile. The shops were full of beautiful handmade art, jewelry, and furniture. Hazel even bought a few things—an old black and white photo of two horse-drawn carriages parked along main street in Maple

Bay, as well as an antique silver serving tray. She thought both would fit perfectly in the carriage house. Even if she couldn't be the one to see the carriage house through to a bed-and-breakfast, she figured the art and serving tray would be nice decorative touches for when she staged the building and put it on the market.

Now, as she stood in Frankie's bedroom, curling her hair for tonight's barn dance, Hazel's heart sank as she thought of selling the carriage house. Hazel had put so much of herself into the renovations. And she'd created memories that would last a lifetime—with Grace, with Frankie . . . with Jesse. Hazel could see her and Grace staying there, making the carriage house their home. Hazel would love to run a bed-and-breakfast—to rent out the four rooms, to wake up early every morning and make a glorious breakfast for her guests. Furthermore, she would have her very own home that overlooked a beautiful lake, was surrounded by a sweet town, and could be filled with even sweeter family and friends. And, if she stayed, Hazel could have a real shot at a relationship with Jesse.

"Are you okay?" Frankie asked, breaking into Hazel's thoughts. She was rummaging around in her walk-in closet. The kids were in the front yard, playing kick-the-can. Hazel could see them out the bedroom window and faintly hear their laughs.

"Yeah," Hazel replied, setting the curling iron down on the dresser and brushing away her conflicted thoughts.

"You sure? You look like you're trying to solve a Rubik's cube in your head." Frankie stepped out of her walk-in closet wearing a flowy sundress and cowboy boots that sparkled with crystals and studs.

"I'm fine." Hazel gave her a soft grin. She didn't want to upset Frankie. They were growing close, and Hazel didn't want to remind her that she'd be selling the carriage house come fall. "By the way, you look gorgeous." Frankie was a natural beauty. She was stunning in her everyday barn-wear, but today she looked like a country music star ready for the stage.

"Thanks," Frankie smiled. "You do too. That green dress is absolute fire on you. Your eyes match your dress almost exactly. I don't think you even need any jewelry other than some simple earrings."

Hazel's mom had packed a few things that Hazel didn't think she'd have any use for during her time in Maple Bay. She was wrong and silently thanked her mom for having the insight to pack a knee-length emerald green dress she'd worn one time at a friend's wedding. The top fell off her shoulders. The skirt swished at her knees. Her hair fell in curls down her back and she'd used lipstick for the first time since she left the city.

"It's nice to get dressed up every now and then." Hazel smiled.

"This is about the only time of the year Garrett sees me in a dress," Frankie laughed. "And I don't know what to do with my hair. I kind of forgot how long it is since I throw it in a ponytail every day." She shrugged her shoulders and looked at herself in the dresser mirror.

"I could braid it if you like." Hazel had become a braiding expert over the years, doing Grace's hair any time she let her.

Frankie's face brightened. "Sure." She sat down on the edge of the bed and Hazel grabbed a brush from the dresser. She brushed Frankie's strawberry-blonde hair which fell to the middle of her back. It was maybe a few inches longer than her own. Then she started weaving it into a fishtail braid.

"Do you want me to read another one of Mom's letters while you braid?" Frankie asked.

"Not today." The box of letters sat on the dresser. Hazel had brought the box over from the carriage house, and they'd read two of the letters together before getting dressed. In the past few weeks, Hazel and Frankie had read fifteen of Rose's birthday letters. Sharing the experience had brought them close, threaded them together like a quilt. She looked up and met Frankie's eyes in the mirror. They looked so much alike. The red tone of their hair. Their freckles. They had the same green eyes. Only now, their insides were starting to match their outsides. Frankie was starting to feel like a real sister.

"Tomorrow then?" Frankie asked.

Hazel continued weaving Frankie's silky hair. "Yes, I think we should end the weekend with a campfire and s'mores. We can read a few more letters while the kids play a game."

"Maybe a glass of vino?"

"Of course." Hazel wrapped a hair tie around the end of Frankie's braid. "I've still got that bottle of pinot at my place."

"At where?" Frankie shot back.

Hazel looked up, meeting a lively look from Frankie in the mirror. "At my place," she repeated, and instantly realized what she said. "At the carriage house, I mean." She couldn't believe how easily the words had rolled off her tongue, like she'd been living there for years.

"No, you had it right the first time. At *your* place." Frankie genuinely smiled and held Hazel's stare in the mirror.

"We should get going." Hazel looked away, guilt riddling her, and moved across the room to grab the kitten heels she brought to wear tonight. "Jesse will be here any minute."

Hazel sat on the bed, next to Frankie, to slide the black heels onto her feet. Frankie didn't stay put. Instead, she disappeared into her closet again.

When she reappeared, Frankie was holding a pair of cowboy boots.

"It's time you got your own boots," Frankie said. "You and Mom were the same size. I think these need to be yours." The boots were chocolate brown. Beautiful floral embroidery filled the tall shafts. Burnt orange and ivory flowers were delicately stitched into the leather, surrounded by emerald green leaves which matched Hazel's dress. The boots were a piece of art.

"What?" Hazel choked out. "No." She was taken aback by the offer.

"Yes."

"I can't."

"You can," Frankie insisted and brought them over to her. "Mom would want you to have them. I want you to have them."

Hazel couldn't find words.

"Put them on." Frankie set the boots on the carpet, next to Hazel's feet. Then she opened a dresser drawer and pulled out a pair of tall socks. She handed the socks to Hazel. "Here. You'll need these if you're going to be dancing in those boots."

Hazel took the socks and picked up one of the boots. They were well taken care of. The leather was oiled and clean, but there were slight creases where the toe had been bent over the years—as Rose had walked, or danced, or rode a horse. Hazel ran her fingers over the creases and embroidery and thought of what Rose had said in her letters. Rose was born in Minneapolis, a true city girl until her finger landed on the map dot of Maple Bay. She moved to Maple Bay, by herself, looking to start her life anew. It was in Maple

Bay that she found family and eventually found herself. Hazel and Rose were more alike than Hazel would've ever guessed. Knowing that, Hazel put the boot back on the ground.

Then she put the boots on. After the socks, of course.

They fit her perfectly.

"Now you're officially a country girl," Frankie said, and pulled Hazel into a hug.

Hazel hugged her sister back, tears welling in her eyes. She'd been walking in Rose's shoes as she read her letters, but now, Hazel literally stood in her boots.

The dance was at an old barn on the edge of the fairgrounds. The barn's weather-whipped wood and peaked roof were backdropped by swaying corn fields and the setting sun. Hazel wanted to take a picture, to remember the beauty and perfection of the evening. But more than that, she wanted to hold Jesse's hand as they walked toward the dance. Her fingers itched to grab it, but she wasn't ready to announce their budding romance to the whole town, especially because Grace was walking just a few steps in front of them, with Frankie and Garrett.

"You girls all look so pretty," Jesse said as Charlie skipped a circle around them. She was toting hot pink leggings, a rainbow tutu, and cowboy boots. Hazel adored the fact that Jesse let his daughter wear whatever she fancied. "Stunning, actually."

He caught Hazel's eye and his stare forced her to face to warm. Jesse had nearly driven into the ditch a few times on the way over as he stole glances at Hazel. She felt like a queen. Maybe even a rodeo queen. Jesse had a way of making her feel like the center of his world.

"You're looking pretty handsome yourself." Hazel thought Jesse seemed even *more* tall, dark, and handsome tonight. His dark jeans and crisp black dress shirt showed off how lean and fit his work kept him. Her mind flitted to the other day when she'd seen him stacking haybales in the barn with Frankie. She caught herself gawking at his strong arms, and only looked away when he caught her stare and gave her a wide grin.

Charlie skipped between them. Noah chased her, giggling in his tiny Wranglers and boots. They wound around them again and made a circle around Grace, taunting her to chase them as well.

"I think you two need to get on the dance floor." Hazel chuckled as the kids made another loop and they all entered the barn.

The old barn was open at both ends, a sweet summer breeze floating through. White lights hung from the rafters, casting a warm glow over a bustling, happy crowd. On one side of the barn, a flatbed trailer was decorated with streamers and balloons, serving as a stage for the band that was strumming guitars and filling the space with a fast-paced melody.

"And how about you, Miss Hazel?" Jesse asked as Frankie gathered the scampering kiddos and directed them toward the dance floor. A new song started, and the crowd was forming lines and synchronizing dance moves. "Do you know how to line dance?"

"This might surprise you, but Grace and I are pretty much experts at the *Electric Slide* and the *Macarena*." Hazel had taught Grace and a few of her daughter's friends both dances during a slumber party last year, and they'd danced the night away.

Grace laughed. "Mom, that's not the same."

"We just have to follow what the crowd is doing. It's kind of the same." Hazel squeezed her daughter's shoulders. "Let's try it."

"If you guys can do the Electric Slide, you'll have no problem line dancing." There was a gleam in Jesse's eyes. "Come on. Both of you."

He took Hazel's hand like it was the most natural reaction. Hazel's heart jumped and for a second, she stiffened. Then Grace took Hazel's other hand, and the worry eased right out of her. Jesse led them both to the dance floor, making a human rope that weaved through the crowd.

He pulled them right into the mix, and Hazel was happy to see the friendly faces she was coming to love. Frankie waved at her excitedly but didn't miss a beat as she kicked up her heels next to her husband. All three of Frankie's boys were lined up next to her, doing their own versions of what they thought they should be doing. Tommy was following along with the steps. Wyatt and Noah were jumping and wiggling their butts. A laugh bubbled out of Hazel at their cuteness.

Creed was behind them, dancing with a Hollywood smile. His thumbs were in his belt loops, framing the buckle he'd won at the rodeo. There were three women practically fighting to get the spot closest to him. He was eating up the attention. Evan was next to Creed, belly laughing at something he'd just said to his friend. At the front of the pack, Myra looked to be leading the whole crowd with some fancy moves and a couple of hoots. Even Joyce and Gene were kicking up their boot heels. Charlie was dancing between her grandparents, shaking her little tutu.

"You're here!" Joyce sashayed over and gave Jesse, Hazel, and Grace each a grandma-sized hug. Her short silver hair was curled tight, and her red lipstick accented her checkered shirt. She left a mark on Grace's cheek where she kissed her.

"Just in time for my favorite song!" Joyce took Grace's hand and pulled her right into the mix of family. Hazel almost cried at the sight of it.

Hazel had learned a lot about Joyce through Rose's letters—what a kind, caring, and accepting friend she'd been. She'd taken Rose under her wing and shown her the love Rose had never received from her own family. Hazel had learned that Joyce and Rose were like sisters, even though they hadn't grown up together. One day Hazel wanted to share Rose's letters with Joyce so she could see her friend's words for herself.

But now? Now she would dance.

Jesse fell right in line next to Garrett, and he obviously knew the dance moves. He jumped right into the steps, but then slowed and broke down the pattern for Hazel.

"Kick and kick and kick and kick." Jesse tapped his boot heels out, alternating legs. "Then crossover, rock back, and face the next wall." He did the pattern again and Hazel loved seeing this side of him—footloose and fancy free. Not to mention, sexy. Hazel had no idea how good line dancing could look on Jesse, but he was a sight to behold—all bright smile and confident dance moves.

Hazel followed Jesse and by the next round, she had it. She fell into step with Jesse and all of Maple Bay. They kicked and stomped to the beat of the music, letting all their cares float away. After the last note, Hazel cheered and clapped for the band, along with rest of the crowd.

The lead singer tipped his cowboy hat and put a hand on the microphone. "All right, ladies and gents. It's time to slow it down for a few songs, so grab that special someone."

Hazel's hands were at her chest, clasped together in post-clapping mode. They felt glued there as the slow song started and everyone paired off. Gene sashayed Joyce into a slow two-step. Frankie wrapped her hands around Garrett's neck. Creed picked up Charlie and put her on his hip. She giggled as he carried her into a dance. Evan twirled Grace.

"May I have this dance?" Jesse asked.

Hazel wasn't sure she could mask her growing feelings for Jesse if she was wrapped in his arms, but she nodded. He took her hand and led them into the beat.

Frankie laughed and Hazel looked at her sister, grateful for the distraction. Garrett was leaning down, close to Frankie's ear, and had said something that sent them both into wide smiles. They were tangled up around each other.

"They really are in love, aren't they?" Hazel asked, but knew the answer.

"Have been since the eighth grade."

"Really?" She looked back at Jesse.

"Really."

"I wasn't sure because he hasn't been around much. They spend a lot of time apart."

"They're both hard workers. And the past few years Garrett's been putting in a ton of hours. They're saving up to buy the excavating business from his uncle."

Hazel gave a soft smile, longing for the type of relationship Frankie and Garrett had. Someone to navigate life with—through the good times and the bad. Someone that wouldn't run when things got tough. Was it possible that Jesse could be that man? He was proving to be someone that held the qualities she longed for in a partner, but could they make a relationship work after Hazel moved back to the city? Hazel looked around, at Jesse's family, at the life he had here in Maple Bay. She couldn't ask him to give this up. That wasn't even a question. And she needed to be where her daughter was—in Haven Hills and close to her father. The only way they could make a relationship work would be to do it long-distance.

"What's on your mind?" Jesse whispered, and she ran her fingers over his strong shoulder.

Grace was ten years old. For the next eight years, Hazel would be tied to Haven Hills. She'd gladly make that sacrifice for her daughter, but she couldn't ask Jesse to wait eight years to have a real relationship. Honestly, she couldn't ask that of herself. She wanted a husband to share her life with—not just someone to spend a weekend with here or there. She wanted more kids. She wanted a family.

Hazel swallowed and shook her head. This wasn't the place to say any of that, and when Charlie ran across the dance floor and attached herself to her dad's leg, Hazel wasn't sure her heart could take another whack. But she kept on dancing. The three of them swayed together, and as the song ended, Charlie looked up at Jesse with her innocent blue eyes and curly pigtails.

Then, with a big smile, Charlie yelled, "Daddy, kiss her again! Like you did in the truck!" Her little voice bellowed out just as the band stopped playing. Her words echoed through the crowd.

Hazel glanced up to find plenty of eyes looking her way. The most important were Grace's. Grace's brow furrowed in confusion, and when she turned and walked off the dance floor, Hazel let go of Jesse.

She cursed herself for getting lost in a fantasy. "I need to go talk to her."

Jesse didn't protest, but his glimmering smile had faded.

"What wrong?" Charlie asked. Hazel bent down to her, making sure Charlie didn't get upset as well.

"Nothing, sweetie." Hazel gave Charlie's arm a little squeeze. "I'm just going to go talk to Grace for a few minutes, okay? You stay here with your daddy."

Charlie nodded, but when Hazel left the dance floor, Charlie scooted after her. Hazel saw her out the corner of her eye and stopped, intending to gather Charlie and send her back to Jesse. Just then, a hand reached out of the crowd and landed on Hazel's arm.

"I can take her to Jesse," a pretty brunette woman offered. Before Hazel could reply, the woman scooped Charlie up and set her on her hip.

Charlie smiled at the woman, obviously knowing her. "Hi, Emily," Charlie said, and hugged the woman's neck.

Emily. The name resonated with Hazel, because Myra had mentioned an Emily in the coffee trailer yesterday. She'd said that Emily was the last person Jesse had brought to Sunday family dinner. Was this *that* Emily?

Emily reached out her hand. "I'm Emily. A friend of Jesse's."

Hazel's stomach clenched, but she shook her hand. "Hazel."

Emily cocked her head and wrinkled her nose. "I didn't know Jesse was dating someone. At least, he didn't mention that when I was at his place for dinner the other night."

"The other night?" Hazel asked, dumbfounded. Jesse had dinner with this woman? At his home?

"A couple of nights ago." There was a gleam in Emily's eye that felt like a dagger. "And then we painted your nails. Didn't we, Charlie?" She scrunched her face at Charlie. The little girl giggled and nodded.

Hazel was certain something had pierced her heart.

She managed a one-word response, "Oh." Looking back toward the dance floor, Hazel got confirmation of her suspicions. Jesse was a stone's throw away, standing still as a fence post. He looked like both feet were stuck in a sink hole.

Hazel looked back at Emily, feeling like the ground was swallowing her up as well. "Excuse me." Then she went to find her daughter.

CHAPTER TWENTY-TWO

"Grace," Hazel said as she walked out of the barn. Her daughter hadn't gone far. She was sitting on a haybale, looking forlorn in her lilac dress—the one she'd been laughing and dancing in just a few minutes ago. "Oh, baby. I'm sorry, but it's not what you think." Hazel sat on the haybale next to her daughter, not wanting to be the cause of Grace's frown.

"Why would you keep that from me, Mom? Why didn't you tell me?"

"I didn't," Hazel started and stopped, not sure how to explain what had just happened. This was the reason she didn't want to act on her feelings for Jesse. "We didn't kiss. Charlie thought she saw something that didn't happen." That was true enough, though Charlie had seen the intention behind Jesse's gesture in the truck. And Hazel and Jesse had definitely kissed. Just not in the truck.

Grace furrowed her brow again, like she was frustrated. "You obviously like him. Why wouldn't you just tell me? I don't keep secrets from you. You shouldn't keep secrets from me."

Hazel's mom-brain scrambled for an appropriate way to explain her actions to her daughter, and ultimately concluded that Grace was right. Hazel didn't have to tell Grace everything, but her daughter didn't deserve to feel like her mother was keeping secrets from her. "I wasn't keeping a secret from you. I was protecting you. I wanted to be sure of my feelings for Jesse before I told you anything. Does that make sense? I won't date just anyone. I want to make sure that person is someone I want in our lives for a long time . . . that *we* want in our lives for a long time."

"Mom, you can date. You're allowed to."

Hazel was shocked by her daughter's frank response. She gathered her thoughts. "I know how upset you've been after meeting your dad's last few girlfriends. I didn't want you to feel like that with me too." She didn't want to cause Grace any more pain than she'd already endured through the divorce.

Grace gave her a look like Hazel had just added ketchup to cake batter. "That's not the same. Dad picks bad."

"He *picks* bad?"

"Yeah, he picks bad. I don't know what he's looking for in a girlfriend, but I do *not* approve of any of the girlfriends I've met so far."

Hazel almost laughed, but suppressed the urge. She knew exactly what Bill had seen in his last few girlfriends, and it didn't have a thing to do with their brains or how sweet they were.

Hazel placed her hand over Grace's. "Your dad is finding his way in life, just as I am. He's trying the best he knows how, and I don't think he's intended to upset you with any of his choices."

"I guess." Grace looked back at the barn and peered into the open door. "I like Jesse. He's really nice. To you. And me. To everyone. Even total strangers."

Hazel gave a half-smile at her daughter's observations. "I'm glad you like him."

"Do you *like* him?" Grace prodded, looking curious.

Hazel sighed. She thought she did. She thought she really liked Jesse . . . that she was starting to feel the stirring emotions of love she'd been missing for years. She should be happy that her daughter was more upset about not being told about Jesse than the idea of a new relationship for her mother.

But Hazel wasn't about to fall for someone that might rip her heart to shreds. If Jesse was still involved with someone from a past relationship, Hazel had been reading him wrong all along. Now her doubts were smashing any fleeting thought of a possible long-distance relationship. If Jesse would have dinner with an ex and not mention that fact to her, what would he do when they lived in separate towns?

Hazel squeezed her daughter's hand. "I'm not sure."

Jesse put his truck in drive and pulled out of the fairgrounds. The barn dance faded in his rearview mirror.

"What'd you do?" Noah called to Jesse from the backseat. Noah, Tommy, and Wyatt were lined up on the bench seat of his truck. Garrett was next to Jesse, in the passenger seat. Frankie had all the girls in her truck.

Jesse saw the little man's confused face staring back at him in the mirror, waiting for an answer.

Garrett piped in, "That's none of your business, Noah."

"But you always ask me that question when I get in trouble," Noah challenged his dad. "And Momma definitely gave Jesse a look like he was in trouble."

Garrett scrubbed his hand over his face and Jesse winced, but Noah was right. Hazel must've told Frankie what happened.

When Charlie had chased Hazel as she left the dance floor, Jesse had followed, intending to grab Charlie. Hazel needed some time alone with Grace, to talk with her. But when Jesse found Charlie in the crowd, she was in Emily's arms and Hazel looked like she'd gone back in time—to the woman he'd met a month ago in front of Frankie's house.

Hazel couldn't get away from him fast enough. Jesse wanted to talk to Hazel, to explain, but after her encounter with Emily, Hazel avoided Jesse like the plague. When it was time to go, Frankie claimed all the girls needed to get in her truck and all the boys would be riding with Jesse. Frankie gave Jesse a look like she was going to give him a piece of her mind later.

"Just something really stupid," Jesse replied to Noah.

Noah shook his head, like he knew what Jesse meant. "Yeah. I do that sometimes too."

CHAPTER TWENTY-THREE

Last night, when Jesse dropped Garrett and the boys off at home, he wanted to talk to Hazel. He wanted to explain whatever Emily had told her, but Frankie intercepted, saying that Hazel needed some time to herself. Frankie looked like she didn't want to give Jesse that news, especially because Jesse could see that the light was still on in Hazel's bedroom. He wanted to go knock on her bedroom door. Instead, he reluctantly drove home and got the worst night of sleep ever.

Today was the last day of Maple Bay Days. With it being Sunday, Cowboy Church was first thing in the morning. Jesse rode in the church service, carrying the flag before the sermon sung out over the arena. After the service, he helped a whole load of excited kids climb aboard sheep for mutton-busting.

Throughout both events, Jesse looked for Hazel. She'd attended the church service, sitting next to Frankie and Joyce in the stands, and he'd caught glimpses of her in Myra's coffee trailer afterward. However, Jesse had yet to talk to Hazel about what happened at the dance. And he needed to. When the rodeo finally ended, Jesse dropped Charlie off at his parents' and went straight to Frankie's. Hazel wasn't there. She'd taken Grace into town to get groceries, but Jesse decided to make himself useful until he got a chance to speak with Hazel. By the time she pulled up to the house in Frankie's truck, Jesse had cleaned all the horse stalls. He also had Indy saddled and ready for a ride. He watched from the round pen as Frankie helped Hazel bring bags of groceries inside.

Just as he was about to untack Indy and head to the house, Hazel stepped off the back porch and walked toward the barn. She was carrying a bag of carrots.

When she neared the round pen and saw Jesse, she stopped. He was leaning on the top rail of the fence, watching her.

"Can we talk?" Jesse asked.

Hazel took a breath and walked over. She set the bag of carrots on the ground. "I thought it was weird that Frankie asked me if I could take a bag of carrots out to the round pen for the horses."

Jesse's gaze flicked back to the house. Frankie was peering out a window. She disappeared when he looked her way, and Jesse was thankful for her little scheme. She was a good friend.

Hazel crossed her arms over her chest, and Jesse couldn't tell if she was mad or sad. Either way, he wanted to pull her into a hug and ease her worries.

"Can we talk about last night?" Jesse prodded, and Hazel bite her lower lip. He needed to know what had made her shutdown. "Is Grace okay? Was she upset about what Charlie said?"

"She was upset, but mostly because she thought I was hiding something from her."

Jesse nodded, still leaning on the fence rail. He sympathized with Grace. He didn't like it either—hiding his feelings for Hazel from everyone he cared about. He wanted to show the whole world how he felt. He wanted to hold Hazel's hand in public. He wanted to kiss her goodnight, good morning, and good afternoon. He wanted to be open with Charlie and Grace.

"I don't want to hide anything from the girls," he confessed, and Hazel narrowed her eyes at him. Not the response he was looking for.

"But you want to hide things from me?"

"Hide things?"

"Who is Emily, and why would you have dinner with her and not tell me?" The question spilled out of Hazel, like she'd been sitting on it all night.

Jesse suddenly understood the look Hazel had given him last night, when she'd run into Emily. "She said we had dinner together?" he asked. Hazel tipped her head at him, waiting for more of an explanation. "That would be a bit of an exaggeration. She stopped over Thursday night. I didn't know she was coming. She brought burgers from the diner for Charlie and me."

Hazel's forehead wrinkled. "Why would she do that?"

Jesse ran a hand through his hair. He should've told Hazel about Emily, but he didn't want to rehash the past when it was long gone. "Emily and I were engaged. It was before my sister passed. Before I adopted Charlie. And there's nothing going on between Emily and I. We broke up when Charlie was young—before she could even walk."

"But Charlie acted like she knew her." Hazel's statement sounded like a question. "She hugged her. Emily said she painted her nails."

Jesse's heart sank, realizing how bad this looked. "Charlie knows her, but only as a friend. Emily and her family help with Maple Bay Days as well. I should've known she'd be back in town this weekend and I should've given you a heads-up. I'm sorry about that. I didn't want you to find out this way. She stopped by to say hi. It would have been a very short conversation, but Charlie convinced Emily to paint her nails and I was trying not to be rude." The worry lines on Hazel's forehead were still present. "Hazel, I want you to ask me all of your questions. I want you to feel comfortable knowing that *you* are the one on my mind. No one else."

Hazel was quiet for some time before she asked, "Why'd you break up?"

Jesse shifted against the fence. "She wasn't the one for me. At one time, I thought she could be. She wanted to get married so badly, and I thought that was the next logical step in my life. But I didn't understand what I really wanted or needed in a partner. We were together for five years, but we grew apart. We wanted different things. I was ready for a family, to set down roots and raise Charlie. She wanted to travel and rodeo."

"But . . . is she trying to get you back?"

"She's called a few times in the past year, wanting to start something up again, but we never did. And, frankly, it doesn't matter what she wants. I wish her the best, but I don't want to be with her."

Jesse offered up his hand, over the fence, not wanting to talk about Emily anymore. "Will you come in here with me? Please."

"In the round pen?" Hazel's arms were still crossed over her chest, but the stark tension in her body had loosened.

Jesse moved to the gate and opened it for her like a door. "I want to show you something. With Indy." The buckskin gelding stood behind him, curious as to what Jesse was doing. Indy wore a saddle, but no bridle or halter. Hazel looked skeptical, but walked over and put her hand in

Jesse's. He led her through the gate, closed it, and turned her toward Indy. "When Indy first came to Frankie's barn, he was scared. He'd been hurt in the past and didn't want to trust anyone." Jesse linked his fingers into Hazel's and raised their intertwined hands. He brushed them over Indy's soft nose and the horse blew warm breathes on their hands. Without a bridle or halter, the buckskin gelding wasn't being forced to stay put. He did so voluntarily. "At first, he wouldn't even allow me to touch him or catch him in the field, but look at him now." Jesse rubbed both their hands over Indy's forehead, and then his neck. The gelding stood, eagerly awaiting the scratches.

"Are you comparing me to a horse?" Hazel asked, reading between the lines and getting Jesse's point.

Jesse lowered their linked hands and turned to face Hazel. "I'm trying to tell you that I'm a very patient man. I'll go as slow as you want, but I want to take steps forward with you, Hazel. Even if they're baby steps. I'll take all the time in the world to show you that you can trust me."

Hazel was quiet. Her hair was pulled over one shoulder and fell across her chest, which had started to rise and fall at a faster pace. She looked like she wanted to tell him something.

"What is it?" he asked. "You can tell me."

"My marriage ended when I found out Bill hadn't been faithful to me," she said, looking pained. "I had no idea he was having an affair, but he'd been seeing a woman he worked with for a year. I was completely blindsided when he told me."

Now Jesse felt beyond horrible about not mentioning Emily. He could see why Hazel had recoiled from him, especially if she thought Jesse had met up with his ex-fiancé for some kind of secret dinner date at his house.

"I didn't tell you about Emily only because seeing her didn't matter to me. If I'd known it would bother you this much, I would've run the second I saw her coming. I promise you that." He put his hands on her arms. "And I hate to hear that anyone would hurt you like that. You deserve to be loved by a man that will give you the world."

Hazel glanced up at Jesse. He wanted to be that person for her. He wanted to protect her heart from ever being hurt again, if only she would let him. Jesse slid a hand around Hazel's waist and gently tugged her toward him, knowing that taking it slow with her was difficult, but he'd do anything to make her comfortable.

Hazel set a hand on Jesse's arm. He kept his thoughts to himself, afraid she was going to push away.

Instead, she whispered, "I need you to kiss me."

Jesse obliged without a second thought. Hazel tipped her chin up and he pressed his mouth to hers. She tasted just as sweet as he remembered, but there was something different about this kiss. As soon as their lips touched, Jesse felt like the dirt below his boots disappeared. Hazel ran her hands up his chest and looped them around his neck, and before he knew it, Jesse had one hand wrapped in her silky hair. The other arm pressed her body to his, and he didn't want to ever let her go. He deepened their kiss, and when she returned his need, Jesse thought fireworks lit off inside his chest.

Hazel let a hand fall to his shoulder. She eased back slightly. "Jesse?" she asked, breathless. "I want—"

Jesse hung on each word, needing to hear what Hazel wanted, hoping it was him.

Just then, Indy startled and jumped. Jesse jolted out of his daze and turned so that his back became a barrier between Hazel and the horse, just in case Indy kicked out as he spooked.

As Indy leapt away from them, Hazel buried her head into Jesse's neck. He reveled in her warm breath against his skin. He also discovered the source of Indy's spook. A little silver sports car had driven up alongside the barn. It abruptly stopped, and a well-dressed couple got out. The man and woman started walking toward the round pen. Were they were lost? Jesse wished they'd get back in their car and drive away, so he could go back to kissing Hazel.

"Hazel?" the man called, and Hazel went ridged in Jesse's grip. She peeled herself out of his embrace.

"Bill? What are you doing here?" She stood straight and smoothed down her shirt, which had inched up during their kiss.

This was this Hazel's ex-husband? Jesse eyed Bill like an intruder, especially because Hazel had just told Jesse how badly Bill had hurt her. Why was he here? Bill looked like he'd just walked off a golf course. The woman with him was awkwardly ambling in heels that kept sinking into the grass. Finally, she gave up and let Bill approach the round pen. She waved excitedly from a distance, like she was greeting an old friend. Then she busied herself with her phone.

Bill gave Jesse a once-over and dismissively turned his attention back to Hazel. "Cynthia and I were in Bemidji for the weekend, visiting her parents. We thought we'd swing by on our drive home. I plugged the address you gave me into my GPS. When we pulled in, I saw you over here." He looked around, like he had no idea why Hazel would be standing in the middle of a corral. "This place really is out in the middle of nowhere, isn't it?"

Jesse didn't like Bill's tone.

"What are you doing here, Bill?" Hazel repeated.

"I can't come visit my little girl?"

"Of course, you can. Anytime," Hazel replied. "I just wasn't expecting you."

"Obviously." Bill gave Jesse a leering look, and Jesse checked himself before he said something he might regret.

The backdoor of the house opened, and Grace ran out. "Daddy!"

"There's my little girl!" Bill yelled back and opened his arms wide. When she reached him, he spun Grace into the air. "How are you?"

"So good!" Grace was all smiles, and Jesse forced himself to smile as well. "Now I can show you the barn, and the horses I've been riding, and the lake, and the carriage house." Bill set her back on the ground.

"Grace, go put some boots on," Hazel said. Grace's feet were bare.

Grace gave an excited nod. "Wait here, Daddy. I'll be right back."

"Perfect," Bill said as Grace ran off toward the house. "Then I can see the carriage house and get a better idea of the value. If you want me to put it up for sale in September, we're going to have to take pictures of it by the end of August. Will it be ready then?"

"I-I'm not sure," Hazel replied. "Maybe you could look at it later this summer?"

"That's silly." Bill laughed. "I'm here now. I mean, you're still looking to sell it, aren't you? Like you told me?"

Jesse felt like he'd been punched in the gut. Hazel was already making plans to put the property on the market? She already knew for sure that she wouldn't keep it?

Hazel looked ashen, which was a feat because her cheeks had been flushed a few minutes ago. But she didn't say a word as Jesse backed away. Her silence told him all he needed to know.

Jesse walked over to Indy and haltered him. He tipped his head at Bill as he led Indy out of the round pen. "Sounds like you two have a lot to talk about."

CHAPTER TWENTY-FOUR

It killed Hazel to let Jesse walk away. She'd been on the verge of admitting that she wanted to be with him, that she couldn't stop thinking about him. Then Bill showed up and dropped a bomb all over her happiness. Why did he have a knack for that? He'd stayed away from Maple Bay for an entire month, but decided to show up just as Jesse kissed her like she was his lifeline? Hazel hadn't even noticed Bill's car as it approached the round pen. Her senses had been completely consumed by Jesse.

Now as Hazel walked into the carriage house with her daughter, Bill, and Cynthia, Hazel's eyes shot to the windows on the backside of the building. She searched for any sign of Jesse, but his truck wasn't parked by his house. He'd left Frankie's quickly, and Hazel wondered where he'd gone. She wanted to explain to him *why* she'd told Bill that she would sell the carriage house, why she would give Bill the listing. She'd done it so that she could stay here in Maple Bay, at least for the summer. And she didn't want to mess that up now. Ripping the listing away from Bill would only encourage him to make it difficult for her and Grace to stay.

"Wow," Bill said, his hands on his hips as he slowly spun a circle. "This place has great bones and a beautiful location. You said this is an old carriage house?"

Grace nodded, enthusiastically answering her dad's question. "They used to keep hay in the loft on the second story. The rooms over here were for tack and feed." Grace pointed from one door to the next. "And there were even rooms for stable hands to sleep." She pointed up the narrow staircase that started between the tack and feed rooms and led to the second story.

Bill opened the door to the old feed room and looked inside, making an agreeable sound with his throat. "Converted to a bedroom with a bath?"

Hazel cleared her throat. "All four rooms are. The tack and stable hand rooms are each plumbed for a bath too, though I don't have those rooms finished." Hazel had one room complete—the feed room. It had a half-bath and enough space for a king-sized bed and two tufted chairs, which she and Frankie had picked up at a garage sale last week. Hazel had dreamt of decorating each room in a theme. For the feed room, she wanted to use metal buckets to display fresh roses, burlap throw pillows to embellish the bed, and an accent wall made of old barn wood to complete the look. She had themed ideas for the rest of the rooms as well, but now her ideas seemed insignificant. If she wasn't going to keep the carriage house, she needed to let her decorating ideas slip away like spilled milk.

"I could see a history buff jumping all over this place and converting it into a second-home. Especially because it's right here on the lake." Bill closed the feed room door, and Hazel felt a pang in her chest. She didn't want some stranger buying this place, turning it into a second home that would only be used a few times in the summer; a place that someone showed off to their friends or used to store an expensive, loud boat.

"Or it could be converted into a bed-and-breakfast," Hazel suggested. She wanted to add that she'd thought of keeping the property and doing that herself. It's just that logistics and financials kept getting in her way.

Bill scrunched his face in half-agreeance. "Sure, I guess."

His girlfriend, Cynthia, was on the other side of the carriage house, running her fingers along the stone fireplace. "Is this the original fireplace?" Cynthia asked.

"It is," Hazel replied.

"It's beautiful," Cynthia said. "I can just imagine it with a roaring fire in the winter."

Hazel had met Cynthia a few times before. She was the daughter of one of Bill's clients, and even though Hazel thought she was way too young for Bill, Cynthia had always been nice to her and Grace.

"I plan to restore it to its original glory. That's one of my next projects," Hazel replied. Cynthia's expression held pure excitement.

"Mom has been working really hard," Grace told her dad. "You should see upstairs." She grabbed Bill's hand and pulled him to the loft staircase.

Hazel followed, but hoped this tour would end soon. She needed to find Jesse.

"See, Dad?" Grace said when they were all upstairs. "Mom's been building this place for us to live in. Isn't it great? She refinished the floors, put in a kitchen where we bake treats, and she's building a wall back there to make a bedroom and a bathroom. Hasn't she done such a good job?"

A lump hit Hazel's throat. "Thank you, baby." Hazel really didn't care if Bill thought she'd done a good job. She'd been building this space for her and Grace. She'd learned how to use a sander, nail gun, and a pressure washer—so far. She'd sold her car and budgeted out an entire renovation plan. Now, the loft was nearly ready for her and Grace to move in. The kitchen was complete with shiny, almost-new appliances. The cabinets looked farmhouse chic after Hazel and Frankie painted them using a technique they'd learned on YouTube. The wood floors were refinished and glossy. Jesse and Gene had helped Hazel with her most recent project— framing up walls in the back third of the space, making an area for a bedroom and a bath. Tomorrow, a handy man was coming to complete the framing with drywall.

"I don't think we should sell it, Mom," Grace said. "Can't we keep it and come visit? We could make it *our* second home?" She repeated Bill's suggestion from earlier.

Wheels started turning in Hazel's head. Could she really do that? Could she swing all the expenses of this place without living here fulltime? Would her job as a school secretary be able to pay for property taxes, utilities, gas to drive back and forth from Haven Hills . . . not to mention a new car to put the gas in?

Hazel internally flinched. There was just no way she could swing it. She needed the profits from the sale of the carriage house in order to buy or rent a place for her and Grace in Haven Hills. They couldn't live in her parents' basement forever.

"It's too expensive." Hazel sighed and her daughter politely nodded, accepting a simple answer for a complicated problem. Why did being an adult have to be so hard?

Bill was fiddling with the cabinets. "I could have my photographer here tomorrow to take pictures. I think you should get this on the market as soon as possible, so potential buyers can start looking at it."

"I don't officially own it yet, Bill."

"But you will, right? After Labor Day?"

"As long as I stay here in Maple Bay until then."

He looked at her like she was being difficult, but she wanted to remind him of the clause and obligation she intended to keep. "Then I'd suggest you put it on the market sooner than later. Better to get buyers here in the summer when they can see the full potential of a lake house. Maybe you'll even get a bidding war by the time September rolls around?"

Hazel could see that Bill was getting excited over the possibility of a bidding war and a big commission. "Sure. Call your photographer. Tomorrow works." Why delay the inevitable? She'd have to rip off the Band-Aid at some point.

As Bill got on his phone, Cynthia meandered over to the hay door. "What's this?" she asked.

Hazel ignored the disappointment that washed over her. "It's a hay door. Back when this loft held hay, that's the door they would've used to load the bales through," Hazel replied. "You can open it if you'd like."

Cynthia flipped the latch and pushed open the square door. It exposed all the beauty of the glassy lake and bordering trees. Cynthia gasped. "This view is spectacular."

"It is." Hazel walked toward Cynthia and the hay door. "I'd like to make this into a window. And add big windows on both sides of it." She pictured cooking in the kitchen while Grace did her homework at the kitchen table and rays of sunshine beamed across the floor.

"That's a great idea," Cynthia said, peering outside.

Hazel's eyes fell to Jesse's home, and she searched for one of the major reasons she wanted to stay. When Hazel discovered his truck, she straightened. It was idling in his drive. "Excuse me," she said to Cynthia. "I'll be right back."

"Where you going, Mom?" Grace asked as Hazel headed for the stairs.

"I've got to talk to Jesse. Stay with your dad. I'll be right back."

Hazel sped down the stairs faster than she probably should've, and was amazed she made it downstairs without falling. She lurched out the backdoor just as Jesse was driving past the carriage house. She waved at him, a little frantically. He slowed to a stop. His window was down.

"I just wanted to explain." She jogged up to the truck, but Jesse didn't greet her with his usual warm smile. That threw her off kilter. "About what Bill said."

"You don't have to explain, Hazel." Jesse rested an arm on the door. His tone was strange. It wasn't mad. More disappointed. "You always said you were going back to the city at the end of the summer. I should've listened to your words. I chose not to hear them. I thought time here would change your mind. I thought I could change your mind. That you would want to stay."

Hazel thought the ground shook. "You what?" she asked, not because she didn't hear him. She just wanted to make sure she understood him. "You thought you could change my mind?"

"You needed to take things slow. With us. I honored that. I even understood it. But that doesn't mean that was what I wanted."

Hazel's heart pounded. "What do you want?"

"You." His voice was thick. "Us."

"But how?" All the roadblocks she'd been grinding over rotated through her mind, again. It wasn't like she didn't want to be with Jesse. She was just choosing to put her daughter first. Couldn't he see that? Didn't he understand that?

"Momma!" Grace called and footsteps pattered across the stone patio. "Can Daddy stay here tonight?"

Hazel closed her eyes and gathered her thoughts and patience before Grace joined her at Jesse's truck. "Hey, Jesse!"

"Hey." Jesse managed a soft smile for Grace.

"Can Daddy stay in the carriage house tonight? Then he can watch me ride tomorrow." Grace clasped her hands together in a plea. Hazel turned to find Bill and Cynthia staring at her from the patio. She could've done without Bill's surprise visit today.

"Sorry, I told Grace we could wait until you were done talking, but she was really excited." Bill shrugged apologetically and waved his phone in the air. "My photographer can be here tomorrow, and I thought I'd stick around to help him, and then I could watch Grace ride as well. I started checking around for a hotel, but the closest is an hour away."

"They could stay in the feed room," Grace said, looking up at Hazel. Then she cocked her head. "What's wrong, Mom?"

Everything. Hazel shook her head. "Nothing, baby. That's fine. I'll grab some pillows and blankets from Frankie's."

"Great!" Grace did a little hop. She turned to Jesse. "Hey, where's Charlie?"

Jesse put his hand back on the steering wheel. "At my parents'. Headed there now." He glanced at the clock on his dashboard. "I better get going. Promised Charlie we'd have a tea party when I got there. She's been waiting for twenty minutes and is probably driving my mom crazy. Patience isn't Charlie's strong suit."

"Tell her hi from me," Grace said, and Hazel swallowed the swirl of emotions spinning through her like acid.

"Can we talk? Tomorrow, after work?" Hazel asked Jesse, and he politely nodded before driving off. His truck rolled away, leaving a cloud of dust in the absence of his presence. Her heart screamed at her to run after him. Her head told her to go find pillows and blankets for an ex-husband she wished would go away. Why couldn't her head and her heart get on the same page?

CHAPTER TWENTY-FIVE

Jesse walked into his parents' kitchen and set his keys on the counter, feeling like his future had just been derailed. The briny scent of his mother's homemade gravy filled the air, but Jesse wasn't the least bit hungry. Hazel had burrowed into his heart, one day at a time, until she took up more space than he could stand to lose. And if he let her continue to do so, she'd surely run off with his heart at the end of the summer, leaving him hollow.

Joyce turned from the pot she was stirring on the stove and did a doubletake. "My goodness, what happened?"

Jesse pulled a chair out from the table and sat. "Where's Charlie?"

Joyce set the whisk on the counter and walked toward him. "She's upstairs, with your father. Convinced him to have tea with her, as you were taking too long. What's wrong?"

Jesse put his elbows on the table and scrubbed his face with his hands, knowing there was no easing this by his mom. She'd seen his face and would smoother him with concern until he told her what had run him over like a freight train.

"I think," he said, pausing to really consider what he was about to say, "I think I'm in love with Hazel." It was the first time the thought had manifested through his mouth, and he immediately counteracted it. "But she's planning to sell the property. After the summer is over, she'll be gone. She doesn't want to keep it. She doesn't want to stay here, with me."

Joyce pulled out the chair next to him and sat without saying a word. Jesse expected her to tell him that everything would be fine, that there were plenty of fish in the sea, and if he was ready for a woman to be a part of his life, that he'd find the right one eventually. His mother had seen him through multiple relationships over the years.

Instead, she put her hand on his arm and said, "I know."

Jesse looked at her. "You know? That's she's leaving?"

"That you're in love with her." She gave him a sympathetic smile. "A mother knows."

Jesse thought of all the conscious efforts he'd made to hide his feelings for Hazel, for her sake and his, but were his feelings written all over his face? Was he was too far gone to walk away from Hazel now? Jesse was sitting at his parents' kitchen table, but he felt like he'd just jumped into the middle of the lake, left the safety of solid ground, and was about to sink or swim.

Joyce squeezed his arm. "Love isn't always easy, but it's worth it. Your dad and I have been together for forty-five years. There are ups and downs, and sometimes stuff goes completely sideways, but we made a choice all those years ago to be there for each other, no matter what. Love doesn't just happen. It's a choice. You have to choose it."

Jesse let his mother's advice sink in, and it strengthened what he knew deep inside. He had some choices to make. Tough choices. Decisions that would change his life.

The next morning Hazel sat in the barn office, her gaze rotating between the desk and the clock. It was barely past ten and she couldn't wait until her workday was over. Hazel loved her job. She thoroughly enjoyed all the activities with the horse-camp kids, making lunches, and she even enjoyed the paperwork. Today, however, Hazel couldn't wait to get done with work so she could talk to Jesse. She had a lot on her mind, and a lot to say. All night she'd been grinding over what she should do, and by the morning she finally let herself see what she really wanted. Hazel wanted to keep the carriage house. And she wanted to truly give her and Jesse a chance.

Last night, after Bill's surprise arrival and proceeding mess, Hazel realized how happy she'd been in Maple Bay. She also realized how miserable she'd be if she moved back to the city and let the carriage house and all the wonderful people that had become part of her life slip away. Maple Bay had breathed new life into her. She'd found a creative outlet in the carriage house—in restoring it, decorating it, planning its future. Her love of cooking and baking had been revived and she had the chance to create a business—a bed-and-breakfast—that would fuel her passions and *could* financially support her and Grace. If she kept the property, finances would be tight, but Hazel had the remainder of the money from selling her car. She'd use that to finish the remodel, best she could. Then she'd open the bed-and-breakfast as quickly as possible. Hopefully, yet this summer. Then, to further cement her plan, Hazel had called Myra first thing this morning and pitched an idea. She offered to provide Perkup Coffee with as many pastries as Myra would take, for as long as she would take them. Myra was delighted with the idea and ordered four dozen of whatever Hazel wanted to bake for tomorrow.

Hazel was starting to make sense of everything in her head, but knew she'd need to scrimp and hustle and save all summer. Then, come fall, she'd buy a cheap car and could travel back and forth between Haven Hills and Maple Bay. She'd stay in Haven Hills during the week, while Grace attended school. She and Grace would continue to live in her parents' basement, and Hazel would keep her job at the elementary school. On the weekends, she and Grace would travel to Maple Bay. When Grace was with Bill, Hazel would put on her big girl panties and leave her be. Because Hazel was starting to understand that if she wasn't happy, her daughter wouldn't be either. This change would be good for them both.

Furthermore, Hazel might be able to rent out rooms in the carriage house even while she was in Haven Hills. If she could hire someone to help her cook and clean, Hazel could manage the reservations and administrative work from afar.

Excitement built inside her, and Hazel couldn't wait to share her news with Jesse. She knew she'd said all the wrong things yesterday, and she wanted to make it right with him. Her fear of failure had blinded her, no matter how worthy or safe Jesse had made her feel. But she didn't want to let her fears keep her from the possibility of love and happiness. Not any longer.

Boot heels clicked down the barn aisle, and Frankie stuck her head in the office. "The kids are tacking up their horses now and I'm going to get them all in the saddle. Do you want to prep lunch while they ride?"

"Already done." Hazel had been wide awake since four o'clock. She'd whipped together sandwiches, apple slices, and cookies by five.

"You're such an overachiever." Frankie winked. "Well, do whatever you like for the next hour. Maybe make a fresh pot of coffee?"

"Sure. I'll bring you a cup when it's brewed. And I'll prep for the craft activity I have planned for this afternoon."

"Great," Frankie replied. "Oh, and I might need your help in a bit. The police finally identified the owner of the last two horses from our rescue."

"Oh, that's great news."

"It is. The owner is driving over from South Dakota. Should be here sometime in the next hour or so. I might need you to supervise the kids while I help her load the horses in her trailer."

Hazel nodded. "No problem."

Frankie smiled and disappeared from the door.

Hazel stood from the desk and walked over to the corner table that served as a coffee station. She opened the coffee maker and removed the full filter. After prepping a fresh pot and pushing the start button, Hazel surveyed the office. What could she do to keep herself busy for the next hour? Prepping for her afternoon activity would only take fifteen minutes. Identifying a light layer of dust on the shelf that held pictures and trophies, Hazel grabbed the duster and started cleaning, but she stopped when she spotted her box sitting next to one of Frankie's trophies. The box of letters from Rose.

Hazel forgot she'd set it there Saturday night, after Hazel and Frankie had read a few of Rose's letters before the barn dance. They'd been outside, watching the kids play while they waited for Jesse and Charlie to arrive. Hazel had intended to take the box back over to the carriage house, but got distracted when Jesse showed up early. She'd set it in the barn office for safe keeping.

Hazel picked up the box. She'd been reading the letters with Frankie, but they'd only made it through about half of them. Curiosity niggled at Hazel. Maybe she could peek at one? Frankie and she could still read the letters together. Hazel would just have a preview.

Deciding Frankie would be fine with that, Hazel sat down at the desk. She opened the box and thumbed through the envelopes. Each was marked with a year and Hazel was surprised by the connection she now felt to the letters—the understanding she had gained of her biological mother. As she flipped through the envelopes, Hazel found herself drawn to the very last one. What were Rose's last words to her? She plucked the soft pink envelope from the box and stared at it. It was written just last fall.

Not able to help herself, Hazel opened the envelope and unfolded the letter.

My Sweet Hazel,

Thirty-seven years ago you came into this world, and I can still remember how you felt in my arms. Since the day I had you, I never set you down. I didn't want to miss one moment with my baby girl. Ever since I left the hospital alone, I've struggled with the pain and guilt of not keeping you as my own, but I've also come to understand that God has a plan for everyone. When you were born, I wasn't ready for you. I couldn't give you a stable home. Instead, I was meant to give you life in order to bless your mother and father with a beautiful daughter of their own. You were meant for their love, though you've never been without mine.

Many times over the years I've wanted to reach out to you, to try to have some kind of relationship, but I never wanted to disrupt the family you already had. Instead, I tried to do you proud by raising Frankie the way I wish I could've raised you.

This may be the last letter I write to you. I've been fighting cancer for over a year and it's taking a toll on my body. By the time you read this letter, I will likely be gone from this earth, but in my absence, I wanted to give you a piece of me. I always intended to leave you these letters so that you could know how much I've loved you and thought about you. I know possessions are not the most important things in life, but I've always wanted to split my belongings between you and Frankie. I've left you each adjoining properties and special mementos from my life. In my will, I have set forth a clause, asking that both you and Frankie live on your properties for whatever length of time Frankie requires. You may not see this as a gift at first, but this is my gift to my daughters, in hopes that you will become sisters.

I will love you always,
Rose

Hazel's throat closed. She felt paralyzed, but managed to blink. Tears dripped off her lashes onto the letter, and Hazel read it one more time. Frozen to the chair, she focused on the last few lines.

I have set forth a clause, asking that both you and Frankie live on your properties for whatever length of time Frankie requires . . . Frankie was who determined that Hazel live here for the summer? She had set the timeline?

Betrayal crept in like smoke, clouding the time Hazel had shared with Frankie, making it feel murky. Hazel remembered the pity she'd felt for Frankie at the reading of the will, how she couldn't understand why Rose would put Frankie in a spot where she'd be vulnerable and could possibly lose her house, barn, and business. Then Frankie had basically begged Hazel to stay. Frankie had cried. All of that was a lie? Frankie had the power all along to end the clause? To change the terms of the will?

Hazel slowly rose from the chair and walked out of the office, still holding the letter. She left the barn and moved toward the arena like a car through fog—not really seeing anything outside what was right in front of her. Her sights were set on Frankie.

Frankie stood near the arena fence. She was saying something to the kids who were in the arena, saddling up their horses which were all tied to the fence. She must've heard Hazel approaching, because she turned. Her face was bright and cheery and the second she saw Hazel, confusion grabbed Frankie's features. Her eyes flicked to what Hazel held in her hand and Frankie's eyes widened.

Hazel stopped in front of Frankie. "You lied to me."

"I—" Frankie started. "I didn't—"

"You *lied*, Frankie. I actually trusted you and you lied." Did everyone in her life like to hide things? Her parents hid her adoption until she was a teenager. Bill hid all his stupid financial decisions and then his affair. Her biological mother hid from Hazel all her life. Now her sister—someone she thought she could trust—lied to her face? Hid the truth? Even after they grew close? "I rooted up my entire life and moved here at a moment's notice *with my daughter* because that's what I thought I had to do. But you had the ability all along to put an end to the clause?"

Frankie's chin moved for a bit before she sputtered out words. "It's not like that."

"What's it like then?"

"I was going to tell you. I planned to tell you before we got through all the letters. Why were you reading them without me?"

A painful bubble of anger shot up Hazel's throat. That's what Frankie had to say for herself? "The letters were written to me. *Not to us*. I can read them as I see fit."

Frankie looked like Hazel had slapped her. "I thought—"

"You thought wrong." Hazel stared at Frankie. "You watched me struggle and still chose to hold Rose's will over my head?" Tears sprung to Hazel's eyes. She thought she'd gained a sister this summer. Now she didn't know what to think. "Why wouldn't you just tell me the truth? Why did I have to read it here?" Hazel raised the letter in her hand and shook it like a rattle, angry at the strong twinge of pain wringing through her.

"Stop!" Frankie called sharply. She snatched Hazel's wrist, pulled it down, and removed the letter from Hazel's hand before stuffing the paper in her back jeans pocket.

For a second, Hazel was stunned by Frankie's knee-jerk reaction, but quickly realized a horse behind her was scrambling on gravel. Hazel turned to see hooves in the air.

There was a strange truck and trailer parked next to the barn, and the last two rescue horses were walking toward it. Jesse led one. Tommy had ahold of the other, kind of. The waving letter must've spooked them.

"Easy," Jesse repeated a few times as both horses continued scattering backward. He had a firm hold on his horse, even as it jumped, and tried to grab Tommy's horse's lead rope as well, but the horse was too quick. It reared and jerked backward, pulling Tommy to the ground.

"Let go, Tommy!" Frankie shouted. Her son held tight to the rope, and the horse yanked him across the grass like a sled on snow until he couldn't hold on any longer. The rope shot out of Tommy's hands like a rubber band and whipped the already frightened horse across the chest.

Frankie swore and moved toward the running horse. Hazel heard Frankie tell the kids in the arena to move away from their horses and stay calm, but everything happened so fast. The frightened, loose horse galloped away from Tommy and through an open gate on the other end of the arena. He tore across the arena sand, bucking and running as the lead rope slapped against his side. The kids backed away from the horses that were tied to the fence, which was good because the horses danced around and whinnied. But Hazel quickly realized there was one rider that was already in the saddle—her daughter.

Grace must've mounted up on her own while Frankie and Hazel were talking. She sat on the horse she'd be assigned for the day—Patches—in the middle of the arena, looking terrified as the loose, bucking horse ran straight for her.

Hazel had no idea what to do. She only knew that she had to get to Grace.

Scrambling through the arena fence, Hazel made it between the boards just as the loose horse neared Grace and Patches. To Hazel's horror, Patches lurched forward, trying to get away from the loose horse. The sudden movement knocked Grace off balance and out of the saddle. She fell to the ground with a *thud* and the loose horse raced by, just feet from where Grace lay in the sand.

Dear God. Hazel ran toward Grace, quieting every ounce of her that wanted to shout out. She didn't want to scare Grace or the horses any more than she already had. When Hazel reached her daughter, she kneeled beside her.

"Tell me what hurts."

Grace looked stunned, but when she saw her mom, the tears came. She was obviously in pain.

Hazel unclipped the chin strap of Grace's helmet, unbelievably grateful that Frankie required helmets of all her riders. "It's okay, baby. Everything will be okay. Now, tell me where you're hurt." Hazel's heart raced and she tried to calm all her own fears so she could be fully present for Grace.

"My arm," Grace sobbed and grabbed one arm with the other. It looked like she'd fallen on her side, maybe taken the brunt of the tumble on her shoulder.

"Don't move her," Jesse shouted, and Hazel looked up. He was running across the arena toward them. "The ambulance is on its way."

CHAPTER TWENTY-SIX

Jesse had gone to his client's barn first thing Monday morning, but he couldn't focus on training horses. His mind was stuck on Hazel and he needed to talk to her. He couldn't wait to say his piece, so he got in his truck and drove to Frankie's. When he arrived, Frankie called for him from the arena and asked if he could go with Tommy to grab the two rescue horses. Their owner had just arrived. But what should've been a fifteen-minute chore turned into a full-on disaster.

As he and Tommy led the two horses to their awaiting trailer, Hazel appeared from the barn. She wore jeans, a t-shirt, and Rose's cowboy boots. Her red hair gleamed in the sun and was twirled into a bun at the nape of her neck. She looked beautiful, as always, but seemed preoccupied. She didn't look his way and walked toward Frankie with papers in her hand. Hazel and Frankie exchanged words, and the conversation seemed off. Were they fighting about something? Just as Jesse contemplated what they could be arguing about, Hazel waved the paper in her hand like a flag. It couldn't have happened at a worse time. Jesse and Tommy were directly behind Hazel, leading the horses toward an open trailer. The horses were already on alert, and their owner had mentioned they weren't the best loaders. The flailing paper tipped Tommy's horse over the edge and he reared up. Jesse's horse reacted to his horse-buddy's explosion.

In a matter of seconds, Tommy was being dragged along the ground, and the horse got loose. Jesse quickly handed his horse off to its owner and went to make sure Tommy was okay, but the little boy was already on his feet, reassuring Frankie that he'd only skinned his elbows. By that time, the loose horse had made a grand entrance into the arena and Jesse lost his breath, knowing they were in an emergency situation. The horse was frantically running, and all the camp kids were in the arena, way too close to danger. Jesse and Frankie moved fast, jumping into the arena as they told the kids to get out of it, but they couldn't stop the loose horse from sprinting toward Patches and Grace.

Patches moved out of the way of the stampeding horse, but the movement was too quick for Grace, and she ended up in the dirt. Jesse saw Hazel running for her daughter, and he went with Frankie to corner the loose horse. As soon as he had ahold of it, he handed the horse off to Frankie, pulled his phone from his pocket, and dialed 9-1-1.

"Don't move her. The ambulance is on its way," Jesse shouted as he got close to Hazel and Grace. Jesse knew Hazel was only trying to help by loosening her daughter's helmet, but Jesse didn't take chances with unplanned dismounts. Not after what happened to his sister.

Hazel hovered over Grace and looked at Jesse like she was scared out of her mind. "I think she broke her arm."

Jesse wanted to scoop them both up and cradle them to his chest. Instead, he knelt over Grace. "Hey, Grace," he forced his voice to stay even and calm. She was on her back, holding her arm, and grimacing. "I'm going to need you to stay still until the EMTs get here. Can you do that for me?"

"Yeah," she squeaked through tears. Hazel wiped them away with her thumbs.

"The ambulance will be here really fast," he added. He knew every EMT in the Maple Bay unit, and they all drove like they were NASCAR racers. "Can you wiggle your toes for me?" Jesse grabbed her boot and felt Grace's toes move. "Great. Now, how about your fingers?" Grace did the same with her fingers, and Jesse felt a little tension ease from his chest.

"It's my arm that hurts real bad." Grace's bottom lip trembled, and Jesse went into story-mode. It was a trick he'd discovered with Charlie. If Charlie was upset, Jesse could tell a story and, if the story was interesting enough, it would distract her from her tears.

"You know what happened to me the very first time I fell off a horse?" he asked. Grace sniffled, but her big brown eyes were on him. "I tried to make my horse go across a big mud puddle. My sister, Kat, had her horse trotting through the puddle and I wasn't going to let her one-up me. So, I spent what felt like forever trying to coax my stubborn horse into the water. When he finally gave in, he jumped into the puddle and I plopped right off his back and into the water. I can still remember the sound of my sister laughing when I stood up with a face full of mud."

Grace blinked her teary eyes, but she was paying attention to him. "You've fallen off too?"

More times than he could count, but he wasn't about to admit that fact right now and push Hazel to never let her daughter on a horse again. "Sure have. Everyone falls off at some point, but it's what you learn after the fall that matters. You know what I learned after I took a nosedive into a puddle?"

"What?"

"To have one hand on the saddle horn the next time I asked my horse to go into water. That way I could hang on if he decided to jump."

Grace's trembling lips slid into the slightest of grins, and Jesse heard sirens in the distance.

"The ambulance is almost here, baby," Hazel said. "We're going to go to the hospital and get you checked out, okay?"

Jesse looked up to see flashing lights coming down the driveway and Frankie waving the ambulance over to the arena. "Looks like my friend, Bubba, is driving. You'll like him. He's super funny and he'll tell you all about his silly goats if you just ask him. Don't forget to ask him, okay?"

"Okay," Grace said, and she looked a little calmer.

Jesse stayed with Grace and Hazel while Bubba and the other EMT checked Grace over and put her on a stretcher. However, when they loaded Grace into the ambulance, Jesse's body went cold. Memories he'd suppressed for quite some time snatched up his mind. He'd watched his sister, Sarah, get loaded into an ambulance as well, but Sarah wasn't crying. She wasn't breathing either. It was an image he knew he wouldn't forget until the day he died.

"Jesse?" Hazel put a hand on his arm. He jerked out of his glazed stare. "Thank you for being there for us."

"Of course. What else can I do?"

"Do you think you could come with me to the hospital?"

"In the ambulance?"

Hazel nodded, and Jesse was touched that she wanted him with her. "Of course, I can."

Just then, a little silver car pulled up to the barn and Bill jumped out of the driver's side door. "Hazel? Grace? What happened?" Fear was etched on his features as he ran toward the ambulance.

"Grace fell off her horse. We think she broke her arm," Hazel said to Bill as her hand dropped from Jesse's arm.

Bill raced to the back of the ambulance and Jesse heard him talking with Grace. Then he climbed in and turned back to Hazel, "Let's go. They're ready." He waved Hazel over. By this time, Bill's girlfriend had joined them at the ambulance.

"Go," Jesse said to Hazel. "I'll follow you. I can drive Bill's girlfriend as well."

"Thank you." Hazel turned away and climbed up into the ambulance. Bubba shut the doors.

CHAPTER TWENTY-SEVEN

A few hours later, Hazel and Bill walked with Grace down the hospital hallway, toward the lobby. Grace had her arm in a sling and a purple cast on her hand, wrist, and forearm. She'd fractured her wrist, but was otherwise okay. Her sweet smile was back on her face, but Hazel still felt terrible, knowing she'd started the catastrophe by carelessly waving Rose's letter in Frankie's face. She never would've done that if she'd known the rescue horses were behind her, but in that moment, she had tunnel vision. She wasn't paying attention to what was around her. A pit had grown in her stomach as she thought about what could have happened, and she was incredibly thankful that Frankie and Jesse were there to control the situation.

"You might need to pick a sport that's a little less dangerous," Bill said to Grace as a nurse passed them.

Grace looked at her dad, astonished. "No way. I could get hurt in another sport too. Remember when my friend from school broke her leg in gymnastics? Or that other girl got hit in the face with a baseball?"

Hazel cringed at the visual, but agreed with Grace's point. No matter how desperately Hazel wanted to protect Grace from even the slightest pain, she was starting to accept that she couldn't keep her daughter in a bubble. If she did, Hazel *might* protect Grace from the lows of life, but she'd also deny her the highs. She didn't want to do that. Life was bumpy. There would be bruises and falls—literally and figuratively. Hazel only hoped each bump would make her daughter stronger.

"She really loves to ride, Bill. She's really good at it too." Grace smiled up at Hazel, silently thanking her mom for the backup. "And I know she'll be as safe as she can possibly be."

"I will. I promise." Grace glanced back and forth between her parents. "And next time, I'll grab the saddle horn if something scary happens. That way I can hang on better." Grace looked proud of her conclusion and Hazel grinned, knowing Grace was repeating what she'd learned from Jesse.

Bill still looked unsure. "I don't know—"

"Let's talk about it later. Okay?" Hazel gave Bill a look that said she wanted to talk to him about it in private. She'd explain how much the horses and riding had made their daughter bloom this summer, and Hazel was sure she could convince Bill to allow Grace to continue to ride. Hazel had a few other things to talk to Bill about as well—like the fact that she was going to keep the carriage house. Before Bill could rebut her, Hazel pushed open the double doors and stepped into the hospital lobby, finding it full of familiar faces. Her heart swelled at the sight.

Frankie and Garrett stood near the coffee pot, Styrofoam cups in their hands. Tommy, Wyatt, Noah, and Charlie were sitting in a circle on the white tile floor, playing a board game. Joyce and Gene sat behind them, watching the kids from waiting room chairs. Bill's girlfriend, Cynthia, sat next to Joyce.

Frankie was the first to see them. Her face lit up and she strode over, leaning down to give Grace a big hug, though she was careful of her casted arm.

"There's my tough cowgirl," Frankie said to Grace. She also slid Hazel a sympathetic smile, as though Hazel hadn't thrown harsh words at her just a few hours ago.

In a matter of seconds, everyone circled around, fussing over Grace.

"Doctor said I have to wear the cast for six weeks, but I can still use my fingers, so I should be able to ride," Grace announced.

Grace would need a little time out of the saddle in order to heal, but Hazel decided to tackle that topic for another day. "You guys were waiting here the whole time?" Hazel asked.

Joyce made a strange expression. "Where else would we go? We had to make sure our girls were all right."

"I think I drank a whole pot of coffee myself while we waited to see you guys," Frankie added.

"And we got to pick out candy bars from the vending machine!" Noah announced. "I got one for you too." He ran back to the plastic chairs and grabbed a pack of Skittles that was sitting by Joyce's purse. Enthusiastically, he raced to Grace and offered it up. "I know they're your favorite."

Grace smiled and took the candy. "Thanks!"

Hot tears sprang to Hazel's eyes, and she finally let herself accept what everyone here was trying to give her. She'd discovered a second family here in Maple Bay. A group of wonderful people that wanted to love her and Grace. "Thank you," she repeated, blinking away tears.

"It's just Skittles," Noah said, concerned. "You don't have to cry."

Hazel laughed and wiped at her eyes. She ruffled Noah's hair. "Thanks, buddy. That was really sweet of you." She found herself looking for the only other face she yearned to see. "Where's Jesse?"

Frankie stood from her crouched position in front of Grace. "We weren't sure when you guys would be done, so Jesse ran out to get lunch for everyone."

"Oh." Hazel tried to keep her disappointment from showing. She also knew she had some unresolved issues to talk with Frankie about. "Can I talk to you? Alone?"

"Sure," Frankie replied, looking uncertain.

Hazel and Frankie walked to the other side of the waiting room, closer to the entrance.

Hazel started the conversation. "Look, I've had some time to think about the letter, and what I said to you."

Frankie didn't let her finish. "I'm sorry for keeping that secret for so long, but I'm not sorry I did it," Frankie blurted. "I wanted to get to know you. You're my sister. And I thought the clause was the only way I could be sure you'd stick around. After I got to know you, I should've told you the truth, but the more time I spent with you, the more I didn't want you to leave."

Hazel found herself crying again. "I know," she choked out. While Grace was being doctored, Hazel had plenty of time to think, and she wished she hadn't reacted so rashly after reading Rose's letter. "Honestly, if the will hadn't required that I stay for the summer, I'm not sure that I would've."

Hazel might've sold the property immediately and scampered back to Haven Hills, to a life that wasn't fulfilling her. It's possible she would've taken the time to get to know Frankie later, but Hazel was certain nothing could've forced her and Frankie closer than living together and sharing all the experiences of the summer. "I'm glad you lied."

Frankie huffed a laugh like she'd been holding her breath. "I won't lie to you ever again."

"You don't need to lie to keep me here. I want to be here, Frankie. I want to be your big sister." Hazel opened her arms, and they grabbed each other into a hug. "I'm sorry too. I wasn't thinking straight. And I'm *really* sorry I caused both of our kids to get hurt. Is Tommy okay?"

Hazel and Frankie stayed clasped in their hug as Frankie replied, "Oh, goodness. He's fine. He thinks the scrapes on his arms are cool, and now Noah's trying to figure out how to get matching injuries."

Hazel laughed, thankful Tommy was okay.

Frankie pulled back from their hug and looked Hazel in the face. "Did we just have our first sister-fight?"

"I think so." Hazel grinned and brushed a strand of hair from Frankie's face. "And our first sister-reconciliation."

"I really like this sister thing."

"Me too," Hazel replied, and squeezed Frankie's shoulders. As she did, Hazel caught a glimpse of Jesse's red truck pulling into a parking spot just outside the glass doors. "Hold that thought. I've got one more person I need to makeup with."

Frankie glanced outside and her smile widened. "Go get 'em, Sis."

Hazel started toward the automatic glass doors and they whooshed open. By the time she moved through them, she was running. Jesse walked toward the ER. He was carrying two brown bags. When he saw her, he faltered, looking alarmed. Hazel hoped her big smile would reassure him that nothing was wrong. She just needed to get to him. She needed to be in his arms and tell him everything she'd been thinking of.

As Hazel neared, Jesse dropped the bags to the pavement. Hazel jumped into his arms. She linked her hands around his neck and clamped her cowboy-booted legs around his waist. Jesse pulled her to his chest, and they stared at each other in stunned silence for a few breathes—until Hazel kissed him. She planted a kiss on him like he'd just come home from war, not from McDonald's.

They kissed like the world might end and Hazel lost herself in Jesse's lips, in his strong embrace and the way he made her feel. Then she eased back and looked at Jesse. His blue eyes were hazy.

After a few beats, he said, "Wow, you must really like chicken nuggets."

Hazel giggled and kissed him one more time, just because he was so cute.

"I want to tell you something." Hazel was done fighting with herself. She was done pushing away this wonderful man because she was scared.

He stopped her. "I'd love to be a gentleman and listen to what you have to say, but I need to tell you something too."

Hazel searched his baby blue eyes. The determination in them made her hold her tongue. "You go first."

"Life is short," he said, holding her against him with his strong arms. "I know that firsthand, and I don't want to waste one more day wondering what our life could be like together. I understand what you've been trying to tell me, and I don't expect you to change your entire life to be with me. I want you to know I'm willing to change too. I'll do whatever it takes to make us work. We can share our time between Haven Hills and Maple Bay. I'll move to the city. Charlie could even enroll in kindergarten in Haven Hills next year, if that's what we decide."

It took Hazel a few seconds to find words. "You'd move to the suburbs?"

"For you, I would."

"What about your horses? The business you've built?" If Hazel knew one thing, it was that horses and city life didn't mix. Hazel wasn't about to ask Jesse to give up his passion in life. She knew all too well what that did to a person.

"I could pick up some clients closer to Minneapolis. I already called an old friend that has a show barn in the area. He said he'd have plenty of work for me if I wanted it. I also talked to Evan, Mom, and Dad about possibly taking some time off from training colts for the family business. They understand and can hire extra help if needed. It also helps that my entire family is crazy about you." He clasped his hands tighter around her waist. "All I want is you. I want to keep you, me, Grace, and Charlie together. I want us to have a life together. Whatever that takes, I'll make it happen."

Hazel didn't even have her feet on the ground, but her pulse picked up like she'd just run a country mile. With her own plans and what Jesse had just offered, they could make it work, even if they had to bounce back and forth between two towns. "You know what you told Grace after she fell off today?"

Jesse quirked an eyebrow, not quite sure where she was going with their conversation. "About holding onto the saddle horn?"

She shook her head. "About hitting the ground. You told her that everyone falls off at some point and it's what you learn after the fall that matters."

"I did say that, didn't I?"

"You give good advice." Hazel ran her fingers up his neck and into his hair. "I realized that all this time I've been scared of the fall. I've been scared of hitting the ground and getting hurt. But being scared has never done anything good for me." She ran her knuckles across his dark stubble. "If I never take a chance, I'll never get what I want. And I want you, Jesse. I want to fight to make us work." She placed a hand over his heart. "I love you, Jesse. I can't promise I'll be perfect, but I'll—."

"I don't want perfect." The conviction in his voice was like an exclamation point. "I want to be together through the good times *and* the bad times, no matter what. I love you too, Hazel."

They shared a smile that spread and surged through their whole beings. Then Jesse leaned in and kissed her again—until there was a faint shouting noise that caught their attention. Following the noise, Jesse spun and gave Hazel a view of the hospital.

Pressed up against the waiting room window was an audience of their family. Joyce had her hands clasped together at her heart like she might burst of happiness. Gene bounced Charlie in his arms, and she flailed with glee. Frankie was clapping, her arms above her head, and Garrett gave a few fist pumps and some hoots. Grace, Tommy, Wyatt, and Noah were at the open automatic glass doors, looking like they were having a little dance party. Bill was behind them, scowling. His girlfriend was excitedly clapping.

Hazel placed her head in the crook of Jesse's neck and laughed, knowing exactly how lucky she was. "Doesn't look like we were fooling anyone."

She picked her head up and Jesse touched his forehead to hers. "I just want to *make sure* everyone knows how I feel about you." Then Jesse kissed Hazel one more time, for everyone to see.

EPILOGUE

Snow fell outside the carriage house, twinkling though the windows and covering Maple Bay in a fresh, white blanket. Flakes glittered against the dark New Year's Eve sky, but Jesse's gaze was ripped from the windows as Hazel started down the carriage house stairs.

He clutched his chest.

Hazel wore a glossy emerald green dress—his absolute favorite color on her. The dress hugged her curves and was topped off with a white faux fur shawl and dangling gold earrings. Her red hair fell in waves that reminded Jesse of a fifty's pinup girl.

"You look like an angel." He met her at the bottom of the stairs and took her hand, leading her down the last few steps and twirling her toward him. Her laugh made him high.

"You look mighty handsome yourself." Hazel took hold of the lapels of his black blazer, her eyes sparkling like jewels. "Do you think anyone would notice if we were late to dinner?"

He grinned and ran his hands up her arms and under her shawl. "I'd gladly miss out on dinner just to stay here and kiss you senseless, but I don't think the girls will feel the same, and they'll be here any minute." Frankie had taken Charlie and Grace, keeping them busy while Hazel finished getting dressed for dinner.

Over the last half of the summer, Hazel had gone into overdrive, finishing the carriage house remodel. She had lots of help from Jesse, Frankie, and her Maple Bay family—as she lovingly referred to Jesse's parents, siblings, and cousins—and *The Carriage House Bed-and-Breakfast* was officially opened for business by the end of August. As soon as Hazel started taking reservations, bookings filled the calendar. Most all the rooms were rented every weekend through the fall and winter so Hazel and Jesse stayed busy, spending their weekends in Maple Bay. Their weekdays were spent in Haven Hills, where Grace attended school and spent time with her father. Frankie, Joyce, and Myra all pitched in to clean and cook for guests when Hazel and Jesse couldn't, but they wouldn't have to juggle back and forth between two towns any longer. After Christmas break, Hazel and Grace would make their permanent home in Maple Bay.

When Bill was in Maple Bay for his first impromptu visit, he did quite a bit of research on the local housing market. By the time Hazel told Bill she wouldn't be selling the carriage house, he'd already picked up another listing in the area. It sold in a few days, and he landed another listing quickly. Word of mouth was a strong marketing tool in Maple Bay, and Bill quickly built a reputation for his strong negotiation skills. Over the fall, Bill traveled back and forth to Maple Bay as much as Hazel did and he was able to spend a lot of time with Grace. By Thanksgiving, Bill decided to move his real estate business to Maple Bay and buy a house in the small town. His girlfriend, Cynthia moved with him. In a few short months, she'd become enamored with the quaint, small town as well. After that, Hazel had no reason to keep roots in Haven Hills.

"Everyone else already left for dinner?" Hazel asked as she looked around the carriage house's lower level, which had been transformed into a living and dining area for guests. A long wooden table sat along the backside of the building, bordering the windows and view of the lake. An overstuffed couch and chairs circled the stone fireplace. Hazel had everything decorated beautifully for the holidays. Garland, holly, candles and bows were strung along tables, mantles, windows and doors. A twelve foot Christmas tree filled the corner, decked out with white lights and shiny bulbs. Jesse smiled as he remembered just a few days ago when the girls had opened their Christmas gifts, sitting cross-legged in matching plaid pajamas at the base of the sprawling fir.

"Everyone is meeting us at the restaurant. Your parents left just a few minutes ago." Hazel's parents, Sandy and Peter, were staying in the carriage house for the holidays and wouldn't be headed back to Haven Hills until next week. It was wonderful to have the space to allow them to visit whenever they wanted to, and Jesse knew they'd be here often. The other rooms were full of family as well—Jesse's aunts, uncles, and cousins that had traveled home for the holidays.

"We should get going, then," Hazel said, but tipped her head like she might've heard something out of place. Jesse caught the faint jingle-jangle as well. "Do I hear jingle bells?" she asked, quirking her brow. "Is Santa coming for a second visit?"

Jesse acted like he didn't know what could possibly make that noise. "It sounds like it's coming from out front. Let's go see." He swooped his hand around Hazel's back and guided her to the front door, excited nerves bundling in his chest.

When Jesse opened the front door and they stepped into the brisk evening air, Hazel gasped. A horse-drawn sleigh was gliding through the snow.

"Oh, my goodness." Hazel's hands covered her mouth in astonishment.

The red lacquered sleigh skated toward them, pulled by the beautiful buckskin gelding that had won Jesse's heart—Indy. After working with Indy for months, Jesse found he couldn't stand to part with the horse and ended up adopting Indy for himself. Now, Indy trotted down the snowy driveway, gracefully pulling some of the most important people in Jesse's life—Charlie, Grace, and Frankie.

"I got us a sleigh," Jesse announced. "I thought your carriage house needed one for the snowy Minnesota winters. And I taught Indy to pull it. We can take guests out for winter sleigh rides."

Hazel still had her hands over her mouth, her eyes wide. "I can't believe it. I love it. I simply love it."

"And I'm going to get you a carriage as well. Because you obviously need one of those." The glee on Hazel's face warmed Jesse's insides.

"Did somebody say they needed a ride?" Frankie called from the front of the sleigh before using the black leather reins to pull Indy and the sled to a sliding stop in front of Jesse and Hazel. The bells on Indy's harness jingled as he halted. Charlie and Grace waved excitedly from the back seat, warm and smiley in purple velvet cloaks. Frankie wore a matching cloak as well.

Hazel laughed with pure joy. "All you ladies look absolutely beautiful."

"Your chariot awaits, Sis," Frankie exclaimed. "We're sure going to turn some heads on main street."

"We sure are," Hazel agreed and turned to Jesse. "Thank you. I love, love, love the sleigh. That was so thoughtful of you."

Jesse took both Hazel's hands in his, knowing the horse-drawn sleigh was just the start of his plan for tonight. "I have one more gift for you before we go." Under the moonlight and snowflakes, Jesse reached inside his jacket and pulled out the little box. Blood pounded in his ears, but as Jesse went onto a knee in the snow, he'd never been more certain of anything in his entire life.

"Oh my—" Hazel's hands flew back to her face and tears instantly sprang to her eyes.

"Hazel, you bring so much joy and happiness into my life, and I try every day to do the same for you. I know without a doubt that I want to spend the New Year and every single year after that by your side. I want to make you, me, Charlie, and Grace a family. I already asked the girls for their blessing and they both support what I'm about to ask you."

Hazel glanced over at Grace and Charlie who were now standing at the edge of the sleigh. "You both knew?"

"We kept this secret for a whole week!" Charlie shouted, like she'd been waiting to get that off her chest. Grace laughed and put her arm around Charlie, squeezing her shoulders. In the embrace, both girls tipped their heads toward each other. The sight nearly knocked Jesse from his knees.

"Say yes, Momma," Grace said, a huge smile on her face.

"May I have your hand?" Jesse asked. Hazel's red stained lips hung open and she shakily offered Jesse her hand. "Will you make me the happiest man in the entire world and be my wife?"

She was nodding her head before Jesse finished his sentence. "Yes, yes, yes."

Jesse's heart felt like it might explode as he slipped the sparkling diamond ring onto Hazel's finger and stood to kiss her. The girls and Frankie squealed in delight.

"Come on, you two lovebirds," Frankie said through a smile. "Don't want to be late for your own party."

Hazel reluctantly eased back from Jesse's kiss, though her arms stayed wrapped tightly around his shoulders and neck. "I thought we were going to a New Year's Eve party."

Jesse wiped happy tears from her cheeks and then kissed them. "We're going to our engagement party."

Then Jesse helped his fiancé into the sleigh, and they jingled off to main street.

THE END

HAZEL'S PEANUT BUTTER PIE

1 cup peanut butter (creamy or crunchy)

1 cup powdered sugar

8 oz cream cheese (softened)

¼ cup milk

1 teaspon vanilla extract

1 store-bought graham cracker pie crust

2 (8 oz) cool whips (thawed)

chocolate chips

1. Get out your electric mixer. Add peanut butter, powdered sugar, cream cheese, milk, & vanilla to a mixing bowl. Mix until creamy.

2. Add one of the 8oz cool whips to the mixture (save the second container for when you serve the pie) and gently mix with a rubber spatula.

3. Pour mixture into the graham cracker crust.

4. Slide the pie into the refrigerator and hide it behind something so no one gets sneaky and digs into it early. Keep in fridge for 4 hours or overnight.

5. When ready to serve, top with cool whip and sprinkle chocolate chips on top of cool whip.
6. Enjoy!

SECOND CHANCE IN MAPLE BAY

(A Maple Bay Novel, Book 2)

Running from the past is easier than facing it...

Kat swore off horses after a riding accident took her sister. Five years later she still blames herself and deals with the guilt by losing herself in city lights, a corporate job, and a sham of an engagement. But when Kat returns home for her brother Jesse's wedding, the past comes creeping back. She's not sure she can face the memories, especially because she shared many of them with her brother's best friend, Creed—a man Kat's been in love with since high school and who was with her that fateful night.

Creed lives for one thing—rodeo—and he learned long ago that family is more than blood. Creed's best friend's parents took him under their wing when he was a teenager, treating him like a son. Which is why Kat, his best friend's little sister, has always been off-limits. When Kat comes home to Maple Bay, a ring on her hand and sadness in her heart,

Creed is pulled to her once again. But is she worth the risk of losing the only family he's got?

A feel-good story of second chances and how love, family, and friendship can heal all hearts.

Please join Brittney's newsletter to be notified as soon as book 2 is available:

http://www.brittneyjoybooks.com/newsletter

Author's Note
Brittney Joy

I've wanted to write a sweet adult romance for years now, but 2020 was the year that finally nudged (or, more properly, pushed) me to write it. Twenty-twenty was hard, for many reasons, and I found myself wanting to escape to a simpler time. I've lived in Oregon for over a decade, but I'm originally from Minnesota and much of my family still lives there. We visit each other often, but 2020 put a pause on face-to-face visits. As I'm sure you all know, phone calls and video chats simply don't fill the void of physically being with loved ones, so while the world lost its mind for a year, I turned to my writing to find peace.

Maple Bay is a fictional town, but it is very much inspired by the small town I was born in (Wells) and the town I grew up in (Winona). The characters were also highly inspired by my wonderful extended family and the many memories I have with them. This book is a romance, but it is also a love letter to my hometowns and my family. My hope is that this story has made you laugh, smile, and cry. I hope it warmed your heart. It certainly did that for me.

Sending you love and best wishes,
Brittney

www.brittneyjoybooks.com

If you have a few minutes, I'd love your honest review of Starting Over in Maple Bay on Amazon, GoodReads, or anywhere you purchased your book. Reviews help me understand what stories readers enjoy. They also help me decide what to write next. Please leave a review if you'd like to see more of Maple Bay.

Books by Brittney Joy

Sweet Young Adult Contemporary:
Lucy's Chance (Red Rock Ranch, book 1)
Showdown (Red Rock Ranch, book 2)
Rodeo Daze (Red Rock Ranch, book 3)

Clean Young Adult Fantasy:
OverRuled (The OverRuled Series, book 1)
OverRun (The OverRuled Series, book 2)
OverThrown (The OverRuled Series, book 3)

Sweet Adult Romance:
Starting Over in Maple Bay (book 1)
Second Chance in Maple Bay (book 2)
Country Stars in Maple Bay (book 3 ~ coming soon)

www.brittneyjoybooks.com

Printed in Great Britain
by Amazon

58886266R00192